The Otley Murders

ALSO BY J. R. ELLIS

The Otley Murders

A YORKSHIRE MURDER MYSTERY

J.R. ELLIS

THOMAS & MERCER

Text copyright © 2025 by J. R. Ellis
All rights reserved.

Published by Thomas & Mercer, Seattle

www.apub.com

Amazon, the Amazon logo, and Thomas & Mercer are trademarks of Amazon.com, Inc., or its affiliates.

EU Product Safety contact:
Amazon Publishing, Amazon Media EU S.à r.l.
38, avenue John F. Kennedy, L-1855 Luxembourg
amazonpublishing-gpsr@amazon.com

ISBN-13: 9781662515910
eISBN: 9781662515903

Cover design by @blacksheep-uk.com
Cover images: © rafal.dlugosz © Florin Danilet / Shutterstock;
© Les Wagstaff / Alamy Stock Photo

Printed in the United States of America

The Otley Murders

Prologue

2013

Detective Chief Inspector Oldroyd of the West Riding Police in Harrogate sat in the courtroom feeling the tension mount. The jury were filing back in, about to announce their verdict in a sensational case that had gripped the nation. The public gallery was full.

The accused sat impassively in the dock, watching as the jury members resumed their seats. Adam Blake was a good-looking man of forty with dark, wavy hair and a neatly trimmed beard. He smiled a lot, showing his perfect teeth. He had a pleasant voice and a very pleasant manner. It was only when you looked carefully into his cold blue eyes that you had any idea of the clever, manipulative and violent psychopath that lurked beneath his attractive, carefully curated exterior.

Blake was a serial killer who had befriended, betrayed and killed women – mostly elderly and vulnerable. His victims had lived in remote farmhouses, luxury apartments, beautiful cottages, even minor stately homes. What they all had in common was their wealth and their loneliness. Blake charmed them into his confidence and persuaded them to leave him money in their wills before disposing of them, faking their deaths as accidents or suicide.

He cold-bloodedly studied each victim carefully to establish that they had the right level of unhappiness and isolation to make them credulous – an appropriate victim. He rejected the ones who had close friends or relatives – people who could have sensed that something was wrong and sounded the alarm. It was not known just how many women had been potential victims before he discarded them to save his own skin.

His methods of dispatch varied so as to avoid the appearance of a pattern, but included drowning, overdoses, and falls from height. Often there were poignant suicide notes explaining why the women had decided to end their lives, often citing depression and loneliness. He'd strung one woman up in a barn and left her hanging while he forged a note that claimed she felt she had nothing to live for. Another was burned to death in her cottage; an electrical fault was blamed. The petrol-soaked rags that Blake had used were completely obliterated.

He had moved around a broad area in the affluent parts of East Yorkshire and Lincolnshire, forging his terrible career of deceit and death. He constantly made slight changes to his appearance and altered his name after each death. He was very careful to leave no evidence behind. His rampage had lasted for some years before links were finally made between his crimes. The person who had made these links was DCI Oldroyd.

Oldroyd watched Blake as he sat awaiting his fate and for a moment their eyes met. The killer frowned and turned away. Oldroyd was one of the very few people whom Blake had been unable to outwit. The malice in Blake's eyes had a satanic intensity about it, which unnerved even Oldroyd. The experienced detective thought back several months, to the climax of his investigation and the questioning of Blake after he had finally been apprehended.

Blake's last murder had been of an elderly woman called Frieda Ascomb. Oldroyd had been called on to the investigation after a local detective had been unhappy with the verdict of suicide or accidental death. Oldroyd was immediately suspicious. He had previous experience of patterns within crimes, and – as was his usual habit – he referred to this particular pattern by an acronym of his own invention. He had filed Blake's crimes under SSMK. This stood for Serial 'Sugar Mummy' Killer: a younger man who inveigles older, vulnerable women into his power, gets them to gift him money or leave it to him in their will, and then murders them, staging the death to look like suicide or an accident.

Oldroyd's team investigated details of other deaths of elderly women in the area, and eventually a pattern emerged. Oldroyd considered it very likely that a killer was indeed on the loose, especially after he realised that most of the women who had died seemed to have a new relationship with a younger man in the period before their death. A number of photographs were acquired of these men, and despite the changes in appearance and name, it was clear to Oldroyd that each image was of the same man. Once this had been established, it became possible to gather the evidence that eventually trapped Blake.

Oldroyd had found it quite unnerving to be so close to Blake in the interview room. The man emanated a sense of evil and danger, but he didn't admit to any part in the deaths of his victims. Yes, he had befriended these women, he said, but he never meant them any harm. In fact, his intention was always to bring some happiness to their lives. If they wanted to give him gifts or leave him money then, he claimed, surely that was testimony to how much they valued his friendship. It was true that he had changed his identity many times, but he stated that was due to his own insecurities. He had never felt happy in his own skin and so he kept moving around and reinventing himself. He admitted that he should probably have therapy about this, but maintained there was no sinister reason as to why he lived the life he did.

Oldroyd was not convinced by Blake's account, but no forensic digital evidence to link him with any of the crimes could be found. He had been particularly clever in avoiding any kind of banking trail so that the police could not link him to any money from the victims.

For once in his career, Oldroyd had felt that he was up against a mind as sharp as his. He had no doubt that Blake was guilty, but proving it was not easy.

In the end, it was the evidence of a handwriting expert that proved crucial. Oldroyd reached out to her for assistance, and she established that the wills and notes left by some of the women were forged. Starting from this, Oldroyd was able to prove that Blake had practised handwriting styles from material found in his home. Finally, a footprint was found on the bank of the river near where Frieda Ascomb was assumed to have entered the water that matched shoes owned by Blake. Ultimately, it was the near impossibility of removing every possible piece of incriminating evidence from so many scenes once they were linked that brought Blake down. Dogged and diligent work by forensics discovered Blake's fingerprints in different locations associated with his victims.

Oldroyd brought his attention back to the courtroom. The evidence against Blake was not overwhelmingly strong, but he was certain it would be enough to secure a conviction.

The foreman rose to deliver the verdict: guilty of all charges. Shouts and applause came from the relatives of some of Blake's victims. Oldroyd breathed a sigh of relief but Blake suddenly and unexpectedly erupted. It was a terrifying moment that reminded Oldroyd of the moment in *The Lord of the Rings*, when Galadriel is briefly tempted by the chance to possess the ring of power and becomes a horrifying figure.

Blake stood up, his eyes blazing, and pointed towards Oldroyd. All his smiling charm had gone, his face distorted. 'You think you're

Sherlock bloody Holmes,' he sneered, 'but I'm your Professor Moriarty. I'll get you back – don't think I'll ever forget.' He had to be dragged from the courtroom still shouting to await sentencing the next day.

It was a terrible confirmation of the kind of person he really was. Oldroyd had encountered blustery, empty threats from criminals before, but in that moment he found Blake truly chilling. The man really meant what he said, and there was something almost inhumanly deadly about the way he glared at the detective as he was pulled from the room.

The courtroom appeared to breathe a collective sigh of relief when Blake was finally removed. The newspaper reports the next day contained lurid accounts of Blake's outburst but as it was the end of the trial, the papers and television news soon moved on to the next story.

The experience reverberated in Oldroyd's memory for some time afterwards, but eventually he was able to banish it to the back of his mind, secure in the knowledge that his greatest foe was behind bars after having received a life sentence.

2023

Stansfield Prison in Yorkshire, in the small town of the same name, holds some dangerous criminals, and therefore the public are entitled to assume that it has very careful rules when it comes to moving prisoners around. But despite the procedures in place, one quiet day in early autumn, things went badly wrong.

Adam Blake had been incarcerated in this prison for ten years, largely forgotten by the outside world. This was about to change.

On this particular morning he was being taken to court in Leeds, where he faced charges in connection with yet another cold case – the suspected murder of an elderly lady, this one in Lincolnshire, in which – of course – he denied any involvement.

When the two escorting officers came to his cell, he greeted them with his usual conviviality. They suspected nothing. The prisoner transport van arrived at the prison gates and Blake was led out handcuffed. As soon as he appeared outside the gates, there was shouting a little way down the street – two men appeared to be fighting. One of them had a half brick in his hand and threw it. It missed the other man but landed not far from the van. The attention of all the officers was now on this scuffle, and one officer walked towards the fighters and shouted at them to stop. At that moment, a car came quickly around the corner from the other direction.

Blake lifted his handcuffed arms, smashed them into the face of one of the officers, and ran towards the car, which had screeched to a stop. A hooded figure got out of the passenger side of the car and pointed a gun towards the two officers pursuing their prisoner. The figure shouted at them to stop, and they froze as Blake hurriedly climbed into the back seat of the car, which immediately drove off at high speed.

The 'fighters', having provided the distraction, were already sprinting away. Some officers attempted to pursue, but the men quickly disappeared. The getaway car would later be found abandoned and burnt out some distance from Stansfield. It was assumed that Blake and his accomplices had transferred to another car.

It was all over very quickly. Much to the consternation and embarrassment of the prison, one of the most notorious prisoners at Stansfield had escaped in a very well-planned operation. The consequences of this would be dire for all concerned.

A couple of evenings later, in the Wharfedale village of Menston, near Otley, a man was walking down a quiet street towards a local pub. He was hardly aware that a vehicle had pulled up just behind him. A figure dressed in black, and wearing a balaclava, got out and checked that there was nobody around then walked quickly and quietly up behind the man, slipped a cord around his neck, and pulled it tight. There was a short struggle until the man passed out.

When he regained consciousness, he found himself bound and gagged and being driven. He was taken at knifepoint into a house and tied to a wooden chair. His abductor sat opposite and took off the balaclava.

The victim's eyes widened with shock. 'You!' he said, and the other person smiled.

'I'm glad you recognise me. I suppose you thought you'd never see me again. You were wrong.'

One

Otley is an ancient town on the River Wharfe, north of Leeds. Its name derives from Otta, a Saxon personal name, and the Old English word 'leah', meaning a wooded clearing. It was recorded as 'Otlelai' or 'Othelia' in the Domesday Book of 1086. There is evidence of prehistoric settlement on both sides of the River Wharfe and it is believed this part of Lower Wharfedale has been settled since the Bronze Age.

It was a crisp October Thursday morning in the small town of Otley, West Yorkshire. Abigail Wilson walked the short distance from her terraced house along the road that in pre-Beeching times had led to the railway station. In her late thirties, she hummed a tune as she walked briskly, her route taking her down the busy main street, across the cobbled market square, past the Buttercross and through one of the town's many narrow alleyways. She enjoyed the sunshine and the cool air and was dressed simply in skinny jeans and an oversized woolly jumper. It was a pleasant morning, and she greeted a number of people she met on the way. One of the things she liked about living in Otley was that you got to know a lot of the locals, especially if you were in a public role, like being the manager of the Courthouse Arts Centre.

It was 8.45 a.m. when she arrived at the centre. As the name suggested, the popular local arts venue had been created by converting an old courthouse into a performance space with tiered seating, and separate rooms for a variety of courses, group meetings and activities. The entrance was through a modern glass and steel extension, which housed a reception area. Displays of art by local artists filled the walls and there was a collection of books by local authors. The second floor housed a row of rather sinister-looking barred windows set into the old wall. These were the cells in which prisoners had been held before their appearance in the courtroom.

Still humming, Abigail fumbled with the key and opened the door. She was always first at the centre before the rest of the staff arrived. As soon as she entered the building, she stopped abruptly by the reception desk. A sixth sense was telling her that something was wrong. Looking around, she noticed one or two books had fallen on to the floor from a small display on the history of the Courthouse. Where the staircase to the cells was lined with framed photographs and more artworks, one of the pictures was hanging at a strange angle.

Her first thought was that there had been a break-in. She went around checking, but no windows had been broken and no doors had been forced on the ground floor, including the one to the office. As she examined the office itself, finding everything apparently in order, she heard a cheery voice.

'Morning!' The voice belonged to Hillary Sands, the volunteer coordinator, an energetic woman in her forties. She'd already been to the shops and walked her dog on the Chevin – her face had the healthy glow of a person who spent a lot of time being active outdoors. She burst into the office with a wide smile on her face, apologising for the mud on her trousers. She carried two large bags full of groceries. 'I've got the stuff for the café we talked about yesterday,' she said. 'I'll take it up there – some of it needs to go in the fridge.'

'Morning, Hillary,' Abigail said. 'Hold on just a moment.' She explained about the things she'd seen, which still didn't seem right.

'I see,' said Hillary. 'That is strange. Mice wouldn't knock books on to the floor or move a painting, would they? Perhaps Wendy did it without realising.' Wendy, the cleaner, came into the Courthouse in the early evening.

'Maybe . . . I'm just going to pop upstairs to have a look round there. Perhaps we've got a poltergeist.'

'Very unlikely!' Hillary laughed as she went back past reception and up to the café area.

Abigail climbed the stairs to the first floor and turned left on to a corridor with a high ceiling and walls constructed of white glazed bricks. With its row of sturdy doors leading to the cells, it had a Victorian institutional feel. As part of the Courthouse's display of its heritage, one of these stark cells was left open to the public and still had its original fittings. The white bricks continued into the cell where there was a cracked, greyish concrete floor and a wooden pallet bed. In one corner was a primitive-looking toilet bowl with a wooden seat.

But today, when Abigail glanced into the cell, she noticed there was also something else in the space: a strong, well-built man with short dark hair. He was fully clothed and lying on the floor with his legs stretched out and his back against the wall. His head had slumped to one side, though she could see his face sported a neat moustache. Abigail's first thought was that somehow a homeless person had managed to get into the centre and slept in the cell.

'Hello,' she called tentatively, but there was no response. She went across and touched his face. It was cold. She drew back and put her hand to her mouth. Then she saw that on his forehead was scrawled the word, *Vindicta*. Abigail felt her legs go weak. She stumbled back down the corridor, shouting to Hillary, who came to the bottom of the staircase and stopped when she saw Abigail's white face staring down at her.

'Ring for the police,' Abigail said. 'There's the body of a man in the heritage cell!'

~

'Well, Jim, this is all very curious, isn't it? You've got the victim in the cell and not the perpetrator.' The tall, lean figure of Tim Groves, wearing protective clothing, crouched over the body in the cell at the Courthouse. Groves was the chief forensic pathologist attached to West Riding Police in the Harrogate and Lower Wharfedale area. His remark was addressed to DCI Oldroyd, who had been called out to investigate the murder scene. Oldroyd and Groves had worked together for many years, and Groves liked to tease Oldroyd whenever he got the chance. 'What do you make of a body being left here? Odd place, isn't it?'

Oldroyd was a man of medium height and powerful build. He had a craggy face with striking grey eyes, which at this moment were roving around the old prison cell, assessing the situation.

'I don't know what I make of it yet, Tim,' he said, his voice deep with its pronounced Yorkshire accent. 'What can you tell me about the victim?'

Groves was packing up his instruments as he spoke. 'The SOCOs have removed his wallet and various other items from his pocket. No phone though – the killer must have taken it. Looks as if he's in his forties. Been dead about twelve hours, I would say. I'll confirm that later when I get the body to the lab. He was strangled by some kind of cord – you can see the marks around the neck. I imagine he would have struggled but there's no sign of that in this room, so it seems he was killed elsewhere before the body was brought here. I've no idea why. Maybe the murderer was making some kind of statement.'

'Possibly,' replied Oldroyd. 'But the most interesting thing is the writing on the forehead.'

'Ah yes, *vindicta*. That is "revenge", if I remember my Latin correctly. It was written with a black marker pen, most probably after he was dead. No sign of the pen, I'm afraid.'

'Hmm. Yes, revenge for what, I wonder?' Oldroyd looked around the cell in case something else caught his eye. 'So we may have a motive, but unspecified. Unless that's just been put there to mislead us, but we have no details and no suspects yet of course.' Another pause, and then: 'What do you make of it, Steph?'

This question was addressed to Detective Sergeant Stephanie Johnson, a regular member of Oldroyd's team along with her colleague and partner Detective Sergeant Andy Carter, who today was working at Harrogate station. Now in her thirties, Steph had worked at Harrogate since leaving school. Andy Carter had moved up from Croydon to join West Riding Police some years before, but was as devoted as Steph to their boss.

'There must be some reason why the body was brought here, sir,' Steph said. 'It would have been a real effort to get it up the stairs, which suggests that there may be more than one person involved, but also that this cell has some significance. I agree with Mr Groves.'

'Yes,' replied Oldroyd, a little distracted as he screwed up his face and looked around the cell again. 'The other question is, how did they get here? There was no sign of a break-in.'

'Does that mean the people who work here and had keys are suspects?' asked Steph.

'Maybe, but it's a bit obvious, isn't it? Would you bring the body of someone you'd killed to your place of work, and also make it clear that a door key had been used? We need to talk to the centre manager.'

Downstairs in the small office, the atmosphere was sombre. Abigail Wilson and Hillary Sands had been joined by Dylan Hardy, who worked part-time as an administrator. The centre had remained closed to the public – a police car was parked outside, and a uniformed officer stood by the door. This was all causing intrigue and concern – people were starting to call the centre to find out what had happened. There was also a steady stream of people walking slowly past the Courthouse to have a good look in. After fielding several calls from concerned customers and local reporters, Abigail had had enough and was now allowing them to proceed to voicemail.

'You didn't recognise the person in the cell?' asked Dylan, as the phone rang yet again.

Abigail, sitting at the desk, held her head in her shaking hands. The shock of discovering the body had been greater than she had originally thought. 'Nope,' she murmured through her fingers. 'His face was vaguely familiar. If he lives in the area, I've probably seen him around the town.'

'Oh, I'd better message today's volunteers and explain what's happened,' Hillary whispered to Abigail, reaching for her phone.

'Be careful what you say,' said Abigail. 'The police haven't made an official statement yet and they may not want details revealed. Just tell them not to come in because there's been an incident and the police will say more about it later.'

'OK,' Hillary said, as she began to text the first number.

∾

Upstairs, Oldroyd was speaking to DC David Hall from the small Otley police station. Hall had been directing the SOCOs in their investigation of the scene. He was a lean, energetic character with alert eyes. He impressed Oldroyd, as he was clearly someone keen to work hard with them on the investigation.

'There were various cards and some money in his wallet, sir,' said Hall. 'It doesn't look as if the motive was robbery. His name was Tony Lowell, and we've got an address for him in Menston. His wife called this morning to report him missing, so it seems we now know what happened to him.'

'Good work. Stay here and see if the SOCOs find anything else. And you'd better give me that address so I can visit the poor widow.' Oldroyd turned to Steph. 'We need to talk to them downstairs . . .' He looked at Hall. 'By the way . . . would there be CCTV footage of this place?'

'There is, sir,' replied Hall. 'Just one camera trained on the entrance area, but it's been knocked out, I'm afraid.'

'Right, further evidence that the person was familiar with the Courthouse. Let's see if the stuff you found on him can shed any further light.'

In the office, Oldroyd could see that all the staff – who had now gathered together in one space – were shaken. 'I know this is difficult for you all,' he said kindly, 'but I'm afraid I have to ask you some questions. As there is no evidence of a break-in, we have to assume that whoever brought the body here had a key for the centre, so can you provide me with a list of all the key holders? I assume that there is more than one entrance?'

'Yes,' replied Abigail. 'There's another door at the back and one at the side, but they're emergency exit doors and alarmed. They're not for normal use. People don't carry keys for them. I checked the other doors, but no one seemed to have tampered with them.'

'Has anyone reported keys stolen?'

'No,' Abigail told him.

'OK,' continued Oldroyd. 'The victim's name was Tony Lowell, and he lived in Menston. Did any of you know him?'

They all shook their heads.

'I was telling the others that I thought his face was vaguely familiar,' Abigail said. 'He had no connection to the centre that I know of.'

'OK. Can you tell me exactly what you saw when you came in this morning?'

Abigail took a deep breath. 'The door was locked, but as soon as I opened it, I sensed something was wrong.' She explained about the books and the picture.

'Yes, those things must have been disturbed when the body was dragged up to the cell. So . . . nothing else has been interfered with, and nothing is missing?'

'It's a bit early to be completely sure, but no money or any other items have been stolen as far as we can see.'

'So it appears as if someone unlocked the door, brought in the victim, and then went out again, locking the door behind them.'

'Yes, but I can't imagine that anybody who works here and has a set of keys would have done something like that.'

Oldroyd nodded. 'No, but has anyone noticed anyone acting strangely around here recently? Maybe someone who works here behaving in an unusual way or a member of the public whose behaviour stood out during their visit?'

Abigail, Hillary and Dylan looked at each other and Abigail shrugged her shoulders. 'We're the only three regular members of staff, Chief Inspector. Although we do have a lot of volunteers who come in to do jobs, and a board of trustees who drop in regularly. But I don't think any of us have noticed anything unusual.' She looked around at the others, who nodded their assent.

'OK. We need to establish an incident room here, and I'd prefer not to take over your office if there's an alternative.'

'I think the robing room would be suitable,' said Wilson. 'It's where judges used to put on their attire before going into the courtroom. I'll show you.' She got up and led the detectives out of the glass entrance door, across the courtyard and through a solid wooden doorway in the corner. The square room was set out with chairs and tables. 'We use this room for classes and the writers' group on Fridays. There's a toilet and a little kitchen area.'

'This will do fine,' said Oldroyd. 'Thank you.'

After Wilson had left, Oldroyd and Steph were settling in when Oldroyd's phone went.

'I'll have to take this,' he said. 'It's DCS Walker.'

'OK, sir,' replied Steph, and she left the room.

Detective Chief Superintendent Tom Walker was Oldroyd's boss at the Harrogate station. Walker was several years older than Oldroyd but showed no inclination to retire. He could be a curmudgeonly character, especially when he embarked on one of his frequent rants against his hate figure: the trendy, managerial Matthew Watkins, chief constable of West Riding Police. But he was very supportive of his officers who worked in the field. He and Oldroyd shared the same values regarding policing and a deep pride in their Yorkshire identity. They were on first name terms in private.

'Morning, Tom. To what do I owe the privilege?' said Oldroyd, his tone cheery.

'Morning, Jim. It's not good news, I'm afraid.' Oldroyd flinched. Walker's tone was uncharacteristically sombre. This was going to be something more serious than an angry update on Watkins' latest management antics. 'You remember Adam Blake?'

A shudder went through Oldroyd. 'Of course, Tom, how could I ever forget?'

'The bastard's escaped from prison.'

Oldroyd felt this bald statement like a physical blow. He remembered sitting in the courtroom when Adam Blake had threatened him before being sentenced to life imprisonment.

'What?'

'Yes, believe it or not. They were supposed to be taking him from Stansfield to the court in Leeds, but they never got further than the prison gates. He managed to get away with the help of a bunch of clever thugs; they put on a bit of a skirmish and then he was whisked away in a car. I don't know what the hell was going on with the prison wardens. It should be routine moving prisoners around; sounds like a Mickey Mouse operation to me or, more likely, bent. There must have been somebody working for him on the inside. Anyway, the point is, however he did it, he's escaped . . . and there's been no sign of him since.'

'When was this?'

'This is another outrage: three days ago. The governor of Stansfield, James Perry – he's a damned lightweight, like Watkins – contacted me earlier on. He said he'd been confident that Blake would be quickly recaptured, but now of course he had to admit to me that he was still at large. He was trying to contain the consequences of their cock-up and keep it quiet and out of the press. Then he waffled on about wanting to establish exactly what had happened but not jumping to any conclusions,' Walker grunted. 'And that's also a load of tosh. He knows something's gone badly wrong and he'll be trying to keep anything embarrassing about his staff from the public, but it won't wash. There will have to be a thorough independent inquiry into this and there will be an outcry if there are some corrupt prison warders involved. And he hasn't heard the last of it from me, I can tell you – especially as it's putting you in danger, never mind the public generally. He should be damn well sacked for not informing us earlier and I told him so. We all remember what Blake said to you.'

Oldroyd didn't reply. He was thinking about the events of a decade ago, and the moment when Blake had sworn his revenge. Of course, he had come to terms with all the details of those terrible crimes and the threats to him made by Blake over the years. Blake had been given a full life tariff, and no one believed that he would ever be let out of prison; he was far too dangerous. His escape was a big surprise to Oldroyd, and now he had to wonder how long Blake had been planning it, and whether it was connected to his threat of revenge against Oldroyd – the man who had put an end to his criminal career.

'Are you there, Jim?'

Oldroyd was brought back to the present with a jolt. 'Yes, Tom. I have to admit it's a bit of a shock.'

'I'll bet it is. He should never have been in Stansfield anyway; he should have been in a higher security prison, but he's been very well behaved since his conviction, and he'd lured some gullible twit of a psychiatrist into believing that he was no longer a high-risk prisoner.'

'Is there any information about where he might be?'

'No, but there's a team of detectives from Stansfield pursuing all leads, and because you're involved, I'm going to get Andy Carter to liaise with them and get our people to be on the lookout in case he pops up around here. Obviously you, Deborah and your family need to be careful but I'm sure he'll be caught before he can track you down, if he even still wants to after all this time.'

'Right.' Oldroyd was not convinced by this. Walker was trying to reassure him but they both knew that Blake was a real threat and quite capable of finding out where Oldroyd lived. And he wasn't the kind of person who would forget a serious grudge. He wanted to get his own back, and Oldroyd smiled grimly as he remembered the word *vindicta* written on the forehead of the victim. He shuddered as he imagined that word written on himself. And then the thought occurred: could Blake be involved in this Otley murder? It seemed too much of a coincidence.

'Anyway,' continued Walker. 'What have you discovered in Otley?'

Oldroyd explained about the body in the cell. Walker grunted. 'It sounds as if you've got quite a job on. You've got Stephanie Johnson there, haven't you?'

'Yes.'

'Well, look, if you think you're in danger, I'm quite happy for you to take some time off and lie low until Blake's been recaptured. I can get someone else to take over this Otley case. It has crossed my mind,' said Walker, echoing Oldroyd's thought, 'that Blake could be involved in this murder, as it was committed after his release. I don't suppose you've seen any evidence of that?'

'No, Tom.'

'Good, well, if you do, you will definitely have to stand down. It would be too dangerous for you to continue.'

Oldroyd thought about this for a moment. 'OK, thanks, Tom, but in the meantime, why should I let that man stop me from doing my job? He'd be delighted if he thought I was frightened of him and cowering away somewhere. I'd rather continue.'

'As you wish – but for goodness' sake, be careful. We both know what he is capable of. Let me know if you change your mind at any point. And you'll have to inform your family and tell them to take care too. I'll be arranging protection for you all, don't worry.'

This was a further blow, but Walker was right: characters like Blake often attacked you through the people you cared about.

Steph had remained outside when she heard that Oldroyd was still on the phone, watching the body be taken away to the mortuary. When she came into the room, she found her boss sitting

19

in a chair and gazing into space. He told her about Blake's escape and how the killer had threatened him in the past.

'Oh, bloody hell, sir – that's not good news. He's an absolute psycho, isn't he? How on earth did he escape?'

Oldroyd shook his head. 'I don't know, Superintendent Walker is sure he had help from someone inside the prison. Anyway, however it happened, the fact is: Blake's free.'

Steph sat down. 'Do you really think he'll come for you, sir?'

Oldroyd shrugged. 'I think there's a good chance he'll try.'

Steph looked at him. It was rare to see anxiety or fear on his face, but it was there now.

'I'm more concerned about Deborah and the rest of my family. I can look after myself, but I worry about them.'

'I know, sir, but you'll all get protection, and it surely won't be long before they recapture him.'

'I hope so,' said Oldroyd, but he didn't sound very convinced.

Steph had the same thought as her boss had earlier. 'If Blake escaped a few days ago, sir, you don't think he could have had anything to do with the murder here? You know, with this vengeance business.'

'It doesn't seem likely but it's not impossible, I suppose. We need to find out who this dead person is and whether he did have some connection to Blake. I'll be very surprised if that's the case, but nothing's beyond that man and I find the writing of that word *vindicta* on the victim unsettling because he would certainly be seeking revenge after being in prison for so long.'

'Surely Blake couldn't have got keys to the Courthouse, sir.'

Oldroyd took a deep breath. 'Again, it seems unlikely but it's a big coincidence, isn't it? And don't underestimate Adam Blake, he's what you might call an evil genius: extremely devious and intelligent. He's probably spent years planning this escape, and whatever he has in mind to do now. Acting alone is his usual modus operandi.'

'He obviously had a number of accomplices to help him break out of jail, and then to disappear. Maybe they obtained keys for the Courthouse for him?'

'Yes, he will have used people for specific purposes. And we know he had money stashed away from his crimes that nobody could track down. He'll be paying them handsomely. Damn!' he shouted, suddenly angry, and brought his fist down on the table. 'This is going to make things so difficult, get people anxious and waste so much time. I'll have to call Deborah and my sister and my son and daughter. Bloody hell! What on earth were they thinking of at that prison?'

'Surely Superintendent Walker is right, sir – Blake must have had some help on the inside as well as out.'

Oldroyd rubbed his forehead with the fingers of his right hand. 'I know, I know. But it's not good enough; it just makes things so awkward and difficult, as if police work isn't hard enough as it is. And now people close to me could be in danger. It's just a bloody awful mess!' He shook his head. 'But I told Superintendent Walker that I want to continue with this case; I'm not going to let Blake stop me. And by the way, Superintendent Walker is getting Andy to liaise with the detectives looking for Blake.'

'He'll enjoy that, sir – and it will be good experience.'

Oldroyd got up. 'Go and see how they're getting on with the key holder list, will you, while I make some calls. And find out a bit more about the history of this place. It might give us a clue as to why the killer chose it to dump the body.'

'OK, sir.' Steph looked at her boss with concern. He really was under pressure now. There was a threat to his life. 'You know we're all here to support you?' she said.

'I know, thanks,' replied Oldroyd with a tight little smile.

When Steph had left, Oldroyd sighed and reluctantly picked up his phone. He rang his partner Deborah, who was at home at their house in the village of New Bridge, near Harrogate.

'Well, what an unexpected pleasure to hear from you at this time in the morning,' she said with her usual playfulness. 'Haven't you got enough to do today? You'll have to be quick; I've got a client coming soon.' Deborah was a psychotherapist who worked mostly from home.

Oldroyd felt bad puncturing her cheerful mood with the news about Blake's escape.

After he'd finished speaking, there was a short pause before she replied. 'Bloody hell, Jim! So they've no idea where this bloke is?'

'Apparently not. It's a huge cock-up and heads will no doubt roll, but I'm afraid he's on the loose and very dangerous. It will mean that we will all have to have police protection until he's caught.'

Deborah sighed. 'Well, I suppose I knew what I was taking on when I got into a relationship with a detective – especially a successful one. I've already suffered for it once.'

Oldroyd winced at this reference to a case in which Deborah had been taken hostage. His sister Alison and his daughter Louise had also once been in serious danger. It made him feel guilty to know that his work had placed people he loved in jeopardy.

'I know; I'm sorry.'

'OK,' Deborah said, taking a deep breath. 'Well, I suppose I'll manage.' Her voice took a lighter tone. 'Just make sure that the officers assigned to protect us are attractive young men. There have to be some compensations for being in fear of your life.'

Oldroyd laughed. He loved her because she was so brave and good humoured in the face of such danger. He promised they would talk about it more when he got back before ending the call.

Next he tried to call his sister Alison in Leeds, his son Robert in Birmingham and his daughter Louise in London. He spoke briefly to Robert, explaining the situation regarding Adam Blake. He emphasised that the threat to his son and his family was minimal, but that police would be coming round to arrange protection. There was no answer from Alison or Louise, so he left messages.

After making the calls, he felt exhausted. He wondered if Blake knew the kind of stress this escape was putting him under. Probably he did and would delay any action he was planning to take in order to increase the pressure. It would satisfy his sadistic impulses.

Steph came back into the room. 'All right, sir?'

'Yes. I've spoken to them or left messages. Obviously they're worried. I tried to reassure them as much as I could.' He gave Steph a determined look. 'I think we should just carry on and not let this interfere with the investigation.'

'OK, sir.'

'Did you find out anything useful?'

'Well, I think you'll find it interesting from a historical point of view, sir, but I'm not sure of the relevance to this case.' Steph referred to her notebook. 'Those cells were built in the 1850s and the Courthouse in the 1870s. It was used by the County Court, the Magistrates' Court and the Probation Service until it was all closed in 1997 and everything was moved to Leeds. There used to be a police station in one wing of this building.'

'Hmm . . . Maybe the revenge was for a sentence that was handed down here. Did Lowell have any connection with this place when it was a law court? Did he ever have anything to do with law enforcement, I wonder? Maybe he even had something to do with Adam Blake's case sentencing.'

'It doesn't seem likely, sir, but we'll definitely find out.'

'One thing I'm wondering is why the killer bothered locking the door of the building behind them when they left.'

Steph thought for a moment. 'Maybe out of habit, sir? If they use their key regularly, they would be used to locking up when they left, which suggests that the killer may have a close connection with this place.'

'That's a good theory. To me it also suggests that maybe they didn't want to cause any real harm to the Courthouse, supported by the fact that nothing was taken from here. And if they'd left the door open, there could have been a burglary. You could say that they were being polite. The killer wanted to put their victim in a cell for some reason. It's difficult to think of anywhere else round here where that would be possible short of breaking into a prison.'

Steph nodded. 'So Mr Groves could be right, sir? The killer was making some kind of statement?'

Oldroyd nodded. 'Yes, but we don't know precisely what and for whom it was intended, but I'm thinking if all this is about revenge, then it's very possible that Blake is involved. I'm sure I wasn't the only person he swore revenge on. When I speak to the press, which I'm sure I will be doing soon, I'm going to give them all the details. It might make someone come forward with information.'

At Harrogate HQ, Andy Carter was called to Superintendent Walker's office. He was quite nervous as he knocked on the door. Walker's often gruff Yorkshireness and his broad accent were sometimes difficult for him to deal with as a Londoner, though he had great respect for the older man's experience of policing – which exceeded even that of his immediate boss and mentor DCI Oldroyd.

'Come in,' he heard Walker say. Inside he found the super sitting at his desk, wearing his reading glasses. He looked up and took the glasses off. 'Ah, Carter – sit down, lad.' Andy sat down at the other side of the desk. Walker sat back in his chair. 'I'm sure you've already heard from Chief Inspector Oldroyd or Detective Sergeant Johnson about the escape from Stansfield Prison.'

'Yes, sir. I understand that Chief Inspector Oldroyd could be in danger.'

Walker smiled. 'Well, you've got straight to the issue. I like officers who are sharp and on the ball. I won't go into all the background details now, you probably know a lot of it anyway. Adam Blake is a very nasty piece of work. When he was sentenced, he made serious threats against Chief Inspector Oldroyd. We have to assume that he meant them and that Chief Inspector Oldroyd's family could also be at risk.'

Andy flinched, thinking about Oldroyd's partner, Deborah, as well as his sister Alison and his daughter Louise – all of whom Andy had met and liked. He knew how close they were as a family.

Walker continued. 'Now, obviously, there's a full-scale manhunt going on, but after the complete mess the prison over there made of things, not to mention the strong possibility that Blake had help on the inside, I've insisted with the chief constable that we have some involvement here from the Harrogate station, given that one of our key officers is personally affected by this escape.

'At the moment all my inspectors are occupied, so I want you to liaise with the team at Stansfield and help them where you can, but stay around here because Blake is likely to turn up looking for Inspector Oldroyd. I'm going to give you DC Warner and DC Hardiman to work with you on this.'

Andy was pleased. Sharon Warner was a young DC who had been a protégée of Steph's when she had joined the force. She excelled in tracking down information online. Alan Hardiman was also quite young but had already proved himself to be a reliable detective. They would form a good team.

'Your contact over at Stansfield is Inspector Hamish McNiven and he'll be expecting a call from you. I assume that he'll welcome the extra support that you can give, but if you find that there's any resistance to your being involved, let me know. That man has got to be caught and we can't tolerate any inter-station rivalry or nonsense like that.'

'OK, sir.'

'Right. So, I'm leaving it entirely up to you to decide how you play this. Talk to McNiven and work out a strategy. I want you to report back to me regularly.' Walker looked at Andy. 'Chief Inspector Oldroyd is a first-rate detective and he's been a great asset to this station. I've known him for a long time, and I know Stephanie Johnson and yourself have worked with him a lot over recent years and you've formed a special bond. I know you will want to do everything you can to protect him and his family.'

Andy was quite moved by this. 'I will, sir, and can I just thank you for selecting me for this responsibility.'

Walker waved his hand at him. 'Never mind that, you are the right person for the job. Now off you go and get on with it.'

≈

Oldroyd and Steph drove out from Otley to the nearby village of Menston. They found the address, which was a small semi-detached house in a new development. Lowell's wife, Alice, answered the door. She was a small woman with long, unbrushed, knotty dark hair; she wore patterned leggings and a stained sweatshirt – clothes that were easy to put on. Her eyes were red from crying and the right sleeve of her top was damp with tears. She led the detectives into a neat sitting room.

'I'm sorry to have to ask you questions at a time like this,' said Oldroyd kindly. 'I know it's been a huge shock.'

Alice hung her head and seemed unable to say anything.

'When did you last see your husband?'

'Last night,' she began in a quiet, wavering voice. 'He left here about seven o'clock, said he was going to our local pub down the road – The King's Arms. He meets a friend in there every Wednesday evening. I don't wait up for him. I went to bed at about half past ten. I work in a nursing home and it's a tiring job.' She faltered for a moment and put a handkerchief to her eye. 'When I woke up in the morning, he wasn't there. I rang him but there was no answer, so I contacted his friend, who said that Tony had never appeared at the pub. I panicked and rang the police straight away. And then . . .' She stopped and burst into tears. Oldroyd waited for her to recover.

'Had your husband been behaving at all strangely recently? Did he appear anxious or distressed?' asked Steph.

'No, I didn't notice anything different about him.'

'Where did your husband work?'

'At an estate agent's office over in Guiseley. It's called Westwood's.'

'Was he happy there?'

'As far as I know, yes.' She shook her head and couldn't say anything for a few moments. 'This is . . . a complete shock. I don't know what I'll . . .' She seemed on the verge of tears again.

'How long have you been married?' asked Steph.

'Five years; we met in our late thirties. We don't have any children. Tony always said he didn't want them, and I was happy to go along with that.'

Steph gave her a sympathetic smile. 'Did you meet around here?'

'Yes, I've lived around Menston and Burley in Wharfedale all my life. Tony was brought up in the Leeds area, but he has no family there now. He spent some time away from Yorkshire when he was younger. He'd been back a few years when we met and . . .' Her voice trailed off as she remembered those times and she was near to tears again. 'I'm close to my brother and his wife. They live in Ilkley. I know they'll . . . they'll help me.'

'How much did he tell you about his life from before you met? What did he do?' asked Oldroyd.

'He didn't tell me much. Just a series of odd jobs, I think, after he left school. He said he was a bit of a mixed-up character in those days. He did things he wasn't proud of. He didn't really want to talk about it much, so I never pressed him. It didn't bother me what he'd done in the past, I was just pleased to be with him now.'

'Did he have any family? Brothers and sisters? Parents still alive?'

'No. He was an only child. His parents were dead when we met.'

'Did he have any enemies? Anyone who would wish him harm?'

She shook her head and looked perplexed, as if she was still finding it difficult to register what had happened. 'No. Tony was a quiet man. He got on with everybody. It's . . .' She was unable to continue.

'I'm sorry again, Mrs Lowell,' said Oldroyd. 'But I have to ask you, were you and your husband getting on well together?'

She looked at Oldroyd. 'Yes, we were – and we always did. I'm going to miss him terribly.'

'Did he have any friends? People he spent a lot of time with?'

'He used to go cycling a lot. He liked to keep fit. He was a member of the Airedale Cycling Club. They meet over in Bingley. The leader is Richard King; he's a nice chap. I can give you his number.'

'Thank you. You've been very helpful. An officer will come round to take a statement from you. Other than that, I don't think that we will have to bother you again. Please don't get up, we'll see ourselves out.'

~

In Courthouse Street, people were walking slowly past the blue and white police tape and gazing curiously towards the closed arts centre. Small groups were huddled and talking in hushed voices. A nearby café was doing excellent trade.

A van arrived and pulled up by the entrance. A man dressed in paint-stained overalls got out and spoke to the police officer on duty. The officer then spoke on his radio and the new arrival was let through the cordon. He went into the building and made for the office.

Abigail, Hillary and Dylan were still fielding phone calls from the press and the public. They were even trying to do some work, although it was almost impossible to concentrate.

'Morning, everybody,' said the workman, whose name was Scott Evans, trying to be cheery. 'What the hell's going on?'

'Hi, Scott,' said Hillary. 'Abigail found a body in the heritage cell this morning. It's been terrible.'

'What? Bloody hell! The police officer just told me that there has been a serious incident, but nothing about dead bodies. He didn't really want to let me in. I had to explain I was doing some painting in the courtroom before he got permission to let me through to speak to you and collect my stuff. I'm not allowed to stay. Was it anybody you know?'

'According to the police, it was somebody called Tony Lowell. I think they've gone up to Menston to talk to his wife. But none of us knew him.'

'Right.' Evans shook his head. 'Body in an old prison cell . . . weird or what? Anyway, I'll be back as soon as I can, when the police give me permission. I've got another job I can be getting on with.'

'OK,' said Hillary, and Scott went to collect his stepladder and a bucket full of brushes from a storage cupboard.

'It won't be long before the press turn up,' said Dylan. 'We're not telling them anything over the phone. I hope the detectives are back before then.' He turned to Abigail. 'I don't think we should talk to reporters if they turn up, do you?'

'Absolutely not. Not until we get some guidance from the police. The media are likely to twist anything you say.'

'I think I'd like to go and listen to what the chief inspector says to them,' said Hillary.

'Would you?' said Dylan.

'Yes, I want to find out more about what's happened and what they're letting the public know.'

'Good idea,' said Abigail. 'I'll come with you.'

'Not much there, I'm afraid,' said Oldroyd as he and Steph left the victim's forlorn wife and drove down towards Burley in Wharfedale. They were in Oldroyd's Saab, which was now so old that it was almost vintage. Oldroyd wasn't interested in cars, but he liked the Saab. He said getting into it was like putting on an old pair of slippers. Steph had arrived separately in Otley in a police car, but her boss preferred his own car and had offered to give her a ride back to the station. 'Except for what she said about his early life. We'll have to look into what was going on recently, but I'm already beginning to feel that the answer to why he was killed probably lies in the past, as it so often does in mysterious cases like this.'

'She mentioned that he said he'd done things that he wasn't proud of, sir. I wonder what she meant?'

'Yes – tantalising, wasn't it?'

'She didn't seem very curious about it. Unless, perhaps, she's keeping something from us?'

'If she was, I don't think she would have mentioned it at all. We urgently need to find out more about his past. It would be a good job for young Sharon Warner, but I think DCS Walker has assigned her to work with Andy. Maybe she can do a bit of work for us too.'

They were now driving along the bottom of Wharfedale near to the river. Ahead and above the town of Otley was a steep hillside known as the Chevin. It was covered in woodland, which was slowly assuming the beautiful colours of autumn.

'There are some great walks up there on the Chevin, and then you can come down into Otley and take your pick from its many pubs. Did you know Otley has a claim to be the town in Britain with the most pubs per person?'

Steph laughed. Her boss's enthusiasm for all things Yorkshire and his tendency to deliver little lectures on some aspect of his beloved county was famous among anyone who'd worked with him. It seemed to her, however, that on this occasion, talking about Yorkshire was a distraction from the anxiety he must be under due to the threat from Blake. He clearly didn't want to talk about it. She decided that it was better to go along with him at this point, but she was watching him very closely for signs of stress.

'Yes, sir. Mum used to take Lisa and I walking on the Chevin when we were little. I remember we used to pick bilberries. It's a good place for those. There's an open area that is full of bilberry bushes. She didn't take us into the pubs though.'

'No, but it was good that she made the effort to take you walking up there,' said Oldroyd. He glanced at Steph. 'She brought you up well, you and your sister, didn't she? It can't have been easy as a single mother.'

'No, I don't think it was, sir.' Steph's violent and alcoholic father had left the family when the girls were young, though they had been reconciled with him in recent years. 'I'm grateful I was brought up in a loving family even though I only had one parent for most of the time.'

'I was fortunate with my family too. It sets you up for life. We see so many examples in our work of people who've been completely screwed up by what happened in their early life. It always makes me think, you know, *there but for the grace of God.*'

'I agree, sir. I know I called Adam Blake a psycho earlier on today, but I don't like that language, really. Something must have happened to him to make him the way he is.'

'Yes – and would you want to be a person like that: cold and calculating? It would be terrible to be inside his head. Unfortunately, he's loose and a threat to us all, so we have to stay on the alert. Anyway, here we are.' They were back at the Courthouse, and Oldroyd noticed a few people hanging around who looked like reporters. 'I suppose I'll have to deal with the press soon. As it's a pleasant day I'll speak to them outside the entrance to the Courthouse. Will you go over and tell them I'll hold a press conference in half an hour?'

'OK, sir.'

≈

At Harrogate HQ, Andy was on the phone with Inspector McNiven, who was briefing him further on Blake's escape. McNiven was a soft-spoken Scotsman with a friendly manner, and sounded like he welcomed the extra help from the Harrogate station.

'There have been no sightings of Blake here in the Stansfield area, or anywhere else,' he said. 'His escape is going to cause some trouble amongst the senior people. In the meantime, we lesser mortals have got to carry on and catch the bugger. I'm glad you're joining us. The more help we get the better.'

'You're welcome, sir,' said Andy. 'I'm sure you've been briefed about the threat to DCI Oldroyd.'

'Yes, and I think it's credible. Apparently Blake swore to get revenge on Oldroyd for putting him away and there's every reason to believe that he will want to carry out his threat. It's good to have you working in the Harrogate area. Blake knows he can't escape recapture for very long and he'll probably try to do as much damage as he can before he's stopped. The first thing I'd like you to do is to get information out to the public that there is a dangerous criminal at large. A brief press conference will be the best thing. Emphasise that while we don't think he's a random killer, he is very dangerous and should not be approached. He will be planning revenge attacks on people who brought him to justice and their families. Anyone in his way will be in danger, so people need to be alert and so on.'

'Will do, sir.'

'Where is Chief Inspector Oldroyd?'

'He and Detective Sergeant Johnson are in Otley, sir. They're on a murder case: a body was found at the Courthouse Arts Centre this morning. He's been informed about Blake's escape. Knowing him, I don't think he'll want to stand down from the investigation and hide away, but he must be under a lot of pressure knowing that Blake is out there.'

'Yes. It can't be pleasant.'

'What about the men who helped Blake? Is there any sign of them?'

'I've got officers working on that. It will probably turn out to be people who are familiar to us in the criminal underworld. We'll leave them to it, and concentrate on finding Blake.'

'Maybe Blake is still with the people who got him out, sir.'

McNiven smiled at Andy's thoughtful approach. 'Yes, perfectly possible, but given that they will probably have done a runner back to hide in London or wherever, I think it's unlikely given that Blake wants to stay around here and be in striking distance of DCI Oldroyd.'

Back in Otley, Oldroyd addressed the press in the small courtyard outside the Courthouse. He felt exposed, and scanned the crowd a little nervously, looking for Blake. There was no sign of the man. Before him was the usual motley collection of reporters and camera people, some of whom he'd seen many times before over the years. He knew which ones were likely to ask sensible questions and which were on the lookout for material they could fashion into a sensational article. He also noted Abigail and Hillary came to the entrance door to listen.

Oldroyd began by explaining how the body of Tony Lowell, a local man from Menston, had been found in the heritage cell in the Courthouse. He didn't say anything about the word *vindicta* written on the victim's forehead; that would only feed their lurid imaginations.

'That's a weird place to find a body, isn't it, Chief Inspector? Do you think he was murdered there or put there after his death?'

'Definitely placed there after his death,' replied Oldroyd. 'We don't know why that location was chosen, but robbery was not the motive as nothing was taken from the victim or from the Courthouse.

'We want to hear from anyone who saw anything suspicious last night, particularly in the Menston area. Mr Lowell left his house in Monroe Gardens, Menston at about seven in the evening. His wife thought he was intending to meet with some friends at The King's Arms pub in the village, which was a regular Wednesday evening social gathering. He never arrived.

'We shall, of course, be releasing a photograph of the victim. If any member of the public recognises Mr Lowell and saw him anywhere last night after 7.00 p.m., we need to hear from them.'

'Chief Inspector, do you think the killer was sending some kind of message by putting the body in a prison cell?' asked one reporter.

This was an insightful question, but Oldroyd didn't want to be drawn into too much speculation.

'It's possible, but it's far too early to say what the killer's motive was in bringing the body here. We're concentrating on the circumstances in which Mr Lowell was killed. We hope that will lead us to the killer, and I want to repeat that members of the public could be very important in providing information.'

'Is there any indication of why he was killed, Chief Inspector?' asked somebody else.

'No, and I don't expect that we will get any until we find out who the murderer is.'

'It must have been a shock to the people who work at the Courthouse,' commented one of the crowd.

'Yes. They will need the support of the community to get through the trauma of it. Hopefully it won't be too long before we can get out of the way and the Courthouse can reopen. Anyway, I think that's as much as I can tell you at the moment. Thank you.' Oldroyd turned round, ignored further questions, and went back inside the Courthouse, followed by Steph.

'That should keep them quiet for a while,' he said when they were inside the entrance foyer. 'We need to check that list of key holders and follow it up. While I'm doing that, could you go and speak to Lowell's employers up in Guiseley? But first, how about a spot of lunch at The Black Raven? They do some good sandwiches.' He frowned. 'They do some good beer as well. Such a shame that I'll have to forego it right now.'

Steph laughed. On many occasions, she had been the driver when her boss had broken the rules and sampled local beers and wines while on duty. But the rules had tightened, and Oldroyd thought it was inappropriate and a bad example for him to continue with his occasional illicit tipple. 'It'll do you good, sir, to avoid alcohol if you're still trying to keep your weight down.'

'Yes, there is that, I suppose,' said Oldroyd, looking glumly at his stubbornly paunchy waistline and thinking about what his partner Deborah would say. For some time now she had been conducting a campaign to get him leaner and fitter. This involved running, including Saturday parkruns in Harrogate, alongside eating and drinking less. The evidence of his waistline was that the campaign had not yet yielded very positive results.

~

When the press conference was over, Abigail and Hillary went back into the office. Dylan was not at his desk.

'Well, that was interesting,' said Abigail. 'I wonder why he didn't tell them about what was written on that man's forehead. Too sensational, I expect.'

'What do you mean?'

'Oh, didn't I tell you? The shock must have made me forget. On that man's forehead was written a word: *vindicta*. I think it means *revenge*. Gruesome, isn't it?'

There was silence. Hillary had looked away. She seemed to have lost her usual cheeriness.

'Are you OK?' asked Abigail.

'Yes, yes. It's nothing. You've just made think about something, that's all.' She turned round and smiled. 'It's nothing. I think we're all suffering from shock.'

They heard voices outside the office and Dylan came in followed by a tall man with greying hair. The man was dressed in blue chinos, white shirt and an expensive-looking jacket. He had a haughty feeling about him.

'What on earth's going on?' he asked. 'I've had a hard job persuading the police to let me in. Something about a murder?'

Abigail looked sombre and Hillary looked away. They could do without this. Edward Brown was chair of the board of trustees at the Courthouse and always took a rather severe approach to the staff who worked there, those paid and volunteering.

'Mr Brown,' said Abigail, 'it's true. A body has been found here in the Courthouse building. In fact, I found it this morning. It was in the heritage cell upstairs.'

Brown looked very grave. 'Good Lord! No wonder the police were reluctant to let me through.'

'Yes, we've got two detectives here from the Harrogate station and one of them is that Detective Chief Inspector Oldroyd. I've seen him several times on television.'

Brown ignored this. 'Someone must have broken in here.'

Abigail explained that there was no sign of a break-in.

'What? Does that mean someone here at the Courthouse was involved?'

'I'm sure that's not the case,' said Abigail.

'Then someone has been lax in the care of their keys. Has anyone reported keys stolen?'

'That's what the police asked me but no, they haven't.'

Brown shook his head, looking irritated. 'We can do without this kind of thing happening. It doesn't do anything for our reputation. Where are the police?'

'They've gone to get some lunch. They'll be back soon and will want to talk to you as you are a key holder for the Courthouse.'

'OK, I'll stick around. I wish I'd come earlier but I've been doing some shopping. I assume the press have been on to it?'

'Yes, the chief inspector spoke to them earlier.'

'You say the victim's name was Tony Lowell?'

'Yes.'

Brown shook his head. 'It doesn't ring a bell. Why was he brought here?'

'I think the police are asking the same thing,' said Dylan.

Brown looked around at them all. 'Well, you've had a difficult time this morning. The centre is shut so I think it would be better if you all go home and leave the police to me. I've got to stay here and wait so I'll deal with any calls or enquiries. When I've spoken to the police, I'll close the office for the day.'

'That might prove difficult,' said Abigail. 'I'm expecting calls from various people, about engagements here at the Courthouse – and I've got other work to do.'

'Never mind,' Brown said. 'You've had a bad shock, and you should be at home. There's nothing that can't wait until tomorrow. I'm sure you could do some work from home if necessary. Things will be difficult here for a while and we're obviously going to be closed to the public. I'll deal with the media. I'm used to that, and we need to protect our reputation.'

Abigail was not happy. She felt that she was being sidelined and that Brown was somehow blaming the staff at the Courthouse for what had happened. But given that he was chair of the board, she didn't feel that she could say anything else. She was about to head home when Oldroyd walked into the office.

'Good afternoon.' Brown introduced himself to the inspector. 'I understand you want to speak to all the people who are key holders here. That would include me.'

'I see, well, let's go over to our incident room. I think you know it as the robing room,' said Oldroyd with a smile as he led Brown across the little courtyard. His smile was not returned. Brown retained a severe expression on his face.

'What exactly is your role here?' asked Oldroyd as they sat at the table in the robing room.

'The arts centre is a charity, mostly run by volunteers, including those of us on the board of trustees. The only people paid a salary are Abigail Wilson as the centre manager, plus the other two people you saw there, Dylan Hardy and Hillary Sands, who are part-time. It's the job of the trustees to supervise and monitor the activities and the management of the place. As chair of the board, I have a key to the centre. I'm sure Abigail will give you a full list but, as far as I'm aware, it's only Abigail, myself and Hillary who are the official key holders.'

'Right,' said Oldroyd, looking thoughtful.

Brown frowned. 'Does that mean we're all suspects, Chief Inspector?'

'Yes,' replied Oldroyd bluntly. 'It's very early stages, but we have to explain how the murderer got in here and left leaving the door locked. They must have had a key. None of you seem like murderers, but then I've had to arrest a lot of people over the years for murder who didn't seem at all likely to be killers.'

Brown nodded. 'I'm sure.'

'So where were you last night?' asked Oldroyd.

'At home all evening. My wife can vouch for me.'

'OK. We'll need statements from you both. Did you hear who the victim was?'

'Apparently a chap called Tony Lowell. I've never heard of him.'

'And have you got your keys to this place? They haven't gone missing?'

Brown produced a set of keys from his pocket. 'No, here they are. I always bring them with me when I visit the Courthouse.'

'OK, now I'm sure you understand that it will be a little while before you can open the Courthouse again to the public. The forensic team are still going over the cell, the entrance and the steps. Once they have finished, people can enter those areas again, but that cell where the body was found will still be taped off.'

'I understand and I'm sure everyone was expecting it.'

~

Steph found Westwood's estate agents in Guiseley quite easily. They were on the Main Street, not far from the police station. There were three people in the office: two agents and a manager. Steph showed her warrant card and explained why she was there. The manager introduced himself and locked the outer door. They all gathered around Steph.

'It was shocking news about Tony. I don't think any of us can believe it,' said the manager, a portly man in his late thirties sporting a moustache.

His colleagues nodded in clear agreement.

'How did you find him to work with?' Steph asked.

'Tony was a good colleague, but he wasn't the easiest person to get to know,' said one of the agents, a young woman smartly dressed in a blue trouser suit and white shirt.

'In what way?' asked Steph.

'He never told you much about himself. I knew he was married and lived in Menston and that's about it. He never talked about personal stuff, and he kept his feelings to himself. I didn't get the impression that he had any friends. He never mentioned anyone, at least.'

'Do you think he had any enemies?'

'Not to my knowledge.' She looked at the others for confirmation.

'Unless it was about something that happened in the past,' said the third person, a young man with ginger hair and freckles. 'I once asked him about what he'd done before he came to work for us. It was the only time I've seen him angry. He told me to mind my own business. It seemed odd.'

'What did he tell you about his past employment history when he came for the job?' Steph asked the manager.

'He'd had some recent experience with another estate agent in Leeds. He wanted to move out here because it was nearer to home. He didn't say anything about any jobs before that. He had a good reference, so I gave him the job. I thought it was a basic position for somebody of his age and I did wonder what other things he'd done in the past; he was well into his forties. But I had all the information I needed, and he proved to be a good member of the team. I decided that what he'd done or where he'd been in the past was his own business. It didn't affect his work.'

'Had he been behaving at all strangely recently?'

'No,' said the manager. 'I suppose, in retrospect, Tony behaved like a man who was lying low. He didn't want to draw attention to himself. I agree with Alan here – this could all be about something related to his past life, but what, I've no idea.'

∿

After he'd spoken to Brown, Oldroyd asked Abigail Wilson and Hillary Sands about their keys to the Courthouse. They both had possession of them and had solid alibis for the night before. At this stage it seemed very unlikely that anyone at the Courthouse was involved in the murder.

Oldroyd was sitting in the incident room waiting for Steph to return when his phone rang. When he answered it, he heard a familiar and chilling voice, which froze him to his core.

'Ah, Chief Inspector Oldroyd, the great man. And how are you this fine day?'

It was very unsettling, but Oldroyd was determined to show that he was not rattled. 'Adam Blake,' he said, keeping his tone even. 'It's been a long time, but I would be lying if I said it was good to hear from you. I have to congratulate you on an ingenious escape from prison. How did you manage it? You must have had help.'

Blake laughed. 'Nice try,' he said. 'A man like me has friends all over the place.'

'Including in the prison?'

'You're wasting your time, Chief Inspector.'

'OK. Well, what do you want?'

'I thought I would just check in with you before things progress any further.'

'Very thoughtful.'

Blake laughed again. 'Yes. I think it's only polite to tell you about what's going to happen.' His tone suddenly changed and became much less jocular. 'Don't think I've forgotten who put me in that prison where I've rotted for all these years.'

'I was just doing my job,' said Oldroyd calmly. He was determined not to say anything to provoke Blake.

'Yes, but the problem was that you were too effective for your own good. It will be a great loss for the West Riding Police . . . but what you did to me has to be avenged, I'm afraid. Remember what I said to you after my so-called trial.'

'I do remember and thank you for informing me,' said Oldroyd, continuing with the surface politeness of the exchange. 'Can I ask you something before you go?'

'I may not answer.'

'OK. Have you been involved in any crimes since you escaped? I'm thinking particularly of murder.'

'Oh! Sounds like you're on a case. Interesting. Is it a difficult one? Not as difficult as mine, I bet, but I'm afraid I'm not about to assist you in your work. You'll have to figure it all out for yourself using that massive brain of yours. So, goodbye for now. When we meet, things will not be so genial. And don't bother tracing this call, I'm using a burner phone.'

Before Oldroyd could reply, Blake laughed again and the call was ended. He frowned and his hand shook a little as he placed the phone back into his pocket. How had Blake managed to get his number? It showed how resourceful and clever he was. Neither he nor Blake had mentioned Oldroyd's family. That didn't mean that they were safe. Blake knew that the best way to hurt Oldroyd was through the people he loved, though that would never be satisfying enough in itself. In the end he would come for the man who had put him away. Blake had always been about the personal touch. He didn't kill from a distance. He liked to be in the room with his victims.

When Steph arrived back at the Courthouse, she found her boss sitting at the table deep in thought.

'Did you find anything significant at the estate agent's?' he asked.

'Only things that confirm what we already suspect. Lowell had worked there for three years. They described him as a quiet character and a good employee who got on with everyone. It's all come as a great shock to them. He wasn't a man who appeared to have any enemies, but not many friends either.'

'Right.'

'They did say that he was very secretive about his past, so we're probably right in thinking that his murder is connected to something that happened a while ago.'

Oldroyd didn't reply.

Steph looked at him, concerned. 'Are you all right, sir? You seem a bit distracted.'

Oldroyd sighed and told her about the call from Blake.

'Bloody hell, sir! How did he get your number?'

'I've been wondering that myself. I've already informed the station. They'll have people getting what information they can using his number, but we know he's cunning enough to make sure it won't lead us anywhere.'

'It sounds as if he is serious after all, sir. I know you said that Superintendent Walker thought that Blake might not be interested in pursuing you after all this time. I think he was trying to reassure you. But maybe you should step back and stay safe until he's caught.'

Oldroyd looked at her with a grim expression and shook his head. 'No. I'm not going to allow him to interfere with our work. That's what he wants me to do; to go into hiding or something, and show that I'm scared of him.'

'OK, sir.' Steph was not sure about the wisdom of this, but didn't feel that she could challenge him. She suspected that Oldroyd's partner, Deborah, would have more to say.

'Anyway, we'd better get on with things. I'm going to give Andy a ring and then I'll go over to Bingley and see if I can find this cycling club that Lowell was a member of. I'd like you to check with DC Hall how the routine stuff is going, taking statements and things like that. From there, I'll probably go home. As you can understand, I need to speak to Deborah about this Blake business.'

'Absolutely, sir. I'll look after things here, no worries.'

~

'I'm sorry to hear that, sir. What a bastard!'

At the Harrogate station, Andy had received a call from Oldroyd as he was driving over to Airedale, telling him about the contact from Blake.

'Yes, not a pleasant individual. He's very polite, even charming, but that just makes him all the more sinister when you know what he's capable of.'

'It does seem as if he's targeting you, then, sir.'

'So it would appear. But a lot of it is bravado, trying to scare me. I don't know whether he would actually have the guts to come for me. He's a coward, really. His victims were all elderly women.'

Andy was concerned that his boss was not taking the threat from Blake sufficiently seriously. 'We still have to take it as a genuine threat, sir. Superintendent Walker has instructed me to help Inspector McNiven at Stansfield to track Blake down. He'll be even more worried when he hears this.'

'I'll give him a quick call to tell him about it. Blake's a clever and very devious psychopath, so I wish you the best of luck with finding him.'

'Thanks. Well, look after yourself, sir. I'm going to speak to the press this afternoon. It's the first time I've led a press conference, but I've learned a lot watching you.'

Oldroyd laughed. 'You'll be fine. Remember you're in charge and don't let them push you into saying anything you don't want to say; stay good humoured and banterous – it's not a good thing to get angry with them, it shows you're insecure. You want to keep them on your side as much as you can, but you have to stay a few steps ahead and show that they can't get one over you.'

'OK, sir. Thanks for the tips.'

Two

The Chevin is a long, steep, wooded ridge above the town of Otley. The name may derive from a word similar to the old Welsh 'cefn' meaning 'ridge of high land' and could be a survivor of the now extinct Cumbric language once spoken in parts of northern England and southern Scotland. It was closely related to Welsh, Cornish and Breton. The Chevin has a number of footpaths and bridleways, and is popular with walkers, runners and riders.

It was late in the afternoon by the time the press conference took place at Harrogate station. Andy was keen to do well leading his first important news conference. Accompanied by DCs Sharon Warner and Alan Hardiman, he entered the room to face the reporters. There was a high level of curiosity amongst the representatives of the press who had turned up – though some suspected they knew the reason for this briefing.

'Sergeant, is this to do with the escape of Adam Blake from Stansfield Prison?' one of them called out pre-emptively.

'Correct,' replied Andy, determined not to be put off his stride. 'Blake escaped three days ago and at present there is no information about where he might be. However, we believe that it is likely that he will come to this area.'

There were some expressions of surprise at this.

'Why's that, then, Sergeant?' called out the same reporter.

'When he was sentenced, Blake made very serious threats against Chief Inspector Oldroyd – the investigating officer who brought him to justice. We believe that it is possible that Blake may try to attack Chief Inspector Oldroyd, which is why we will be searching for him in this area. And we are asking the public to be vigilant. If they see anything unusual, they should report it to us. We will be issuing a photograph of Blake, but it is likely that he will have adopted a disguise after escaping from prison.'

'Do you think he's a threat to members of the public?' asked a reporter from a local paper.

This was always a difficult issue to deal with, as Andy had learned over the years from watching his boss lead press conferences. If you were too alarmist, you ran the risk of creating panic. But if you didn't warn people, and then something happened, you were in trouble.

'Blake is dangerous and should not be approached,' he said. 'But there is no evidence that he will target members of the public at random. I repeat, people should remain alert and report any suspicious activity to us.'

'Is Chief Inspector Oldroyd going into hiding?' asked a lady with a microphone.

This was a question Andy knew he needed to avoid. 'I have nothing to say about the whereabouts or activities of Chief Inspector Oldroyd. The reason for that is obvious.'

'Have you anything to say about how Blake managed to escape?'

Another one to avoid. 'No. All questions on that should be addressed to Stansfield Prison, and to the police in Stansfield.'

Afterwards, Andy was quite pleased at how it had gone. He felt he had handled it well and dealt successfully with the difficult questions.

'You did really well, Sarge,' said Sharon Warner, who knew Andy had been nervous beforehand. 'It could have been DCI Oldroyd standing there.'

'That's what I was thinking, too – well done, Sarge,' said Hardiman.

Andy laughed. 'I don't know about that, but thanks.'

They made their way back into the building and into the general office where Warner had a workstation. 'I'd like you to make a start by doing some research into Blake,' said Andy. 'There should be lots of information – it was a notorious case. See if you can find anything that might give us a clue as to where he might be now.'

'Anything in particular, Sarge?'

'Well, we know he had links with this area. This was where most of his crimes took place. Could there be somebody who's hiding him? Also, he was good at changing his identity and his appearance. Did he have a favourite way of disguising himself? The slightest clue might be helpful.'

'OK, Sarge.'

Andy called DCS Walker to report back. 'Inspector McNiven is pleased that we're helping, sir. I held a press conference on his recommendation, and I think it went well. I got the message across about being vigilant without getting them too worried. We've distributed a photo of Blake, which should be in all the local media.'

'Good. I've arranged for there to be a police presence at DCI Oldroyd's house in New Bridge. He doesn't like it, but he's got no choice, especially after that phone call from Blake – the nerve of the man.'

'I know, sir.'

'All you can do now is wait for any tip-offs from people who've seen something, unless you can locate someone in the area who has links with Blake, which would be the obvious starting point. It might be worth talking to people involved with the criminal community; sometimes they hear things on the underworld grapevine. But it's difficult; he may not come anywhere near this area. He knows we're looking for him.'

'Don't worry, sir, we're on it.'

'Good lad,' concluded Walker.

∼

Oldroyd drove through Menston and on to winding country roads lined with stone walls, over Hawksworth Moor to the town of Bingley in Airedale. He had an officer from the Otley station with him. The extra security annoyed him but he knew that he had to accept it if he was going to continue to work on this case and not go into hiding. The route afforded magnificent views over Airedale which Oldroyd would normally have enjoyed, but today he was too preoccupied with the murder in Otley and the threat from Adam Blake.

He had found the Airedale cycling club on Google Maps and parked at its headquarters at the Sports Club on the outskirts of the town. Passing playing fields and squash courts, he found a door marked *Airedale Cycling,* on which Oldroyd knocked, hoping to find someone there. For the first time that day he was in luck as the door was opened by a lean, athletic-looking man in cycling shorts and a helmet.

Oldroyd and the officer produced their warrant cards. 'We're looking for Richard King – or any member of this club.'

'I'm Richard King. What can I do for you?'

Oldroyd explained about the murder of Tony Lowell.

49

'What? Tony? I can't believe it. He was a good member. Come in,' said Richard. He took off his helmet and shook his head.

Oldroyd followed him into a storage room, where they continued their conversation amongst bikes, wheels, tyres, helmets and other pieces of cycling equipment.

'I'm afraid it's not very comfortable in here. We use this as a store and repair shop. Some members leave their bikes as they think it's safer than leaving them in the open.'

'You said Lowell was a good member of the club?'

'Yes, he turned up regularly and was always ready to help out. He was a keen cyclist.'

'And did he get on well with the other members?'

Richard shrugged. 'As far as I know. Tony was fairly quiet and inoffensive. He didn't have a lot of conversation, but he listened to other people. He never said much about himself.'

'Right. Did it ever strike you as odd that he came right over here from Menston to join a cycle club? I mean, the area around Menston and Otley is famous for cycling. He could have joined a club much nearer to home.'

'I suppose he could. To be honest I've never really considered it. We welcome members wherever they come from in this area – you don't have to live in Bingley.'

'Did he ever say anything about his past? His family or anything like that?'

'Very little. We knew he was married and worked at an estate agent's office, that was about it. But people in a club like this don't talk much about that kind of stuff; it's all bikes and competitions and kit. You know what I mean.'

Oldroyd smiled. 'Yes. When was the last time you saw him?'

'He was at the meeting last weekend. We cycled up to Skipton, and then to Malham and back. We had a great day.'

'Was he his usual self? Did he seem worried about anything?'

Richard shook his head. 'You could ask the other members about Tony. They might know things I don't . . . but as far as I remember, he was just his normal self that day.' He paused. 'I'm really sorry it was his last trip with us. The other club members will feel the same, I'm sure.'

As he drove back to the Otley station, Oldroyd reflected that this trip into Airedale had not revealed anything new, but it had seemed to confirm certain things. It seemed clearer than ever that Lowell was a character who didn't say much or draw attention to himself. Did he join the club in Airedale because he needed to lie low in the Wharfedale area around Otley? If so, what was he trying to avoid? And where might Adam Blake fit into the picture? If they knew the answers to these questions, Oldroyd would be a lot further on in the investigation, and maybe even able to shake his worries about when or where Blake might try to take his long-promised revenge.

∾

When Hillary Sands left the Courthouse that afternoon, she walked into the centre of Otley where her husband Jeremy ran an antiques shop in a narrow lane off Market Square. The shop was crammed with a cornucopia of chairs, lamps, crockery, pictures, walking sticks, mirrors, brasswork, cutlery, wooden boxes and ornaments. There was scarcely room to walk around. Jeremy was dressed in a grey suit with a waistcoat and a tie. He felt that this added to the old-fashioned atmosphere of the shop.

Hillary had been frantically texting him all morning with news about the terrible events at the Courthouse, and she was glad to be able to talk to him about it in person.

'How is everybody over there?' asked Jeremy, who had brewed some tea at the back of the shop. He served it in vintage Wedgwood china cups with saucers. Jeremy was especially keen on fine china. Food and drink served in modern ceramics was an anathema to him and he said it ruined his appreciation of a meal.

Hillary thought this was ridiculous, although she had to concede that fine china seemed to improve the flavour of tea. She took a sip but as soon as she thought about what had happened, she became nervous and jumpy again. The cup rattled on the saucer.

'Are you OK?'

'Yes. It's just that I keep remembering Abigail's face when she came down and told us about discovering the body. She's been amazing. It must have been a terrible shock. Then we've had the police all over the place throughout the day.'

'That's tough. It's the last thing you expect in an arts centre, isn't it?'

'Yes – and then that Edward Brown poked his nose in. We could have done without that.'

'You've never liked him, have you?'

'No, and you know why.'

'That was a long time ago though, wasn't it? And you don't know exactly what his involvement was. He always seems a genial bloke to me, always ready to be of assistance. You need people like that at a time like this.'

Hillary drank some more tea and looked straight ahead. 'Maybe,' she said. 'Another thing that Abigail told me was that someone had written the word – oh, what was it now? Yes – *vindicta,* on the murdered man's forehead.'

'Revenge?' Jeremy looked puzzled. 'That's a macabre thing to do, but what about it?'

'What if the revenge was for something that happened . . . you know?'

'That's a big jump, Hillary. There's no evidence that this murder had any connection with all that stuff in the past.'

'No, but it's a bit weird, isn't it? It's made me think about it all again.'

Jeremy frowned. 'Well, be careful,' he said. 'I heard on the news this morning that a dangerous killer has escaped from prison in Stansfield. That's not far from here. Maybe he was the one who put the body in the Courthouse.'

Hillary raised her eyebrows, but was not convinced. 'I don't know; it sounds a bit far-fetched to me.'

'Well, anyway,' said Jeremy, deciding to distract her from the horror of her experience that morning, 'look at this mahogany Edwardian bedroom chair. I bought it from a chap who came in this morning. It's in beautiful condition.'

~

'Jim!' said Oldroyd's partner, Deborah, when he arrived back at their house in New Bridge. She gave him a big hug and looked at him carefully, alert for any sign of worry in his features, no matter how hard he might try to hide it. 'How are you? It's an awful thing. Imagine allowing that man to escape – what were they thinking?'

Oldroyd gave her a kiss. The welcome was typical of her: strong, selfless, thinking only of him, even though she knew that she could also be a target.

'I don't think they were thinking much at all, and that's the problem. But I'm OK,' he said. 'How are you? How do you feel about police officers being around?' When he drew up outside the house, he'd seen a stationary police car and gone over to thank the officers.

'Well, I suppose it's a good thing that they are there. It makes me feel secure.' She smiled. 'And they are quite nice young men to have around. I can stay here for a while and warn my clients to expect a police presence. That might put some of them off but not all. It's you I'm concerned about. You ought to stay here with me, until they catch this man. But I know you won't want to.'

Oldroyd looked away. It was a big dilemma. He wondered if maybe, after all, he should drop out of the Otley investigation and stay at home in case Blake really did come for those Oldroyd cared about. But he didn't want Blake to win by believing he had him running scared.

As if reading his thoughts, Deborah continued while eyeing him suspiciously. 'Don't make it into some macho thing between you and him. That will not be helpful, Jim. Remember, he's got nothing to lose. He's going back to prison when they catch him, whatever happens. So don't try to prove anything.'

Oldroyd held up his arms. 'You're right. I have to be careful not to make it personal. But this case in Otley needs me. It's a tricky one.'

Deborah frowned at him and continued to speak very directly. 'That might be the case, but you're not indispensable. Someone else could solve it. You're not going to let your ego interfere with your judgement, are you?'

'No, but remember that when I'm on duty I've effectively got a police guard all the time. Blake's not going to risk attacking me in those circumstances. I'm probably as safe at work as anywhere else. There's also the possibility that Blake may have had a hand in the Otley murder. It really should be me who sees the case through.'

'Hmm,' murmured Deborah sceptically as she put her hand on her hip. 'Well, I can see you're not going to change your mind. I just hope you know what you're doing.'

Oldroyd winced. One of the many things he loved about Deborah was the fact that she understood what his job involved. He didn't like to think that her acceptance was being strained.

'Anyway,' she said. 'Come inside, I'm starving. I've made some burritos.'

He smiled, and followed her into the kitchen. Unlike Oldroyd, Deborah was vegetarian, so there'd be no meat in the wrap, but he was quite happy to follow this diet though he often had meat when they ate out.

While they were eating, they discussed what kind of activities they could do in their new circumstances.

'We're not going to barricade ourselves in the house,' said Deborah. 'We'll have a police escort when we go out.' She had a sip of her wine. 'I don't know whether you'll be keen, but Agatha Christie's *The Mousetrap* is on at Harrogate Theatre. It's so famous and I've never seen it. What do you think? Is it too much like a busman's holiday for you?'

Oldroyd took a moment to answer. He was enjoying the spicy bean filling in his wrap and the melted cheese topping. Deborah was a very good cook. He did some cooking himself, but his repertoire was limited compared to hers. He finished chewing a mouthful before replying. 'No, I love watching some of the old classics and I haven't seen that one either, even though it's been on in London – hasn't it? For something like seventy years? Who knows? I might get some ideas.'

Deborah laughed. 'Well, she was one of the most successful writers of all time and knew a thing or two about crime puzzles, so maybe you will. I'll call tomorrow and book the tickets for Saturday. By the way, how did Louise and Robert react to the news about Blake?'

'I couldn't get through to Louise. I think she'll call me back tonight. Robert was very sanguine about it. It's incredibly unlikely Blake will try to track down my son in Birmingham, if he even knows I have a son. I think growing up as the offspring of a detective has made Louise and Robert less disconcerted by things like this. They've always known that something along these lines could happen.'

'That must have been difficult for them when they were growing up.'

'Maybe. Like all children whose parents have potentially dangerous jobs, I suppose. But they seem to have come out of it pretty well. These burritos are fantastic by the way, I've—' Oldroyd's phone rang. He jumped a little, worried for just a moment that it would be Blake again. The police were now monitoring his phone to see if they could trace any of Blake's calls. He made a big effort to remain calm in front of Deborah.

'I'll bet that's Louise.' He looked at the screen and saw that it was.

'So, what kind of a mess have you got yourself into now, Dad?'

It was nice to hear her voice. She didn't seem to be much concerned about the message that he'd left, which had warned her to take special care. Louise managed a refuge for women who were the victims of violence. She was also involved in research at one of the London universities and had completed a master's. Oldroyd was very proud.

'I'm pleased to hear that you're taking it so calmly, love, but there is a threat that you have to take seriously.'

He explained about Blake's escape and intimidation, as well as his current case.

'I saw that on the news and also about the murder in Otley. What on earth is going on there?'

'That's a tricky case, but it's Blake who's truly dangerous. You know that criminals like him may attack families as a way of hurting their real target. I think it's very unlikely that Blake will even try to track you down at that distance, but I have to warn you about it.'

'Well, thanks, Dad,' said Louise with an edge of jokey sarcasm. 'What it is to have a famous detective as a father.'

'We were just talking about that. I'm sorry.'

'Oh, don't worry. Robert and I got a lot of status at school with you on the telly and investigating awful crimes.'

Oldroyd laughed. 'Well, I'm glad there were some advantages.'

'Yes. I'm more concerned about you and Deborah than myself and Robert.'

'Well, don't be. We've got special protection until they catch him, and when I'm at work I've got police officers with me all the time. Anyway, how are you?'

They spent a while catching up with what had been happening in their lives. Louise was as busy as ever; economic conditions were leading to greater hardship in the city, family breakdown and violence against women. Oldroyd knew that her experience meant she understood the danger of Adam Blake being at large and would be unlikely to take any unnecessary risks.

'Bye for now, then, and keep up the good work,' said Oldroyd finally. 'And look after yourself.'

'I will, Dad. Bye.'

∼

In the centre of Otley there is a pedestrianised network of narrow cobbled streets full of cafés and independent shops. There are some small older houses down short alleyways, and Dylan Hardy lived here in a comfortable little terraced house built in the 1840s. He found it a very convenient location as he could walk almost everywhere he needed to go and hardly used his car. There was a regular bus service if he wanted to go into Leeds, or Bradford, or even further down the dale to Ilkley.

Dylan was in his late thirties and had never married or had a long-term partner. There were a number of reasons for this, but one of the main ones was that he was an artist and wanted to spend a lot of time on his paintings. His part-time work at the Courthouse earned him just enough to pay his rent and enable him to live frugally. He also earned some money selling his paintings and doing a small amount of teaching at an adult education centre. It was not a lifestyle compatible with family life, but it suited him.

It had been a long day, and he was pleased that it was darts night at the favourite of his many local pubs – The Star and Garter. Darts night was one of the few social events in his life. The Market Square was quiet as he walked to the pub in the early evening, just as the sun had set. Inside, it was warm and bustling. The Star and Garter was not much of a pub for food; it specialised in good beer and traditional pub games: dominoes, darts and quizzes. There was a TV room with a huge screen for watching sport.

He went to the bar. The darts match was not for another half-hour which gave him time to get a drink in first. As he was taking the first swig from his pint of bitter, he noticed Scott Evans, the decorator, a little further down the bar, so he went to have word with him.

'Hi, Scott. Sorry you couldn't get into the Courthouse today. Did you manage to fill your time?'

Scott was his usual cheery self, sitting on a bar stool, holding his pint glass. 'Yeah, no problem. I had some other jobs that I brought forward. What a bloody carry-on at the Courthouse though, wasn't it? Police all over the place upstairs, entrance cordoned off. Never thought anybody would be murdered like that in Otley.'

'I know. It's going to be a while before the Courthouse gets back to normal.'

'There's a rumour going round that the murder is something to do with the fact that people were in prison at the Courthouse. You know, it's a way of getting back at the place.'

'I could understand that if the victim – this Lowell fella – had something to do with the law, maybe even worked at the

Courthouse in the old days. But I don't think he did, did he? No one seems to know much about him.'

'Who knows? I haven't met anybody who knew him.'

'I suppose that makes it more mysterious. Anyway, it's early days. Are you back in tomorrow?'

'If they will allow me, yes. Still got quite a bit to do. How about you?'

'We're not going back in until Monday. There's nothing happening there and we've been given time off to recover from the shock.'

'In the pub – best way of recovering,' laughed Scott as he finished his pint. 'Can I get you another?'

'No, thanks,' said Dylan. 'The darts team are here. If I drink too much too quick my aim will be well off.'

∾

Next morning, Andy and Steph were having breakfast in their flat in the centre of Leeds, overlooking the River Aire. Andy had nipped out early to buy sourdough and fresh pastries from a local bread co-op. It was a bit of a joke between them that they were paying four quid for a trendy loaf, but they really did appreciate the flavour. It was another warm, sunny morning. The weather seemed to be in an Indian summer phase. As they ate, they were gazing out over the river and watching gulls flying over the water, which still had a hint of early morning mist on the surface. They were also talking about the work they were doing.

'So, I'm working with the boss, and you're trying to keep him safe,' said Steph between mouthfuls of almond croissant. 'Strange, isn't it?'

'It's odd that the body was found in Otley just after Blake escaped from prison. Does the boss think there's any connection?'

Steph shook her head. 'It's early days. We haven't found anything to directly link the victim with Blake but I think we will. It just seems too much of a coincidence that someone is murdered like this just after Blake escapes. How about you?'

'I don't like manhunts. I was involved in quite a few at the Met. There's nothing solid; the person you're looking for could be anywhere and you could never search all possible hiding places. You have to rely on information coming in from the public. A lot of that leads to nothing and you end up wasting time. It's a frustrating business.'

'Not to worry. It's great that Superintendent Walker chose you to lead the hunt in the Harrogate area.'

'I think it was partly because all his inspectors are busy.'

'Maybe, but you should still feel good about it.'

He smiled at her. 'Yes, I do. And we're going to do our best to find him.'

'Have you any idea where you're going to start?'

'I've got Sharon Warner tracking down old associates – seeing if anyone who might have had reason to help him is still in the area. I mean, if he's targeting the boss, he'll need help to do that. But at the same time he has to know we'll be looking, so it's possible he could take a different approach.' Andy sighed. 'That's why it's so difficult.'

'I'll bet you're enjoying the freedom to do your own thing a bit and make some decisions at least?'

'Yeah, that feels good. You realise you've learned a lot over the years.' He shook his head and smiled at her. 'Anyway, how are you getting on?'

'Not much progress so far. It's the opposite of cases where the victim had lots of enemies where you have plenty of people with a motive and lots of leads to follow up. We've not found any suspect with a reason to kill the victim so far. We're in the same position as you, really.'

Andy gathered up the plates and cups. 'Right, well, we'd better go and get on with it then.'

~

In the pretty village of Burley, between Otley and Ilkley, Frances Hughes was watching a morning news bulletin on the television. She'd heard about the murder in Otley the day before and wondered if there was any more information about it. She was a volunteer at the Courthouse. She and her husband lived in a beautiful cottage surrounded by immaculate gardens. Frances had her gardening clothes on: checked brushed cotton shirt, down gilet and a pair of walking trousers. She went for the smart-casual-but-very-expensive country look, even when she was gardening, and bought most of her clothes in independent shops in and around Ilkley. She and her husband Malcolm had retired from their careers in the care industry. They had once owned three care homes in the area, but they had all now been sold. They were both enthusiastic gardeners, especially now they had the time to do everything properly. Malcolm was already outside planting up some pots of winter pansies and shortly she was going to join him.

After the national news came a local bulletin, which featured a piece about the murder of Tony Lowell, including a photograph of the victim. Frances was thinking about what an awful thing it was when the picture came on to the screen. Something immediately struck her about the image. She looked hard at it and frowned. Surely it couldn't be? The photograph disappeared after a few moments, cutting back to the studio, but Frances was certain about what she had seen.

61

She opened her computer and searched the website of a local newspaper. The same photograph was there in an article about the murder. She stared at the screen for a long time. She recognised him, despite the changes he'd made to his appearance. Now he had been found dead in an old police cell at the Courthouse. It was very strange, and it could have very serious implications. She had lived for many years with the feeling at the back of her mind that, one day, something like this might happen. Memories that she'd buried for so long came swarming back. They gave her a sick feeling. And now she had a dilemma: should she go to the police and tell them what she knew or not?

She sat thinking about it for so long that she completely forgot about the gardening, and Malcolm came looking for her. 'I wondered what you were doing,' he said in his cheerful manner. 'Come on, it's a lovely morning out there and I've got to leave soon.'

'It's OK, I'm on my way,' she replied. Malcolm knew nothing about what had happened in the past and she preferred to keep it that way. She put her hands to her face and sighed. She couldn't go to the police; it was too dangerous, and they had all promised to keep what had happened to themselves.

She knew there was someone else she ought to speak to, but again she was very reluctant for the same reason: it would lead to a messy and unpleasant raking over of the past. Something she would definitely prefer to avoid.

∾

Oldroyd, Steph and Andy met up at Harrogate Police HQ before continuing on their separate investigations. Steph was going to drive Oldroyd over to Otley in a police car for greater security. He would have an officer with him now at all times.

'If Blake were to come over to this area,' asked Andy, 'do you have any idea where he might go and who might hide him?'

Oldroyd shook his head. 'Not really. He doesn't come from round here; he was brought up in York. His classic operating area was a bit further to the east. There was no evidence that he had any accomplices in his crimes. He wasn't married and had no family, so it's hard to say who might harbour him.' He pointed a finger at Andy. 'But I'll tell you what might be worth doing. He's been in prison for a few years now and he may well have been making friends in there. Friends that could be useful to him. He's certainly managed somehow to get people to organise his escape. So if you were to look at who has been in prison with him and whether some of those people are now out and living in this area, that could be interesting.'

'Good idea, sir,' replied Andy. 'I'll get Sharon on to it.'

'Ah,' said Oldroyd with a smile. 'About Sharon . . . I was hoping that she could do a bit of research for us too. We need to find out more about the murder victim in Otley, and in particular see if there is any connection with Blake.'

Andy put his head on one side. 'I see, sir. Well, I'm sure she can do some work for both of us, even though Superintendent Walker assigned her to me.'

'Pulling rank on me, are you?!' laughed Oldroyd.

'It might be good idea if I go to speak to her, sir,' said Steph. 'It will be a bit intimidating for her if you both turn up making demands. She's still young and lacking a bit of confidence, though there's no reason for that – she's a brilliant researcher.'

'Good idea,' said Oldroyd, and Steph went through to the general office where she found the detective constable at her workstation. When Sharon had first started at Harrogate station she had been the victim of sexual harassment, and it was Steph who had taken her under her wing.

'Hi, Sarge. I thought you were with DCI Oldroyd in Otley.'

'Hi, Sharon. Yes, we're going back there shortly but we need you to do some research for us.' Steph saw a look of alarm on the young woman's face. 'I know you're already busy working with Sergeant Carter, but you're so highly regarded that lots of people want you to work for them. How good is that? And you were a star on that training course. I don't think it will be that long before you're leading some of the training yourself.'

Sharon relaxed a little on receiving these compliments but still looked a little worried. 'Oh, it's nice of you to say that, Sarge. But it makes me feel a bit under pressure, you know? What if I can't find what you're all looking for?'

'I'm sure you will,' replied Steph reassuringly. 'But if not, it doesn't mean that you're a failure. People won't think the less of you if you don't succeed all the time.'

Sharon nodded and smiled. 'Thanks, Sarge. What is it you want me to do?'

Steph explained about Tony Lowell. 'When we spoke to her, his wife was very vague about her husband's past. We don't know whether she was keeping anything from us or not. Lowell doesn't appear to have had any enemies, but it seems that something has come back to haunt him. It's not going to be easy, but see if you can connect him with any kind of illegal activity or conflict that's happened around here. It may be going back several years, maybe decades, but there has to be something.'

'OK, Sarge.'

'As far as Blake goes, Sergeant Carter asked if you could look into his past and see if anybody around here has a connection with him, any family or places he used to work. It would also be a good idea to investigate any people recently released from Stansfield Prison who are living in this area. The idea is that one of them may have befriended Blake in prison and helped to organise his escape.

Also, if he has come to this area, it may be that he's involved in this murder at Otley so the two investigations could come together.'

Sharon was scribbling notes and still looking a little daunted. 'OK, Sarge, I'll do my best.'

'Good. No one can do more than that. If you think it's too much, let me know, but I think you're more than capable of coping.'

She left, and Sharon prepared to get on with her research.

DC Alan Hardiman was working nearby. He was very fond of Sharon and liked to tease her. 'Someone I know is in the sergeant's good books.'

Sharon smiled. 'No more than you – you've also been selected to work on this case.'

'Yeah, but they don't come fussing around me and making sure I'm OK.'

'Maybe they trust you more to be able to get on and do it.'

'No, it's because I've been around longer than you. And there's no doubt you are an absolute whiz with research, Sharon. I should get you to teach me a bit some time. Where did you learn it?'

'I don't know. I've always been able to find stuff out quickly. Even when I was younger, I always booked our family holidays – found the best flights, accommodation bargains and so on. My dad used to check it all, but he never found any mistakes. The more you do this kind of work, the more you learn about the best sites and what resources there are and things like that. It's amazing what you can find out. I don't know how the police coped in the past without access to digital resources. Everything must have been so slow.'

'It was famously one of the reasons why it took so long to catch the Yorkshire Ripper. All their information was on card indexes and couldn't be properly cross-referenced. The police interviewed him nine times before he was finally arrested.' He looked at Sharon's computer screen. 'I don't think I've been on enough courses.'

Sharon laughed. 'I wouldn't worry about that. I've been on some of them. The instructors are quite old, and I knew more than them. Things often go very slow because the older staff can't deal with the newer methods.'

'Maybe you should be doing the training.'

'Sergeant Johnson mentioned the same. I don't think I'd be confident enough yet.'

'Well, you'd have practice teaching me.'

Sharon smiled. 'OK, it's a deal.'

Inspector Hamish McNiven had worked at Stansfield police station for many years. Stansfield was an ordinary, medium-sized market town north-east of Harrogate on the edge of the Vale of York. But it was also the site of a high-security prison – the presence of which was resented by some who felt that having dangerous criminals in the town was a risk to local people and also lowered the tone of the area.

Normally the prison operated entirely separately from the local police force, but the nature of Blake's escape meant new arrangements. Blake had clearly been helped by somebody on the inside and when news of what had happened reached the Home Office, officials insisted that there should be an immediate preliminary police investigation by the local force. If this proved unsatisfactory, a wider inquiry would be launched into the running of the prison and investigators from outside the area would be sent in.

McNiven was chosen to lead the initial inquiry. This placed him in a difficult position, and he expected to encounter some resistance from staff who might resent the presence of the police. The job of James Perry, the governor, was on the line and McNiven didn't expect a very warm reception from him. McNiven was also tasked with finding Blake, though the two investigations overlapped.

He was called into Perry's office on his first day at the prison. The governor was in his forties and immaculately dressed in an expensive light grey suit. He was overweight and consequently rather red in the face. McNiven, the shrewd Scottish detective, and somewhat shabbily dressed by comparison, sensed that Perry was a blusterer.

'I have to say I don't think that any of this is really necessary,' began Perry, who looked rather uncomfortable. He was aware that his handling of this crisis was already under scrutiny. 'We can manage this ourselves. It's just a question of finding out who the rotten apple is. The system as a whole is fine.'

McNiven had expected this; the 'rotten apple' defence was a classic when an organisation didn't want to admit to systemic failures. 'Maybe, but I'm sure you understand that internal inquiries often lead to the suspicion that they are biased and protecting the institution concerned. Anyway, it's out of our hands; the powers that be have decided,' replied McNiven in his crisp Edinburgh accent.

Perry frowned, realising that McNiven was a tough character, and not someone to be palmed off in any way. 'I assume, then, that you will want to speak to all the staff who had regular contact with Blake?'

'Correct, and I want to see their files, employment history and disciplinary records. The more thorough we are, the less likely there'll be any comeback later saying there was a cover-up or something.'

Perry grunted with contempt. 'The media always find something if they want to run a story.'

'Is there anyone that you suspect?' asked McNiven, ignoring this and changing the subject.

'No,' replied Perry defensively. 'I think I have an excellent staff here.'

But a staff you don't know particularly well and so were not able to pick up any warning signs, thought McNiven. He wondered how often Perry actually went around the prison and spoke to his staff.

'I think Blake intimidated someone,' Perry carried on. 'Maybe he has people on the outside who were threatening that person's family.'

'OK, we'll look for evidence of that,' said McNiven, privately thinking that this was a rather far-fetched idea. It was much more likely that money was involved and that Blake had bribed somebody to help him escape.

McNiven left Perry's office with a list of the people he needed to speak to and access to the information he wanted. It would be interesting to see what the interviews yielded.

~

Despite Edward Brown's advice to take it easy and even stay at home for a while after the traumas of the previous day, Abigail Wilson came into work, though not as early as normal. The police incident tape was still in place and there was a forensic team working in the cell where Lowell's body had been found.

The office was deserted. It was Friday, and Hillary and Dylan were taking the day off as part of a long weekend. Abigail knew that they would be back in to work on Monday. They were dedicated to the Courthouse, as were so many of the people who gave up their time to volunteer. That was why she was so confident that the arts centre would recover from this terrible event. The regular groups would come back: writers, Pilates, choir, children's groups, film society. They would not be deterred by what had happened.

She set about completing essential tasks. There were music and drama groups to book in for future concerts and performances, and she had to liaise with the person who did marketing and promotion. Also, the alcohol licence for the evening bar needed renewing. She was working her way through these jobs when the phone rang.

'Hello, Abigail, it's Frances Hughes.'

'Oh. Hi, Frances,' replied Abigail. Frances was a reliable volunteer and familiar figure at the Courthouse. Abigail had spoken to her many times, often in the evenings when Frances volunteered as a steward for an event and Abigail was doing a stint behind the bar.

'I'm really sorry to hear what happened,' continued Frances. 'It must have been a shock for you all. Who found the body?'

'I did.'

'Oh my God! That's awful!'

'It was.'

'And you found it in the cell?'

'Yes. I thought it was a homeless person sleeping there but when I touched his face it was cold.'

'So, someone had murdered this person, and then taken their body to the Courthouse?'

'It seems like it. The police don't think he was murdered here. It's a mystery. I don't think they have any idea yet about who's done it and why they brought the body here.'

'I'm sorry to be asking about this but I just can't believe it. It's such a grisly thing to find a body like that.'

'Yes. And on the victim's forehead, someone had written the word, *vindicta*.'

'What?'

'*Vindicta*, written in black marker pen. Apparently, it means revenge. Bizarre, isn't it?'

There was a pause before Hughes answered. 'It is. Don't tell me any more. I don't suppose you know when the Courthouse will reopen and things might get back to normal?'

'No, not yet. But Hillary will be back next week. She will contact you all about the situation.'

'Were Hillary and Dylan in the office with you when you discovered the body?'

'Yes.'

'Oh goodness me! Pass on my best wishes to them.'

'I will.'

'Thank you. Bye for now and take it easy – you've had a nasty shock.'

'I will, don't worry.'

≈

When the call ended, Frances sat down. The expression on her face was grim. She had succeeded in getting Abigail to tell her details about the discovery of the body and everything she had told her seemed to confirm her worst fears. Painful memories flooded her mind – things she'd repressed for many years. She had been very weak and . . . she couldn't bear to think about it. She covered her face with her hands.

Her husband, Malcolm, had gone out for the day to meet some friends in Harrogate, and wasn't expected back until the evening. But she couldn't speak to him anyway. He wouldn't understand. What was she going to do?

≈

Oldroyd and Steph arrived to find Otley bustling despite what had happened a few days ago. It was Friday – market day in the little town. The square was full of stalls selling sweets, cheeses, fruit and veg, pies and flowers. In former eras, market day had been a time for buying and selling animals and the many pubs in the town had needed a licence to stay open later in the afternoon when Britain had restrictive opening hours. The small shops and cafés around the square were also busy, including the bookshop.

'Look at that!' said Oldroyd enthusiastically as they drove past. 'The traditional town market. I used to come here with my dad years ago. He'd buy pork pies to warm up for our tea with mushy peas, and there was a sweet stall and he used to buy me torpedoes and midget gems. Then we went for a walk by the river while I ate them.'

'Very bad for your teeth, sir,' observed Steph wryly.

'Probably. Nobody bothered about kids' first teeth in those days. They just went bad, then you had them all pulled out.'

'Ugh!'

Oldroyd laughed. 'Yes . . . I think dental hygiene has progressed a bit.'

'Sounds like parents were a bit irresponsible in those days,' said Steph.

'Not really, they didn't understand. My sister and I were well looked after. I think you'll have to double back here.'

The turning to the Courthouse was cordoned off. There appeared to have been a burst water pipe, so they had to take a different route and ended up driving along Main Street. Straight ahead, above the buildings, was the steep rise of the Chevin. Oldroyd looked up and saw that about halfway up there was a tall dark Victorian Gothic-looking building amongst the colourful autumn trees. He recalled seeing this building years ago on his trips to Otley. Today there was something about it that intrigued him, but also gave him a feeling of deep unease.

~

Frances Hughes was tidying and cleaning the house as a way of taking her mind off her dilemma. It was something that she'd always done to deal with anxiety. The absence of clutter, sparkling clean surfaces and plumped cushions gave her a sense of control. It didn't last long because she kept coming back to the fact that if she was right, she ought to alert people, but it could be hugely embarrassing if she was wrong, and then long-buried things would come to light. Things that she'd promised never to say anything about. But then she'd lived with this burden for so long maybe it would be better if . . . She was still going over it all incessantly in her mind when the doorbell rang.

She was expecting a delivery, so she didn't hesitate before walking down the gleaming oak-floored hall and opening the door.

She hadn't realised that her nemesis had got so close.

~

At Harrogate station, it didn't take Sharon Warner long to find something significant regarding Adam Blake's contacts in the area. She called Andy over to her workstation to show him what she'd found.

'I've got two interesting leads for you, Sarge. First, there's a man called Philip Bryson. He served twenty years for murdering his wife and he was in Stansfield Prison in the last years of his sentence. He served at the same time as Blake. He lives here in Harrogate. There's an address on these prison records but it might be well out of date.'

'Fantastic!' exclaimed Andy. 'Well done!'

'Then there's this.' She switched pages on her computer. 'George Milton, a farmer. He was prosecuted for polluting the land

and the stream that went through it with overuse of pesticides. He refused to change his practices even after many warnings, and he made things a lot worse by resisting arrest and fighting with the police. Apparently, he brandished a shotgun at them, so he has the potential to be violent. He got six years. He was also in Stansfield at the same time as Blake.'

'Right. Amazing! Is there any address for him?'

Sharon looked at the screen. 'New Bridge Farm. It's not far from Harrogate.'

'New Bridge? That's the village where Chief Inspector Oldroyd lives. That could be a crucial link. If this Milton is hiding Blake, the situation could give him good access to DCI Oldroyd.'

Sharon was consulting a map. 'Well, the farm is on the hill above the village. It's only about a mile from the centre.'

'Is it? We need to let the chief inspector know. Thanks again, Sharon, you've done extremely well.'

'I haven't had as much luck with my research for Chief Inspector Oldroyd and Sergeant Johnson. I can't find anything significant. There are lots of people of that name – Lowell – of course, but nothing that links anybody to this area.'

'Well, keep trying. If anybody can find it, you can.'

Sharon smiled and carried on with her work.

∾

When Oldroyd and Steph finally arrived at the Courthouse it was nearly deserted compared to a normal Friday morning. Abigail Wilson came to the robing room to tell the detectives about the call from Frances Hughes.

'She's a volunteer, lives in Burley in Wharfedale,' explained Abigail. 'She rang to ask me about what's happened here, but I felt there was something not quite right. She seemed to be very interested in all the details about the body, who found it and where, but she never struck me as the kind of person who would normally take an interest in such gruesome things. There was anxiety in her voice.' She shook her head. 'Unless I'm just exaggerating all this due to the stress.'

'That's possible,' said Oldroyd. 'But I think you were right to tell us. We'll definitely pursue it. Thank you for the information.'

'It's all so quiet here, it's making me feel uneasy,' she told them. 'I'm going to go out and have a look around the market and browse round the bookshop.'

Almost as soon as Abigail had left them in the robing room, Oldroyd's phone rang – a call from Andy.

'DC Warner is already getting results, sir. She's located two released prisoners who were in Stansfield with Blake.' He explained the details. 'I don't like the sound of the second one, sir. This farmer called Milton . . . his farm is not far from where you live. If Blake is hiding there, he's too close to you for comfort.'

'Yes. Bloody hell! I must say I didn't expect this,' said Oldroyd, thinking about the possible threat to Deborah.

'Don't worry, sir, we'll be around to both properties with a search party. We'll easily get a warrant in the circumstances. Superintendent Walker is right behind us.'

'Good. Well, the best of luck with it. It'll be a great relief if you do manage to track Blake down.'

'How's the Otley investigation going, sir?'

'Slowly. We've got very little to go on. I'm hoping Sharon can discover something that helps us too.'

When the conversation ended, Oldroyd gazed into space with a sombre look on his face. He had the uncomfortable feeling that Blake was moving closer.

～

Andy drove the police car slowly up the bumpy and winding farm track to New Bridge Farm. He had two officers with him and there was another police car behind them. Some of the officers were armed. If they discovered Blake anywhere in the area, they were ready for him.

The farm was in a state of relative neglect. There were abandoned and rusty pieces of farm machinery with grass growing through them at either side of the track. There were holes in the roofs of many sheds and barns. The track ended in a yard in front of the farmhouse, which had some rotting window frames and a battered front door. An old van was parked outside.

Andy looked around the yard and at the upstairs windows of the house. Everything was quiet. He knocked on the door which, after a while, was opened by a man in his late twenties with close-cropped hair.

'Police,' announced Andy. 'We're here to speak with George Milton. Is he your father?'

'Yeah. But he won't want to speak to you. He's had a thing about the police ever since he was in prison.' He hung on to the door frame with one arm, blocking the way, as if he didn't want the police to come inside.

'He doesn't have any choice, I'm afraid; this is a serious matter. Where is he?'

The young man suddenly looked worried and nodded to his left. 'He's feeding t' pigs. He's not in trouble again, is he?'

'Not if he cooperates. Stay here,' said Andy to the other officers, and walked across to a narrow passage between two outbuildings. It was very muddy and full of animal dung, but Andy was wearing stout walking shoes. He'd long ago learned the necessity of proper footwear when you were in the countryside – particularly at farms. He smiled as he thought of his early days in Yorkshire when he would often turn up to a place like this in his smart designer shoes.

He reached a small field that was little more than a grassless, wet quagmire with some rudimentary low wooden shelters with curved corrugated iron roofs. Grunting and squealing came from a corner of the field by a gate. Black and white pigs smeared with mud huddled by some metal troughs and furiously wagged their curly little tails. A ruddy-faced, powerful man was pouring feed into the troughs. He wore a ragged mud-streaked jacket and rubber boots. His hair was wild, and he had a greyish beard.

'Mr Milton,' called Andy, stopping at the edge of the field to avoid walking into the stinking mud. The man turned towards him. 'I'm Sergeant Carter.' He held up his warrant card and Milton scowled and bared his teeth like an animal.

'What the hell do you want? I've had enough o' t' police,' he demanded as he frowned at Andy.

'We're investigating Adam Blake's escape from Stansfield Prison.'

'What the hell do I know about that?'

'Do you know where he is?'

Milton put his head back and laughed contemptuously. 'No, I bloody don't. But I wish him the best of luck in keeping away from you lot.' He turned away and continued to fill the troughs.

'I think we need to go inside,' said Andy.

'Do we? I'm busy.'

'Yes,' replied Andy, as he squared up to Milton. He was a tall and powerful man himself. 'This is a serious business. A dangerous criminal has escaped – someone you knew in prison – and we need to ask you about that. My advice is not to make things difficult for us. We already have a warrant to search your premises.' He was about to speak when Andy cut him off. 'I've got a number of officers with me, some of them armed, so don't do anything stupid. We're looking for Blake; if he's not here you've got nothing to worry about – but we have to check.'

Milton flung the warrant card back at Andy and then walked out of the field and back to the farmhouse. Andy followed. The door opened straight into a large, untidy kitchen with dirty pots piled high in a very old Belfast sink. The faded lino flooring was worn out in places, and the walls and ceiling were stained yellow by tobacco smoke. A table in the middle of the room was covered with plates of half-finished food, some of it looking very stale. The windows were filthy and the smell of tobacco smoke and congealed food hung in the air. At one end of the room, a wood fire was burning in a grate.

Milton sat down in a rocking chair at the side of the fire. Andy noticed that there was a shotgun propped against the wall behind the chair. He sat down on a wooden chair at the kitchen table. A police officer stood behind him. Milton's son lurked in another corner, leaning against the wall.

Milton rocked gently in the chair and said nothing. Andy was going to have to work hard to winkle any information out of him.

'How well did you know Adam Blake when you were in Stansfield Prison?' he began.

Milton glared as if he didn't want to answer any questions, and shrugged his shoulders. 'I knew him, not that well. He was a bit too posh for me.'

'Did you know what he was inside for?'

'Yeah, he was obviously a bit of a bastard. Unlike people like me, who should never have been there.'

'What do you mean?'

Milton snorted in disgust. 'I was just doing my job: getting the best out of the land. Then I get inspectors round saying I'm polluting the fields and the rivers.'

'I understand you were using illegal pesticides.'

Milton shrugged again. 'It all gets washed away.'

'Yes . . . into the streams and rivers. You had several warnings and refused to pay a fine. Anyway, let's not go into that. I take it you felt it was unfair for you to be sent to jail.'

'You could say that.'

'I'm wondering if it gave you a big chip on your shoulder against authority and the law?'

'So what if it did?'

'You might have been inclined to assist a prisoner to escape in order to get one over the legal system. We know Adam Blake had help when he escaped. Did you help him? Is he hiding here?' Andy had learned from Oldroyd that speaking very directly was often effective. The person being interviewed didn't expect it and was put off guard.

Milton laughed, then coughed, spat into the fire and lit a cigarette. 'And how do you think I managed to do all that?' he said between puffs. Andy winced at the acrid smell. 'I'm not a criminal, even if I went to jail. I don't have any links with the underworld or owt like that. I'm just a farmer trying to make a living.'

'Who looked after this place when you were in jail?'

'My sons.' He nodded to the young man in the corner. 'Jake and Ian. Ian's working up in the top field. We used to grow some barley up there. But if we can't deal with the pests there's no point.'

Andy wanted to ask him how he thought other farmers managed, but he desisted.

'So, you didn't form any kind of friendship with Blake?'

'No.'

'Were you aware of any plans to spring him from prison?'

Milton laughed again. 'No. But I'll say this: anyone who manages to escape like that is a clever sod and deserves a bit of freedom.'

'Even somebody like Blake? A con man and multiple murderer?'

Milton shrugged yet again.

'OK,' said Andy, and he got up from his chair. 'You're not going to like this, but my officers are going to search these premises. We have to make sure that Blake is not hiding here.'

Milton glared at Andy. He finished his cigarette, then flung the butt into the fire. 'You can look where the bloody hell you like,' he snarled, 'but you won't find anything. Anyway, I'm off back out; I've got work to do.' He walked out of the house and headed towards the pigs. His son was still lurking in the corner, but Andy ignored him, called his team together and organised the search.

Over the next hour, Andy and his team went through the house, including its gloomy cellars, and all the outbuildings, including some remote barns in fields. They had to avoid some vicious dogs, and trudge through some stinking piles of manure. Milton's son Jake followed them around, keeping his distance. Occasionally they got him to unlock a door. But the search proved fruitless. There was no sign of Blake or of anyone having stayed anywhere on the farm.

'I don't think there's anyone hiding here,' said Jake, breaking his silence. 'I'd tell you if there was. I don't want my father getting into trouble again.'

'OK,' said Andy. 'We just have to make sure.'

As they were about to leave, Milton showed up again with a satisfied smile on his face. 'Happy, then? Even though you've wasted your bloody time,' he said.

'Yes,' said Andy through gritted teeth. 'Thank you for your cooperation,' he remarked sarcastically.

~

It was a very frustrating day for Oldroyd and Steph at the Courthouse. They had no leads in the murder of Tony Lowell. Apart from his wife and work colleagues, Lowell seemed to have no connections with anyone in the area and no family. The friend he met regularly at the pub turned out to be someone who had once worked with him at the estate agent's. This man was now being checked out by a member of DC David Hall's team. Hall had taken a wide range of statements from everyone at the Courthouse, Lowell's wife and the people who worked with him. Oldroyd had pored over these statements, but they had revealed nothing.

The two detectives were sitting in their room at the Courthouse listlessly drinking tea.

'It looks as if we're waiting for Sharon Warner to come up with something,' observed Oldroyd. 'The very fact that Lowell seemed so disconnected from everything is suspicious, as if he was deliberately leading a very quiet life for some reason, unless I'm reading too much into it. He may just have been a quiet sort of chap.'

'Maybe we should consider his wife, sir,' said Steph, who had also looked at the statements. 'She's the only one without an alibi. She seemed a very quiet and inoffensive person – but that could be a front.'

Oldroyd frowned. 'I suppose you're right. But what would be her motive? Is there any evidence they weren't getting on together? Any reports of arguments or violence? Any large sums of money involved for insurance or something? Did she have a lover? Did he?'

'No evidence for any of that, sir, but we could get David Hall to talk to the neighbours and look into Lowell's will, see if we can find some kind of a motive.'

'Perhaps, but I can't imagine her taking the body to the Courthouse. If it was her, it's likely she had some help. I'm not sure she could have carried her husband's body up the stairs to that cell.'

'True.'

'It just doesn't seem likely somehow, but . . .'

Oldroyd's phone rang.

'We've been to Milton's farm, sir,' Andy said. 'He wasn't very cooperative; got a huge chip on his shoulder against the law. He felt he was unfairly treated, being sent to prison for what he did. So, there is a kind of motive there, but he's not a criminal-underworld type; can't see him organising the busting of anybody out of prison. But of course his role could be hiding Blake after his escape. His farm would be a good place to hide for anyone who wanted to stay off the radar. We searched it as thoroughly as we could, but unfortunately didn't find anything.'

'Good work, nevertheless,' Oldroyd said. 'But I understand you've got another lead?'

'Yes. We're on our way to an address in Harrogate. A bloke called Philip Bryson; he was also in Stansfield with Blake.'

'OK – best of luck with it.'

'Thanks, sir. Someone must be hiding him. I can't imagine him just living rough in a shed somewhere.'

'I agree. The problem is where.'

'Don't worry, we'll keep at it until we find him, sir.' Andy rang off.

Oldroyd was impressed. 'Well, I must say, Andy is really stepping up on this one. He seems very well organised and determined.'

'He is, sir. It's not just a question of catching Blake. Your safety is in jeopardy too,' replied Steph.

'Right,' said Oldroyd, nodding. He was genuinely moved by how much his team cared about his welfare. He was very conscious of the danger that Blake represented. It was never very far from his mind, but he was trying not to show his fear to the people in his team.

'The one thing we can do, I suppose,' he said, 'is follow up that report we had from the head of staff here about the woman who rang up and asked questions.' He grimaced. 'I'm not sure I attach much significance to it, but we might as well go and speak to her since we've nothing else to do. Ask DC Hall for the woman's address, will you?'

'OK, sir,' Steph said. But Oldroyd could still see the worry in her eyes.

~

Andy and his team drove straight from Milton's farm to an address in Harrogate. It was a small, rather neglected-looking semi-detached house in the Prioryfields estate. Andy knocked on the door, a DC beside him, hoping that they would be lucky twice and Philip Bryson would be at home.

The door was opened by a pale, thin-faced bespectacled man with straggly hair.

'Yes,' he said in a quiet voice. He had the air of a person who'd had all the vitality drained from them. Having established that they were talking to Bryson, Andy showed his warrant card and explained why they were there. Bryson rolled his eyes and beckoned the detectives in with a gesture that was weary and cynical. The sitting room into which he took them was shabby, cold and had a fusty smell, as if it had been uninhabited for a long time. The furnishings were of good quality and the room looked as if it could have once been part of a warm comfortable home, but that would have been a long time ago.

Andy and the DC sat on the sofa while Bryson sank into an armchair. He raised his thin arms, put his hands behind his head and closed his eyes as if he might fall asleep. 'Yes, I knew Adam Blake,' he said. 'Not for very long, though. I was in jail for fifteen years and was moved around to different prisons. The last one was Stansfield, where I served at the same time as Blake. I heard that he'd escaped. Just a few days ago, wasn't it?'

'How did you get on with him?'

'OK. He was friendly enough. I don't think he was the kind of person you wanted to get close to. You had to keep reminding yourself what he'd done.'

'Did you do anything to help him escape?' said Andy, taking the direct approach again.

Bryson opened his eyes. 'Why on earth would I do that?'

'Maybe you sympathised with him in some way? Or he offered you money.'

Bryson shook his head. 'I'm not sure why you think I would have any sympathy for a psychopathic murderer who preyed on defenceless women. Yes, the money would be useful. I don't have much of it, can't get a job and I'm living on meagre benefits. But I'm not somebody who would have any idea about how to organise a prison break. Do I look like that kind of person who has links with the criminal world?'

Andy had to admit that he didn't, but he wanted to probe a bit deeper.

'You served a prison sentence for murdering your wife.'

'Correct. It sounds terrible, but she was a terrible woman. At the trial nobody seemed to take into account the way she behaved. She provoked me beyond endurance: endless affairs humiliating me in front of our friends; overspending with our joint credit card; getting us into serious debt then expecting me to foot the bill. Do you want me to go on? Eventually I lost it. I stabbed her with a kitchen knife. But I called the police right after I did it. I hoped what I'd done might be regarded as manslaughter. Even my friends testified about how out of character it was.'

'But the jury didn't agree?'

'No, the more my defence pleaded provocation, the more the prosecution twisted this into evidence of why I'd planned to kill her. I was found guilty of murder. I think the judge was sympathetic towards me. He had to pass a life sentence but his recommendation of the number of years I should serve was low.'

'Even so, did you feel resentful about being found guilty of murder? Did it make you hate the system?'

Bryson laughed grimly. 'Not enough to want to help Blake get out of prison, if that's what you're driving at. Actually, the worst part of it all was how my family disowned me, even though they knew what Caroline was like. I can understand why her family might've taken against me, but even my son and daughter both sided with her. I don't think they made an effort to see it from my point of view.'

'You had killed their mother.'

Bryson shrugged. 'Yes, but she wasn't blameless. She drove me to it – and they knew it.'

'OK,' said Andy, moving on. He didn't have time to listen to a long account of how Bryson thought that he had been badly treated, but he noted that the man seemed very bitter. 'Blake is on the run. We have to search places where he might be hiding. You and he knew each other in prison. I have a warrant to search this house.' He produced it, but Bryson waved it away.

'Go ahead,' he said in the same flat tone. 'You won't find anything. I don't intend to get involved in anything criminal again. I've spent enough time in prison. When I can summon up the will and the energy, I'm going to sell this house and move away; have a fresh start.'

Andy didn't answer. He called in the rest of the team and allocated them to different parts of the house. A thorough search was conducted, but nothing was found. Andy was left frustrated with this latest blank. The threat to his boss was real, and he desperately wanted to find Blake before the man had a chance to carry out whatever twisted revenge he had planned for over a decade.

Late in the afternoon, Oldroyd and Steph arrived at Frances Hughes' house in Burley, Wharfedale.

Oldroyd had no great enthusiasm for the task of speaking to Hughes. It seemed that they were desperately following any vague semblance of a lead. He walked up to the front door, noticing the picturesque garden with the well-maintained herbaceous borders and clematis climbing over pergolas. This was the kind of effect that Deborah was aiming for in their garden at New Bridge and he had to admit that it looked good.

He knocked on the door several times without response. It was all suspiciously quiet. Then he tried the handle and the door opened. He gave Steph a surprised look but said nothing. They both went inside rather gingerly and immediately discovered signs that something was wrong. There was evidence of a struggle. A small table had been overturned and items scattered in the hallway. The most sinister sight, however, was the blood – a small pool of it on the floor.

'Good God!' said Oldroyd. 'It looks as if Abigail Wilson was right. This woman had good reason to be worried! It looks like we're too late. Get some officers over here; I'll have a check around the house.'

As Steph was on the phone, she heard a voice behind her saying, 'Hello?' She turned towards the front door.

'Who are you?' she demanded.

The man in the doorway looked shocked and puzzled. 'I'm Malcolm Hughes,' he said falteringly. 'Why are you here? Where's Frances?'

'Do you have any identification?' said Steph.

'Yes.' He fumbled for his wallet and took out his driving licence. 'I live here; I'm Frances' husband. Where is she?' His voice was rising in panic.

Steph had a quick look at the licence. 'We don't know. We've just arrived to speak to her. Obviously, something has happened here in the hallway.'

Malcolm came past Steph and noticed the blood for the first time. 'No! Frances!' He staggered back against the wall. Oldroyd returned to the hall, and he and Steph helped Malcolm into the lounge. Steph went to get him a glass of water.

'What . . . what's happened? Where is she?' asked a shocked and perplexed Hughes.

'I'm afraid we don't know anything,' said Oldroyd. 'We only arrived a few minutes ago intending to speak to your wife about a conversation she had with Abigail Wilson at the Courthouse.'

'What conversation? What are you talking about?'

'Let's leave that for the moment,' Oldroyd said, speaking gently to try to calm Hughes down. 'I take it you've been out?'

'Yes, all day, in Harrogate. I'm back a little earlier than I thought. I was expecting her to be here. Where is she?' Hughes asked for the fourth time.

'I'm sorry but can I ask you what you were doing in Harrogate?'

'Just meeting some friends.'

'And they can back you up on that?'

'Yes, what's going on? You don't think I've attacked my own wife?'

'We have to check everything. When was the last time you saw her?'

'This morning. She was in this room reading the newspaper and I said goodbye to her.' He realised the awful implications of what he'd said and suddenly burst into tears.

Steph arrived with the water. Oldroyd frowned and shook his head. He noticed a box of tissues on a coffee table, and handed one to Malcolm.

'I know this is very upsetting for you. It does seem likely that Mrs Hughes has been abducted, but it's not certain. There may be another explanation for what we found in the hall. My officers will start searching immediately. Some of them are here now.'

Oldroyd had seen a police car draw up outside as they were talking. Now he watched out the window as DC Hall and another officer hurried up the garden path.

Oldroyd turned to Steph. 'Explain to them what's happened and get them to organise a search. I'll get a photograph of the victim when I can.' He glanced at the distraught husband. 'Also, we need the forensics team out here asap.'

'Sir.' Steph went out to greet the officers.

Oldroyd waited a moment until Malcolm could compose himself. 'Can you think of anyone who would want to abduct your wife? Did she have any enemies?'

Malcolm dabbed his eyes and shook his head. 'No, nobody. Frances had lots of friends and nobody who wished her harm, as far as I'm aware.'

Oldroyd nodded and let out a deep breath. Was this probable kidnapping related to the murder of Tony Lowell and also to the escape of Adam Blake? If there were connections between these three strange occurrences, then he could not see them yet. He felt totally out of control and at the mercy of events.

∼

It was after midnight, but Deborah was still awake. It had been a stressful day as she tried to adjust to the idea of there being someone out there who was targeting them. There were police officers around all the time now, and a police car was usually parked outside. She was getting accustomed to strange people being in the house, which did unsettle her a little. Of course it was worth it to keep them safe. She smiled as she wondered what the neighbours were making of it. Some knew that Jim was a detective, but some didn't, and they must be very puzzled as to what was going on.

She could hear a tawny owl hooting in the tall trees behind the house. She got up and walked to the window to see if she could spot it. It was a clear night with a large bright harvest moon glowing behind the trees. She scanned the branches but could not see the bird. Then her attention was drawn by movement. Was there someone out there? She looked across the front garden and, yes, there was a dark shape by the hedge. Someone was crouching there.

As she watched, the figure got up and moved stealthily towards the house, dodging between the large shrubs. It looked like a man, but whoever they were, their face was covered. She went back to the bed.

'Jim, wake up!' she said in a loud whisper as she shook his arm. 'There's someone out there!'

'What?' replied Oldroyd sleepily.

'Someone's in our garden! They're coming towards the house.'

Oldroyd, still half asleep, got out of bed and staggered to the window. He stood beside Deborah.

'Where?'

'Behind the camellia. Look.'

They both stood very still, watching the garden. After a few seconds the figure appeared from behind the shrub, looked around and then moved nearer.

'What the hell's going on?' said Oldroyd, now fully awake and pulling on his dressing gown. 'I'm going down to alert the officers on duty.'

'Jim, be careful!'

'I will, don't worry.'

Downstairs, there were no officers in the living room or kitchen.

'What's happening?' said Oldroyd to himself and a spasm of fear went through him. Had Blake entered the house somehow and got rid of the police officers? Then he saw the outline of a figure in the frosted glass of the back door. He hid himself as the door opened. To his relief it was one of the armed officers. He strode out of hiding, startling the officer who was followed in by his colleague.

'Where the hell have you two been? There's someone out there.'

'We've just been patrolling round the back, sir; we didn't see anything.'

'No – they're in the front! We've seen someone from the bedroom window; they're hiding behind the shrubs.'

The officers sprang into action. Wielding their guns, they went quickly through the house and out into the front garden. 'Armed police! Come out with your hands raised!' one of them shouted.

A few seconds passed, during which the interloper seemed to be deciding whether or not to make a run for it and cursing could be heard, then they appeared slowly from behind the camellia with their arms raised.

'Don't shoot,' called a trembling voice. Oldroyd noticed that the arms were shaking, and almost laughed as he realised whoever this was, they were no threat. It was like a scene from a comedy film. The lead officer marched over and pulled off the intruder's hood.

'Well, if it isn't Ian Atkinson,' said Oldroyd with some relief, recognising a well-known local burglar. 'What are you doing here at this time of night? As if I didn't know.'

Atkinson's jaw dropped as he recognised the chief inspector. 'Nowt, just . . .'

'Scoping out the place to see if you can break in? You didn't know I lived here, did you? Unfortunately you've now got yourself involved in something more serious than an aborted B&E. We're going take you in on suspicion of attempted burglary . . . but we'll need to question you about whether you could have been here for some other purpose.'

Atkinson's jaw dropped open even further. 'What other purpose?'

'You'll find out later.' He turned to the officer. 'Call for a car to take him down to Harrogate station. Detective Sergeant Carter will question him tomorrow. I'm off back to bed.'

'Sir.'

Oldroyd chuckled to himself as he went up the stairs. It was actually quite nice to have some comic relief after a tense and frustrating day. Deborah was sitting up in bed.

'What's so funny?' she asked.

'Oh, it's nothing. Don't worry. It was a local burglar. You should have seen his face when we confronted him. It's the last thing you expect when you're carrying out a little bit of burglary in a village near Harrogate: Detective Chief Inspector Oldroyd pops up with an armed officer! It was all I could do to prevent myself from laughing out loud.'

'So you don't think he was any danger, then?'

'No. I'd be astonished if an amateur like Ian Atkinson was working for Adam Blake – and, besides, he wasn't armed. Just a harmless local rogue.'

Deborah sighed. 'Well, that's a relief, but I don't think I'm going to get back to sleep now. I'm wide awake after all that commotion.'

Oldroyd gave her a kiss. 'I'm sorry about this. You said you knew what you were taking on when you became a senior detective's partner.'

'Did I? I'm not sure I thought it would be as exciting as this, for want of a better word.'

'Well, it's worth it to have me, isn't it?'

'Maybe,' she said teasingly. 'As long as you make it up to me after all this is over.'

'How?'

She snuggled up to him. 'You'll have to arrange a nice holiday. Take me somewhere sunny and luxurious. The clocks will be going back soon and it will become dark and probably wet here.'

Oldroyd laughed. 'OK, I promise,' he said, and kissed her again.

Three

Otley has long competed with a number of towns in England for the distinction of having the most pubs per head of population. The town once had over thirty pubs, but this has now dwindled to twenty-one. Nevertheless, with a population of approximately 14,000, this represents roughly one pub for every 700 residents. The reason the town has so many pubs is related to its history as an important market town. Licensing laws allowed pubs to open all day on market days. The number of pubs expanded further in the nineteenth century as the town became an industrial centre.

The next morning was cold and misty in Otley, especially down by the river. A postman on an early round walked over the bridge towards the centre of town. The rowing boats moored nearby were barely visible. The noise of traffic was slightly muted by the mist. He passed St Saviour's church at which there was a very unusual and, in the mist, rather spooky collection of characters on a large grassy area dotted with trees in front of the church building. Children were playing, a gardener held a fork, a woman worked out with weights . . . some of them were characters from nursery rhymes, and they were all still and frozen in a certain pose, because they were all scarecrow figures made by members of the church.

This display was presented each year and had become a local attraction; the postman had seen it many times. He glanced at the fully dressed figures as he walked past, and then stopped. There was something different today about the group formation. Some scarecrow children were gathered around a tree. Leaning against this tree was a female figure. But . . . was that another scarecrow? There was something odd about it.

The postman jumped over a low wall and walked over to the group with some trepidation. As soon as he got close, he realised the truth and staggered back. The woman was not a scarecrow, but a dead body still dressed in gardening clothes. There were marks around her neck and on her forehead was written the word, *Vindicta*.

The postman recognised the woman now. It was Frances Hughes.

∼

Oldroyd surveyed the macabre scene in the church grounds. He found figures like the scarecrows unnerving, and the ones arranged around the grassy area seemed even more sinister than usual after the horrible discovery. It was the same with all mannequins, whether a scarecrow, a large doll or a ventriloquist's dummy. The fixed, exaggerated expression on the face created that uneasy feeling that they could suddenly come to life and it would not be pleasant. He shivered; was it with the cold or the horror of what had happened?

Blue and white tape sealed off the church and police radios were crackling. Tim Groves, dressed in protective clothing, was crouched over the body. As Oldroyd went to speak to him, Groves stood up and stretched his tall, thin frame.

'Well, Jim, it seems you've got a serial killer on your hands. And in Otley, of all places. Same method: strangulation using a cord. She's been dead about fourteen to fifteen hours. She also has quite a deep cut to her arm. Maybe the killer threatened her with a knife? You said there were signs of a struggle in the house so that's when she could have been cut. And the same weird word on the forehead in black marker pen. It must be the work of the same killer, don't you think? No phone or fingerprints again. This killer is thorough.'

'Almost certainly,' replied Oldroyd, still processing the implications this had for the investigation. Groves was right; someone was conducting a campaign of revenge. But for what? And who else was in danger? He sat on a nearby bench to try to gather his thoughts.

Blake escapes and immediately a serial killer starts to operate; surely it was too much of a coincidence. But what was Blake's link to these people? He put his hand to his head. He must be missing something. Was that terrible man, his rival in cleverness, outwitting him? It was an awful thought.

Steph was peering around, looking rather bewildered. She'd never been involved in a case quite like this. She crossed over to her boss. 'Are you OK, sir? It's gruesome, isn't it?'

Oldroyd nodded and came out of his reverie. 'It certainly is, but we have to try to learn from what the killer has done. The first body was placed in a prison cell and the second one here. But I don't think it's anything to do with the church. Look how they've arranged these child scarecrows around the victim.'

'As if it's a family and she's the mother?' suggested Steph.

'Yes, or maybe a teacher. The killer is sending us a message. We know it's about revenge because of the word *vindicta*. But what is this horrible arrangement telling us? And how does it tie in with the body in the Courthouse?' He sighed with frustration.

Steph shook her head. 'No idea, sir. It seems like the work of somebody deranged to me.'

'Maybe,' replied Oldroyd abstractedly. He was deep in thought, unable to escape the feeling that this must be connected to Adam Blake. But how? And why was he going after people seemingly unrelated to Oldroyd? Wasn't he the main target?

'We'll have to work it out as soon as we can, sir. Someone else could be at risk.'

'Yes, I've been thinking about that. We've got to find out what the connection is and who else might be in danger.' He grimaced. The pressure was growing. 'We'll have to get someone straight out to tell the unfortunate husband. He must have spent a terrible night. I feel bad now because I tried to persuade him not to be pessimistic and to believe we might find her. We had officers out looking for her.'

'Surely that was the right thing to say, sir? You have to give people hope.'

'Yes, I know. But it doesn't stop you feeling awful and that you've let people down when things turn out like this.'

'No, I understand.'

Oldroyd looked around, noticing again the other scarecrow figures still frozen in their positions and seemingly indifferent to what had happened. They made him shudder. 'Well, there's nothing more we can do here. DC Hall is going to talk to the people at the church. He'll get officers to go around the houses in this area to see if anybody saw anything.' He frowned and tapped the ground with his foot in frustration. He could see people pausing on the pavement by the blue and white tape, looking into the church grounds and wondering what had happened. It would be a great shock to the community when they found out that there had been another murder.

'Hello, are you the detective in charge?'

Oldroyd turned to see a woman dressed in clerical clothes including a dog collar. She looked shocked but was making a big effort to remain composed. Behind her were two other people in tears, both of whom seemed to be comforting each other.

'I'm Reverend Anderson, priest in charge here at St Saviour's,' she said to Oldroyd, offering her hand. 'Pleased to meet you.'

Reverend Anderson reminded Oldroyd of his sister Alison, who was also a vicar. The resemblance made him think of the danger that Alison could be in and he was momentarily overcome by the terrible feeling that these horrible events were out of his control. He didn't answer the woman for a few seconds. Then he returned to the moment and shook her hand.

'Yes, pardon me . . . I'm Detective Chief Inspector Oldroyd. I'm sorry about all this. It must be very upsetting for you.'

'Oh, it's not your fault,' the woman said, looking at him with some sympathy, realising he was also under great stress. 'But you're right. The church members spend a lot of time each year creating these figures and they give a lot of pleasure to people, including children. It's a terrible desecration of their creativity, to say nothing of the church grounds.'

'I understand. Can you think of any reason why someone would want to do this? Has anyone interfered with the display of the figures before?'

'No, never. It's something that the town values.' She turned towards the two distressed people. 'Anyway, as you can see, there are people I need to attend to. Please don't hesitate to ask if there's anything we can do to help.'

'Thank you.'

The vicar went over to the group of her shocked parishioners, which had now swelled to four.

Oldroyd sighed and turned to Steph. 'It's dreadful, isn't it? This will hit the town very hard. I'll obviously have to speak to the press again. Other than that, I think we'll have to wait to see what DC Warner comes up with. We need to tell her about Frances Hughes and get her to do some research there too. We'll have to go back to the husband and see if we can get more out of him.'

'OK, sir,' said Steph laconically. Her usual brightness had gone, and her expression was sombre. She was feeling the stress too.

~

The horrible news of the second murder didn't take long to spread through the little town. Saturday morning was usually a bustling, lively time in the town centre but instead the atmosphere was very sombre, reflected in the grey, oppressive mist that had settled and showed no sign of lifting. People were gathering in groups on street corners and talking in hushed voices with grave expressions on their faces. The general feeling was that not only were these two murders shockingly gruesome but also they were an outrage. Things like this just didn't happen in a tight community like Otley.

Dylan Hardy and Hillary Sands were both concerned about Abigail but had not yet heard anything about the latest murder.

'She's obviously under enormous pressure,' said Hillary, as they sipped their coffee in a small café down one of the old cobbled streets. It was a relatively new place, brightly painted with a cheerful and welcoming owner. It felt like a refuge from the gloom outside. 'A strange murder delivers an enormous shock to a place like this. It's so unexpected. Rumours will go around, and you'll get someone saying that it was an inside job at the Courthouse or some rubbish. People who come into the Courthouse will be looking around and whispering to each other, "Oh look, that's where they must have taken the body up the stairs."' She grimaced. 'Oh! It's going to be awful for quite a while – especially for Abigail. It's a great strain to be in charge of an organisation when something happens like this.' She took another sip of her coffee.

'I think you're being a little hard on the public,' said Dylan. 'Not everyone is so morbid. Abigail will get a lot of support. She's done a wonderful job and people appreciate it.'

'Maybe, but people also love gossip and scandal. They'll listen to all kinds of ridiculous stuff and—'

'Hillary! Hello.' Hillary looked up to see one of her friends – a woman called Mary West – gesturing from the door. Her expression was very serious. She was dressed in a red puffer jacket and black jeans. 'I didn't expect to see you here,' she said, coming over.

'Hi! No, I don't normally come into Otley on Saturday. Dylan and I were just talking about what happened at the Courthouse on Thursday. We were there when Abigail discovered the body in the cell.'

'Oh, how awful!' She looked from one to the other. 'But have you heard the latest?'

'What?'

'There's been another murder. A body was found this morning in the grounds of St Saviour's.'

'No!'

'Yes.' She leaned forward and lowered her voice as if the next piece of information was too shocking to be heard by anybody else in the café. 'It was a woman, and she was propped against a tree with some of those scarecrow figures around her that they make at the church. Can you imagine? It's like a horror film.' She shuddered. 'There must be some mad person at work in this town.'

Hillary and Dylan were stunned.

'Have the police said anything publicly about it yet?' asked Dylan.

'No, and I don't think they know what to make of it.' She leaned even further forward. 'I heard that there was something written on her forehead. How weird is that?'

'Good God!' exclaimed Dylan. 'Not again.'

There was no response. All three were struck speechless at the prospect.

～

As Hillary and Dylan were receiving the news about the second murder, Abigail Wilson was having an extended lie-in. She was exhausted after the events of the last two days. As it was Saturday morning, her husband Dave, a graphic designer, was at home. Her two primary-school-aged kids Jonathan and Mary had gone for their swimming lesson in Ilkley; a neighbour with kids the same age had taken them all. They had been fascinated by what had happened at the Courthouse and wanted to know a lot more about it than she was prepared to tell them. They had a child's open-mouthed and naive interest in the gruesome.

She was just contemplating getting up when Dave came into the bedroom with a cup of tea.

'How are you feeling?'

She yawned. 'Better for a long rest. Thanks for the tea.' She took a sip.

Dave sat down on the edge of the bed looking concerned. He grimaced. 'Unfortunately, something else has happened. I thought it best to tell you straight away.'

Abigail felt a sharp pang of anxiety and put her mug down on her bedside table. 'What?'

'Jeff rang. He was out early jogging this morning and there was a commotion down by St Saviour's church. Another body has been found.'

Abigail put her hand to her mouth. 'No!'

'I'm afraid so, and it was someone you know. Frances Hughes. She volunteers at the centre, doesn't she?'

'What? No! Where? Where was she found?'

'Jeff saw it. The police were there. She was on that grassy area by the church, propped up among those scarecrow characters that the church makes every year. Jeff caught sight of her before they screened off the body. He said it was awful – made him feel sick.'

Abigail threw herself back on the bed. 'No! That's terrible! What the hell is going on? I was only talking to her yesterday on the phone. I . . . Oh my God! I might have been one of the last people to speak to her. I knew it; there was something wrong. I could hear it in her voice. Oh my God! Maybe I could have done something to save her.'

Dave put his hand on her arm. 'Hey, slow down! You told the police about the conversation, didn't you?'

'Yes, but I think they thought I was just being a bit hysterical.'

'Well, whether they felt that or not, you did what you could, so don't start blaming yourself.'

Abigail groaned. 'This is just getting worse and worse for the Courthouse, too. What are Hillary and the other volunteers going to think? I'll have to ring her. Do you think she will know about it? And maybe I should go down to the Courthouse now and speak to the police again. I—'

Dave laid next to her on the bed and put his arm over her. 'Whoa, hold on! You're going nowhere until Monday at the earliest. You really need to calm down about this or you'll drive yourself to distraction. By all means, call Hillary, but you need to stay here and relax. We'll go for a long walk later. If the police want to speak to you urgently, they'll contact you. There's nothing more you can do.'

She turned over and gave him a kiss. 'Thanks, you're right. And a walk will be nice. The colours on the Chevin are gorgeous at the moment. But what about the kids?'

'I asked Brenda if they could go back to her place after the swimming lesson. She understood that you needed a break after what's happened. They'll play with Tom and Jane; they'll be fine.'

Abigail smiled weakly. 'Thanks for doing that. I'll just drink my tea and then I'll get up. Can you do me a couple of slices of toast?'

'Of course. I'm glad you've got the appetite.'

∾

Malcolm Hughes had collapsed, exhausted with shock, into an armchair in which he could barely sit upright. He had spent a sleepless night worrying about his wife and then in the morning a police officer had brought the news that he had been dreading. Now there were SOCOs examining the hallway and the door.

Oldroyd and Steph sat on the sofa opposite. This was one of the worst aspects of policing: having to ask the bereaved questions at such an appallingly difficult time. It was made much harder if the person was a suspect. Oldroyd always tried to make it as gentle an experience as possible.

'I realise that this is a terrible time for you,' he said, 'but we need to ask some questions, and your answers might help us to find who killed your wife.'

Hughes nodded but didn't say anything.

Oldroyd continued. 'First of all, I'm very sorry about this but I have to ask you about your relationship with her. Was it going well?'

Hughes put his hands to his face. 'Oh God.' He seemed about to turn angry but then said, 'OK, I understand; you're only doing your job, and of course I realise I am still a suspect. The answer is that we got on extremely well and were very close. I think you'll find my alibi stands up. I had no reason to kill my wife.'

'OK. You've already told us that you were not aware of any enemies your wife may have had.'

'As far as I know, she didn't. Couldn't this be the work of some maniac who just enjoys killing, Chief Inspector? There have been two murders in this town now, haven't there? And . . . and arranging the bodies like that; it's horrendous.' He looked away. 'I can't bear to think about it.'

'I understand, but I'm afraid that there is another detail that connects these murders.'

Hughes looked up. 'What is that?'

'Your wife and the first victim Tony Lowell both had the word *vindicta* written on their foreheads.'

Hughes' mouth dropped open. It was shock more than recognition, thought Oldroyd. 'What?'

'I'm sorry, I know it's an awful detail to have to tell you,' Oldroyd said. 'But have you any idea why someone would want to write that word on your wife's body?'

Malcolm seemed to sink further into the armchair after this blow. He shook his head slightly but didn't reply. He looked utterly perplexed and dazed, as if he could not process the information.

'Unfortunately, it suggests that someone may have had a grudge against her. Are you sure you don't know who that might be?'

'No. A grudge? What for? I've no idea at all.'

'It could be connected to something that happened a while ago. How long were you married?'

'Eighteen years. We didn't get married until we were in our early forties. Neither of us had been married before.'

'Did she tell you about her life before she met you?'

'Yes. She was born and brought up in York and moved over here for jobs when she finished at university.'

'What did she do?'

'As far as I know she always worked in the care industry. She was managing a care home when I met her. We set up a care home together and ended up running three until we decided to retire.'

'Do you know the addresses of the places she worked before you knew her?' asked Steph.

'Only where she was working when I met her. That was a care home in Ilkley, but it's closed now. To be honest, I wasn't all that interested in Frances' past – it was our time together that was important to me.' His voice faltered and there were tears in his eyes. 'You see, I'd almost got to the age where I thought I would never meet anyone, you know? And it was wonderful when we got together. She was in the same position as me. We were just right for each other. I . . .' He shook his head and couldn't continue.

'Did she ever mention a man called Adam Blake?' asked Oldroyd.

'No. I . . . Wait a minute, Adam Blake? I've heard that name mentioned on the news. He escaped from Stansfield Prison the other day, didn't he?'

'That's right. Anyone against whom he had a grudge could be in danger while he's on the loose.'

'I see . . . but no, she never mentioned him. I can't see any reason for him to have a grudge against her. She was upset yesterday morning about what happened at the Courthouse, but she said nothing about a prison escape.'

Oldroyd was intrigued by this. 'What did she say about the Courthouse?'

'Just how awful it was – a body placed in the cell. Neither of us could believe it. She was a volunteer at the Courthouse. She was very fond of the place and knew plenty of people there.'

'Did she know Tony Lowell, the victim?'

'If she did, she didn't tell me.'

'Did she seem anxious about anything?' asked Steph.

'No. I told you yesterday, we did some gardening together and then I left for Harrogate.' Hughes paused. 'I didn't realise that I was never going to see her again.' He put his hands to his face and his body convulsed in a sob.

Oldroyd glanced at Steph. 'OK,' he said. 'We won't bother you any more at the moment. I'll send an officer round to take a statement from you. Also, I'm afraid officers will have to search through your wife's things to see if there are any clues about why she was attacked.'

Hughes nodded slightly but again seemed to be beyond speech.

~

Oldroyd and Steph drove back to Otley.

'So Abigail Wilson was right, sir? She picked up on some anxiety about a secret that Frances had succeeded in keeping from her husband.'

'Yes.'

'And I thought it was interesting, sir, that he said he knew very little about his wife's past. Tony Lowell's wife said the same.'

'Yes, I noticed that. If they're both telling the truth, and I think they probably are, it suggests that Tony Lowell and Frances Hughes had things to hide. They seem to have been helped by the fact that their spouses were not particularly interested in their previous lives; in fact, that lack of interest may have been one of the things that made them attractive. If they've both been killed by the same person, it means that it's very likely that they did know each other at some point and that they knew their killer. I still think Blake is a prime suspect; if so, what was his connection to the victims? It must have been important because he's gone for them before me.'

'They were easier to get to, sir. But when and where and in what circumstances could he have known them?'

Oldroyd shook his head. 'We're no nearer to knowing any of that yet.'

Steph looked at him and paused a moment, wondering if his judgement was being affected by his psychological battle with Blake. She knew her boss well enough to be confident that he would accept a comment from her, even if it could be seen as critical.

'Sir,' she said, 'I wonder if this thing with Blake is making you think he might be involved with what's going on here in Otley when really there doesn't seem to be much evidence that he is.'

Oldroyd glanced at her. There was a frown on his face, but a twinkle in his eye. 'Hmm, I see. Well, thank you for being honest. Deborah was saying something similar about not making this a personal thing with Blake. You're both right: the evidence is thin and I must be careful. Let's just say, because it's such a coincidence that these murders began when he escaped, that we can't eliminate him. How's that?'

Steph smiled. 'That's fine, sir, very rational. I wouldn't blame you if you were spooked by all this. It must be a nasty experience feeling that someone like that is out there and could pounce at any time.'

'It is, but in a way it's the price of success. In this job you make enemies by bringing people to justice, so maybe you will face something like this someday, though I hope not.'

'Well, never mind, sir, I'm not going to think about it. The terrible question facing us now is, who's next? Hopefully no one else is in line for this particular kind of revenge but it's a possibility, isn't it?'

'I'm afraid it is,' said Oldroyd, 'and of course, if it is Blake behind them . . . it could be me.'

George Milton sat in the kitchen of his farmhouse smoking and gazing into space with a sour expression on his face. Apart from looking after his pigs, he did less work on the farm these days, leaving a lot of it to his two sons. He was still very resentful that he'd spent five years in prison. It had sapped his energy and drive. Five years just for doing what he considered the best for his farm. It made you wonder whether it was all worth it when the system was against you. Why bother?

Milton's son Jake came in. He stood and looked at his father. 'Are you coming out to give us a hand? We're planting winter wheat in t' top field.'

'You're wasting your bloody time.'

'No, we're not.' He sat down on a chair opposite his father. 'Dad, I know you're still angry about going to prison, but let's face it – you knew using that stuff was against the law. You were taking a big risk. What did you expect was going to happen?'

Milton finished his cigarette and flung the butt into the fire. 'Whose bloody side are you on?'

'It's not a question of sides, is it? You broke the law and you got caught. It's a fact.'

'Huh.' Milton lit another cigarette.

'You can't just sit here all day, smoking. We need your help if we're going to run this farm. What would Mum have thought about it?'

'Why are you bringing her into it? She's been dead for ten years.'

'She wouldn't have wanted the farm to go bust, would she? After she supported you all those years. Times aren't easy. Nobody knows better than you how much work is needed on a farm.'

'Well, you managed OK when I was in prison, so you should be all right now.'

Jake leaned forward to plead with his father. 'Why're you giving up like this?' He looked around the room. 'Look at the state of this place.' Milton lived by himself in the farmhouse. Jake lived with his partner Julie in a small rented house down in New Bridge. When his father got out of prison, Ian had lived at the farmhouse with him for a while, but found it difficult and moved into a shared house in Harrogate. The brothers travelled to the farm each day. The farmhouse seemed to be getting steadily more squalid now that Milton was by himself.

'I'm not,' said Milton. 'Being in that place took a lot out of me. You don't know what it's like behind bars.' He looked at his son. 'I'll be out to help you in a little while. Just go back and get on with it.'

Jake got up, shook his head, and left the house.

Milton continued smoking, and a wry smile came on to his face. He was thinking about the visit from the police. They hadn't found anything and he doubted that they would come back. He was too clever for them; even his sons didn't know about it. He would get one over t' bloody police if it was the last thing he did.

Oldroyd and Steph arrived back at the Courthouse to find it besieged by reporters who rushed forward when they saw the chief inspector, despite the presence of DC Hall and other officers attempting to hold them back. Still, they were unable to enter the building. The story now had national prominence. Television cameras were ready to be trained on Oldroyd, who had decided that he would have to speak to them immediately. He climbed a few steps up a stone staircase which led up to a space used as an artist's studio above the robing room. From here, he addressed the crowd while Steph stood at the bottom of the steps.

'I'll tell you what was discovered earlier today and the implications of this for our investigation into the murder of Tony Lowell,' he said before outlining the circumstances surrounding the discovery of Frances Hughes' body. Then he made the usual request for anyone who saw anything between Friday afternoon and Saturday morning to come forward and report any strange behaviour by anybody they knew.

'Before anyone asks the question, we do believe that these two murders are linked and were most likely committed by the same person. The reasons we are reasonably sure about this are that both victims had the word *vindicta* written on their forehead in black marker pen, the body was staged after death, and the method of killing was the same. This is unlikely to be a copycat murder because, so far, we have not released any information publicly about these details.'

Oldroyd saw one or two of the reporters glance at each other and gritted his teeth. He knew these were the kind of bizarre and horrific details that would send them into ecstasies. Unfortunately, the public now needed to know what had happened because it was entirely possible that another victim would be targeted and someone might have information for which the investigation was desperate. There was a scramble to ask the first question. Microphones were thrust in his direction as cameras roved.

'That's weird, isn't it, Chief Inspector?!' one reporter called out. 'Latin? What the hell does it mean?'

'*Vengeance* or *avenged*. It seems to suggest that the murderer was exacting revenge on the victims, though for what we don't yet know.'

'Unless the killer's just completely bonkers,' piped up another voice. 'Why else would they arrange the body among some scarecrows in the grounds of a church? If that's not mad, what is?'

There were further gasps of surprise from some of the reporters who had been unaware of these details.

Oldroyd took a breath. 'It's true that the body of Frances Hughes was placed in the grounds of St Saviour's church in a ghoulish kind of tableau with scarecrows of children set around her.'

'Bloody hell, that's sick!' someone called out.

'Yes,' continued Oldroyd. 'But we do not yet know the significance of this any more than we know why Tony Lowell was taken to the cell at the Courthouse. We are anxious to hear from anyone who knows about any connection between these two victims. Did they know each other? Did they work together? Who else knew them? It may well relate to events in the distant past.'

'You sound as if you are struggling, Chief Inspector,' suggested one reporter in a slightly mocking tone.

Oldroyd frowned. Why did they seem to take such satisfaction in the police having difficulties? 'We can only work with the information that we have, and this is a very unusual case. We are working very hard to get to the bottom of it, but in the meantime, I have to warn the people of this town and the local area that the killer may strike again, though not completely at random. This killer is not deranged in the sense that they might strike at anybody. There is a pattern to what they are doing. If anyone has reason to think that they may be at risk, then they should come forward immediately.'

'One body in a prison cell and one in the grounds of a church; could it be some nutcase who has a grudge against the police and the church?' someone theorised.

'I think that's rather simplistic and unlikely,' replied Oldroyd, trying to remain patient in the face of the tabloid language. 'The answer will lie with the victims and their relationship with the killer, though, as I said, the killer is making some kind of statement in choosing the places they leave the bodies and in writing something on those bodies.'

'Why in Latin, Chief Inspector? Do you think it's a clue?'

'That's a good question,' said Oldroyd, nodding. 'There's clearly a reason why the killer chose a Latin word – but we don't yet know what it is.'

'The only Latin I knew was on my school motto, and I can't even remember that now,' called out another voice to general laughter.

Oldroyd looked at the speaker thoughtfully for a moment before he brought the conference to an end.

'OK, that's all for now. I hope you will report this sensibly and not indulge in ridiculous flights of fancy concerning scarecrows who speak Latin locked up in prison cells.'

There was laughter at this. Oldroyd always liked to crack a few jokes. It lowered the tension and got them on his side. It was important to try not to antagonise them. After all, they were only doing their job. It was just that sometimes the way they did their job could make his more difficult. He knew a few would ignore his plea and that there would be some sensational writing on the case in tomorrow's papers. Hopefully something useful would also be in their reports.

As he walked over to the incident room, Hillary Sands – who'd been listening to the press conference – stood thinking for a while, then turned and went back into the main building.

∽

Philip Bryson sat in the cold living room of his house in Otley. He'd looked forward to his release from prison but since he'd come back to Otley he'd felt lonely, disconnected and lethargic. He was so unused to freedom that he didn't know what to do with himself, and struggled to organise things off his own bat.

He looked around the room. It held some good memories of when his children were growing up and they were a reasonably happy family. He'd not had the best start in life, and he had been pleased to have a family of his own that he could take care of. It was a torment thinking about how things had gone so badly wrong. It was symbolised by the change in this room. He remembered family Christmases when the room was warm, bright and decorated. How forlorn, quiet and empty it was now; it was enough to reduce him to tears.

It was his wife's fault; she had destroyed their family. But for some reason everyone had seemed to side with her. He now had very little contact with his son and daughter. Perhaps that was understandable. They had still been quite young when the horrible thing had taken place, and understandably they blamed him. But his brother and sister and his wife's family all knew what she was like and yet he'd got very little sympathy from them.

He looked up and shook his head, trying to dismiss these gloomy thoughts, but it was hard when he was in the house. There were too many vivid reminders of the past – and particularly the awful, haunting scene when he'd stabbed her with the knife. As he'd said to Andy, he needed to sell up, move and make a new start somewhere where he wasn't known. He had to make the effort. If he didn't, he was going to sink into a bad depression and maybe never recover.

The gloomy silence was broken by the sound of his phone. 'Hello,' he said, then his head jolted back in surprise. 'What?! How did you get my number? . . . Yes, I've heard all about it . . . Where are you? . . . What makes you think that? . . . I'm sure you are, but why did you think I would be interested? . . . Money? How much? . . . Seriously? I don't know, I'll have to think about it. The police have been round. They're obviously checking everybody in this area who knew you in prison . . . I don't know about that . . . Give me time to think . . . No, I don't know.'

He ended the call and whistled. Adam Blake. He could scarcely believe it. Offering him money if Bryson would conceal him at the house, saying he had to stay on the move. Of course he wouldn't say where he was at the moment.

Bryson sighed. He certainly hadn't expected this, but it was tempting – a quick way to solve his financial problems. But the risk was too great; he loathed the idea of going back to prison. And he didn't want to help that despicable serial killer. It would be better to contact the police. That would gain him some points with them and help to establish his future as a law-abiding citizen. Although he was bitter against people and the system, he wasn't going to behave like a fool. That detective had left his number. He would contact him straight away.

After all, there could be some reward for turning Blake in.

∾

When Oldroyd and Steph finally made it into the Courthouse, the SOCOs had finished their work and the place was deserted. They sat quietly in the robing room for a while and tried to collect their thoughts.

'I've been thinking, sir,' began Steph. 'You know I'm sceptical, but if it is Blake behind these murders, there is a kind of pattern there. Placing the first body in the prison cell could represent him being sent to prison, and I wonder if Frances Hughes represents the kind of older women that he used to trick out of their money. Maybe the scarecrow children represented the families of those women who were denied their inheritance.'

Oldroyd shrugged. 'I can see what you mean, but I'm afraid it's a bit fanciful. I'm not sure that he would want to go to all that trouble just to make points about himself, even if he is a narcissist. I don't think he would just pick victims at random like that. I know how his mind works. All his energy is expended on accumulating things for himself. He wouldn't waste time on making extravagant gestures because he wouldn't gain anything from them, and his emotions are usually well under control. No, we've got to find what the connection is between Frances Hughes and Tony Lowell. Maybe those two are connected to Blake in some way. If we knew how, then we might discover a better motive for Blake to kill them. I don't know. We've got virtually no evidence about anything. We're just speculating.' He threw up his hands in a gesture of frustration at the lack of progress.

Steph looked at a white board, which they had used to put up details of the victims and suspects using photographs and a board marker.

'Of the two, sir, Lowell is the more mysterious. We know virtually nothing of his early life, unless, as we said, his wife is keeping things from us. But somehow I doubt that. So it's possible that he could have changed his name. "Tony Lowell" could be an alias.'

'You're right, but I'm not sure it gets us anywhere unless someone comes forward who knew him under a different name. Anyway—'

He was interrupted by the entrance of DC David Hall, who had some news.

'Sir, we've had reports off someone hanging around Chevin Towers – that's that big mansion up on the Chevin. It's empty but walkers are always going past it.'

'Yes, I know it.'

'I'll send someone up to investigate.'

'Steph and I will have a walk up there. The fresh air will do us good and clear our minds. If you can give us a couple of armed response officers in case Blake is there.'

'OK, sir.'

Oldroyd's phone rang. He wondered if it was Blake again. He was relieved, however, to see that it was Andy's number.

'Hi, sir,' Andy said when Oldroyd answered. 'How's it going over there?'

'I think "slow" is the best answer to that question.'

'Right, sorry to hear that. Well, I've just had a phone call from a bloke called Philip Bryson. He's an ex-prisoner from Stansfield living locally – one of the men that Sharon Warner identified as being in there at the same time as Blake. We went to see him yesterday. He admitted to knowing Blake but said he'd had nothing much to do with him and certainly hadn't helped him to escape. The point is, Blake called him this morning and offered him money if Bryson would allow him to hide at his house.'

Oldroyd whistled. 'Bloody hell! This could be an opportunity to track him down!'

'That's what I thought, sir. What about this? Bryson didn't commit himself to helping Blake, said he needed to think about it. So, what if we set a trap for Blake? Get Bryson to agree for Blake to come to his house in Harrogate and we'll be there to catch him. Blake said he would call back tonight.'

'Well, I like that idea. Blake must trust Bryson.'

'It sounds as if Blake's worried about being found. He wants to stay on the move to avoid being captured. He's prepared to take a risk on it. And if he's currently in the Stansfield area, he must be trying to get closer to you.'

'Probably. Have you got the people you need for an operation like that? Make sure that you consult with Inspector McNiven.

Don't underestimate Blake. He's very mild mannered on the surface but he's a ruthless killer.'

'I think we could pull it off, sir. We need to go for it, get Blake back in prison, and take the pressure off you so you can get on with this Otley case.'

'OK, well, you'd better clear it all with Superintendent Walker as well as McNiven. It's a risky undertaking.'

'I will, sir. I hope you get a breakthrough soon. I know Sharon Warner is working hard for you.'

'Good.'

Andy rang off and Oldroyd explained Andy's scheme to Steph. Then he sighed in exasperation. 'At least they seem to be getting somewhere with the search for Blake. Good for Andy. Whereas we are . . . Oh, I've had enough of this. The fog has lifted. It's a nice day. Let's go out for a walk and see if it clears our minds.' He reached for his jacket and at that moment his phone pinged. He looked at the message, which came from an unknown number.

Getting nearer. Really excited!

His stomach lurched, although in a way it was good news – a sign that Blake was still on the move and could therefore still be caught.

'Ah, a message from Moriarty!' he said light-heartedly, trying to conceal his anxiety as he handed the phone to Steph. 'I think this confirms that he's confident about moving over here and there's a good chance he will fall into Andy's trap.'

'That's good, sir.'

The armed officers arrived and went with Oldroyd and Steph out of the Courthouse and through a narrow, dark passageway on to the busy shopping street of Kirkgate. At the top, they continued up Station Road and Queens Terrace to the site of the former railway station and across a bridge over the modern bypass. A narrow lane took them up towards the Chevin where a long flight of steps reached abruptly up into the woods. The officers went slightly ahead to check for danger.

Oldroyd turned to Steph. 'When we were driving through Otley the other day, I saw a big house up here on the Chevin. I think I remember walking to it once. Let's see if we can find it.'

'OK, sir, but – wow, this is pretty steep,' observed Steph, who was getting out of breath despite the fact that she worked out regularly. Oldroyd was also puffing a bit, though he was fitter than he used to be thanks to parkruns and Deborah's supervision of his diet.

'Yes, it's quite a challenge,' he said with some difficulty. 'It's a long time since I've been up here. I'm sure my dad brought me when I was quite young, and I complained about how tough a climb it was.'

'I'll bet you did, sir.'

They reached the top of the steepest part of the slope and were confronted by a strange-looking barrier made of large flat slabs of stone placed upright in a line.

'Ah! I remember this. It's called the Vacca Wall.'

'The what, sir?'

'*Vacca* – it's from the Latin for cow. They used to think it was Roman or medieval, but I think someone convincingly proved it was from the eighteenth century. But whenever it was built, it was almost certainly there to stop cows or other animals from falling down the slope.'

Steph smiled, used to her boss giving these interesting little bits of explanation about things in Yorkshire.

Oldroyd took a deep breath and looked around. 'It's good to be up here in the woods. I feel better already. Look, there are some bracket fungi on that birch tree . . . and I think that's honey fungus on the ground there.'

They wandered around a little looking for fungi among some rotten tree trunks. Steph found one that looked like human fingers reaching out of the wood.

'Ah!' said Oldroyd. 'I think that's called Dead Moll's Fingers. That's a grisly one to find when you're investigating a murder.' After a while they wandered on until they came to a wide track which led to the large Gothic-style building that Oldroyd had seen from the centre of Otley.

It was even more austere and forbidding when seen close up. The grounds were overgrown and one or two windows were broken. Some of the slates on the steep roofs and ornamental turrets were missing. The doors were secured with planks of wood. The building was clearly empty. In the tall trees behind the house some black crows were cawing, but there were no other birds around, apart from a solitary wren which landed briefly on a branch near to them before fluttering off into the undergrowth.

Oldroyd called to the officers. 'OK, can you look round the building?'

'Sir,' came the reply as they moved off.

Steph looked up at the dark stone walls. 'God, it's spooky, sir. I'm glad we're here while the sun is shining and not when the light is fading.'

'You mean "when the crow makes wing to the rooky wood" – that's a bit of darkness from *Macbeth*.' Oldroyd laughed as he also gazed up at the tall windows and pointed gables. 'Yes, it's full Victorian Gothic, isn't it? I believe it's called Chevin Towers, but I don't know much about it. It's like a building out of an Edgar Allan Poe story, don't you think?'

'He wrote "The Pit and the Pendulum", didn't he, sir?'

'Yes, and a few other horror stories along with several mysteries too. I wonder who used to live here? All I remember as a kid was a big building. It was probably built for some wealthy mill owner, like lots of mansions similar to this in the West Riding. But since that era, most of them have been used for other purposes like schools or nursing homes. Why is this one empty? It still looks basically sound, if it had some refurbishment work done. Maybe it's too big for anyone to want to take it on. The heating bills would be enormous. A lot of these big properties from that era end up being demolished. They had cheap coal and a supply of cheap labour to sustain them in those days.'

The officers reported back. 'No sign of anyone, sir.'

'Good.' He turned to Steph. 'Let's have a closer look.'

They walked across fallen autumn leaves and tried to peer in through a window, but it was so dirty they could see very little with any clarity, just that they were looking into a large empty room with one or two pieces of broken furniture lying around on bare floorboards. Dust lay thick on everything. There were one or two words scrawled on the grubby wall. The handwriting looked like that of a child.

'Oh, sir, look at that,' exclaimed Steph, pointing to an object on the floor. It was a child's teddy bear with a leg missing.

'God, that's sad,' said Oldroyd. 'It's also very intriguing. We must find out about the history of this place. And who knows? It just might prove to be significant. Let's have a look at the front.'

They walked around the house and came across an overgrown lawn and some dilapidated tennis courts which had big holes in the surrounding wire fencing. There were also the remains of a children's playground: an iron framework to which swings would have been attached and places where other equipment, now removed, would have been fixed. There were panoramic views out over Wharfedale partially concealed by the leggy rhododendrons.

'There have definitely been children here at some time in the not-too-distant past,' observed Oldroyd, looking very thoughtful. 'Anyway, we'd better get back. Come on – I think there's a path that winds through the woods and down to the town.'

They pushed their way through the overgrown shrubbery and back up to the path. It was odd, but as soon as they got away from the building there appeared to be more birdsong and a pleasant atmosphere. The sun shone through the trees. Steph paused to have a last look back at the silent and creepy building. The curtainless windows on the upper storeys were like eyes gazing down on the town of Otley – and maybe on them too, as an intruder. She wouldn't have been surprised if there'd been a face up there looking out, as if from some kind of ghost story. Steph shuddered before turning round and catching up with Oldroyd. She felt easier walking next to him with the armed officers just ahead.

∾

Edward Brown lived alone in a rather dilapidated, detached Victorian villa-type house on the outskirts of Otley. It was the family house that his father had bought many years before, but Brown didn't have the resources now to maintain it as it had been in the old days. Nevertheless, he kept it as a house which befitted his position as a local dignitary. His wife had died several years before, but he worked hard to keep up appearances, employing a cleaner and occasionally a gardener for really heavy jobs, though he did most of the work in the garden himself. Like everyone else in the town, he was very shocked when he learned of the murder of Frances Hughes but for him the news had an extra resonance. He was now digging over part of his vegetable plot in an attempt to calm himself down.

He'd known Frances a long time – well before they both became involved in the Courthouse. They had shared a love of gardening. He got on well with Frances's husband Malcolm and they frequently invited each other round for dinner. They were his type: salt of the earth middle class. How would the country manage without them? He stopped digging, put his hands on the spade handle and shook his head. He would have to give Malcolm a call later. Some unpleasant things from the past, which they never talked about, had been largely forgotten. Until now. He'd watched the press conference with DCI Oldroyd in which the gruesome circumstances of Frances' murder had been revealed, including the staging of the body and the writing of *vindicta* on her forehead. It seemed to be the work of a mad person, but the word *vindicta* was chilling. Could it have anything to do with what had happened all those years ago? It was surely completely forgotten about by now.

As he turned over the spadefuls of rich soil, a robin came very close and watched him as it waited for worms to be dug up. Normally he would have welcomed the bird but today he hardly noticed. He was in the same frame of mind as Frances had been before her murder and, like her, he wondered whether he should contact the police. But the possibility in his mind of what and who might be behind these killings seemed so fantastical that it couldn't possibly be true, not after all this time. He shook his head. It would be better to sit tight and wait for them to find the killer. That way he wouldn't have to reveal anything about the past and open up that can of worms. It would shatter the reputation that he had carefully built up over the years, and that was unthinkable.

He carried on digging and with some sadness remembered that he wouldn't be able to talk about gardening to Frances ever again. At that moment, the robin started to sing its melancholy autumn song.

~

In the evening Oldroyd and Deborah drove into Harrogate, still with police protection, to see a performance of Agatha Christie's famous play *The Mousetrap*. The protection team had advised against this, but Oldroyd was insistent. Deborah needed a break, and she was certain it would do him good too.

'I'm really looking forward to this,' said Deborah, who was quite excited at the prospect of getting out of the house; she had had to abandon her walks and runs in the nearby countryside. 'You can't beat a live performance. I just love the atmosphere in a theatre.'

'Me too,' replied Oldroyd, who was driving as the police officers followed in their car.

In the circumstances, they had the luxury of parking just outside the theatre. One officer remained in the foyer as Deborah and Oldroyd took their seats in the beautiful Edwardian theatre. There was the usual hubbub of conversation and sense of anticipation.

Oldroyd looked around approvingly but also with some apprehension. As with the gathering of reporters, there was a feeling of danger being in a public space with lots of people around. Could Blake be among them? It seemed highly unlikely, but the man had changed his appearance frequently as part of his MO. Oldroyd dismissed the thought – he was determined not to communicate any of this anxiety to Deborah. And, besides, they did have police officers close by.

'Do you know this is one of the few hemp house theatres that remain in Britain?' he said to her.

'A what?'

'Hemp house; it refers to the fact that they still use old-fashioned hemp ropes and pulleys tied to sandbags as part of the theatre rigging.'

'Oh, right. I'm not sure I wanted to know that. You're such a mansplainer sometimes, Jim,' said Deborah, looking at her programme.

Oldroyd chuckled and glanced at the programme himself. 'I'm sure it will tell you that *The Mousetrap* is the longest running play in the world. It's been performed in London since nineteen fifty-two. It was originally—'

'Oh, shut up!' whispered Deborah. 'They're starting.'

Oldroyd had to stifle a laugh as the lights went down and the performance began.

Deborah's concerns that her partner would not enjoy the play because it was too much like his work proved to be unfounded. Oldroyd welcomed the opportunity to see this classic for the first time. He loved the way the cosy post-war atmosphere created in the first part of the play changed into something much more sinister and claustrophobic in the second half. He enjoyed the unfolding of the plot in which there was a wonderful twist at the end, so he didn't tell Deborah that he'd worked out who was likely to be the killer. That would definitely feel like bragging.

After the performance they went into the little bar for a drink, accompanied by their officers – one of the advantages to having a police protection officer who could be called upon to drive; normally there'd be a rather heated discussion about whose turn it was. Oldroyd claimed that he did most of the driving and Deborah was so certain that this was not the case, she had started to keep a record on her phone as evidence.

'Oh, that was so good!' exclaimed Deborah, sipping from her glass of wine and looking round with interest at the other members of the audience who were now in the bar. 'I hope you enjoyed it as much as I did, Jim. It wasn't too much like work, was it?'

'No, it was great,' replied Oldroyd, who was also enjoying the post-performance vibe. He was drinking a pint of real ale and had a bit of a twinkle in his eye because he'd not only enjoyed the play in itself, it had also confirmed some of the ideas he'd started to consider about what the case in Otley might be about. He felt more relaxed, and even began to forget about Blake.

~

Andy refused to take the day off on Sunday. He spent the day with his team and Philip Bryson at the latter's house, organising the trap for Adam Blake. He'd spoken to McNiven and Walker, and been given the go-ahead.

It was decided that Bryson would tell Blake that he'd hide him because he needed the money. He would negotiate a price and discuss how long Blake would stay with him. Then he would arrange for the escaped convict to arrive in the late morning on Monday when people had gone to work and it would be quiet in the street. He would give him details of how to get to the house.

'It's very likely that he will be in disguise,' said Andy. 'But that's no problem.'

'How are you going to work it so that I am not at any risk?' asked Bryson.

'Don't worry. You bring him into the house, sit him down in the living room and then go to the kitchen for something. The armed officers will be just outside the room. As soon as you are out of there, they will pounce. You've got nothing to worry about.'

'Am I going to get any reward for doing this? I'm very badly off; it's not easy to get a job when you come out of prison.'

'Well, there's a reward of two thousand pounds for information leading to Blake's recapture, so I'll see to it that you get that money.'

Bryson nodded. In his position, the money was worth the risk.

Before he left the house, Andy paced around, going methodically through the plan. He'd developed this entirely on his own initiative. He was very anxious that it would work, and that he would be able to present a captured Adam Blake to McNiven – and potentially save his boss's life.

~

That evening, when Andy finally arrived home, he and Steph went out for dinner at their favourite Italian restaurant near Leeds Bridge. Some of their friends found the place rather dull and old-fashioned – but with the white tablecloths, family photos on the walls, dark, heavy furniture and somewhat formal waiters, it reminded Andy and Steph of tavernas they'd been to in Palermo. More importantly, the food was freshly cooked and authentic. When they arrived, the place was packed and the atmosphere buzzing. They both ordered a pasta dish and a glass of red wine. Steph sipped her drink and looked at her partner, who was silent and seemed tired and distracted.

'Well, you're not Mr Talkative tonight, are you?' she said teasingly.

Andy rubbed his eyes and shook his head, as if trying to wake himself up.

'No, sorry, I'm knackered, actually. It's been non-stop since Superintendent Walker sent me to work with Inspector McNiven on this investigation into Blake's escape. But I think we've set an effective trap for him.'

'Are you finding it too much? You know, the responsibility?'

'No, I'm enjoying it. But it's hard work and you tend to think about it all the time if you're not careful – wondering if you've made the right decisions, you know?'

'Yes. I suppose that would be the name of the game if either of us went for an inspector's job.'

'You're right, but I think when I got used to it, I would like it. You would too. I think the boss is right; we've got enough experience now to take charge of things.'

She sat back in her chair and looked at him. 'Right, that's interesting. I've not heard you speak so positively about promotion before.'

'No, well, I haven't really done anything like this before now. I'm glad Superintendent Walker gave me the chance.' He sipped his wine. 'You know, doing this has made me think about my dad a lot.' Andy's dad had also been in the police force in London – shot dead by a drug dealer when Andy was eleven.

'Really? In what way?'

'I keep thinking about what he would want me to do. I'm sure he would be proud that I was a detective sergeant, but I reckon he would also want me to go as high as I could in the force.'

'Of course he would, but you have to be sure that you want it for yourself.'

'Yes, I know. I remember telling the boss when I first came to West Yorkshire that I joined the police because of my dad, but it wasn't just because of him; I'd always wanted to be a detective.'

'It's interesting that I've always thought that the boss is a kind of substitute dad for you; someone you look up to.'

'Oh, definitely. And I suppose that's the reason why I'm so concerned to keep him safe. I think I'm afraid of history repeating itself.'

Steph nodded. 'I see. Well, tell me about this trap for Blake.'

Andy explained the details.

'No wonder you're looking a bit stressed,' Steph told him. 'That's a good idea, but also a high-stakes operation. Blake could be dangerous. Have you covered all the bases?'

'Yeah, I think so. I've been over it so many times in my head. There'll be six of us there, most armed. I don't think Blake is going to come to the house waving a gun around. He needs Bryson's cooperation to conceal him and make things appear normal.'

'Well, you never know, so take care.' Steph looked down at her drink and frowned. It was at times like this that you were reminded that their job could be perilous. Lots of things could happen any day and at any moment, but most of the time you forgot about it. You had to. But when there was an operation like this it was impossible not to feel worried. Your partner was going to confront a criminal with a history of violence, and firearms might be involved. Who wouldn't be concerned about that?

'How's it going with the boss?' asked Andy, breaking Steph's reverie.

'Very gentle compared to what you're doing. We had a walk up on the Chevin yesterday. I thought it would clear his mind and it was very pleasant until we got to the building there.' She told him about going up through the woods to Chevin Towers and how sinister it felt. 'The boss seems to think that place could be involved in these murders somehow, but I think that he is clutching at straws, same as his belief that Blake is involved. I know he's very frustrated because we don't have any good leads yet. It feels like we are waiting for the next murder and can't do anything to stop it. At least you've got a clear target.'

'Yes, but if I know the boss, he'll conjure something out of nothing, and the case will be solved.'

'Let's hope so, but as he keeps telling us, he's not invincible,' said Steph as her *spaghetti cozze e vongole* was placed on the table.

Andy winced in mock horror. 'Mussels and clams, yuck! They taste of seaweed and sand. I don't know how you can eat them.'

Steph laughed, wishing she had a pound for the number of times she'd heard him say this. 'Shut up and eat your lasagne,' she said as Andy's more familiar pasta dish arrived.

~

On Monday morning Abigail Wilson, Hillary Sands and Dylan Hardy were reunited in the office at the Courthouse. Although the stairs up to the cells were still taped off, they were able to open the rest of the building. A volunteer was at work in the café and another on reception was receiving calls about bookings for events. At last some sense of normality had been restored. The decorator Scott Evans had been allowed back into the courtroom and was whistling as he worked in his usual cheery way.

'How are you, Abigail?' asked Hillary. Her voice was flat, as if it was an effort to ask the question.

'I was feeling much better for a good rest over the weekend, thanks. But the news about Frances is shattering.'

Hillary looked away and said nothing.

'Yes. We've been very worried about you, especially after the latest crime,' said Dylan. 'Ironically, I think the worst for the Courthouse is over. It sounds an awful thing to say but I think attention has now gone over to the terrible discovery of the body of Frances, which was even more horrific than what happened here. I pity the people at that church now. They'll be getting all the attention we had.'

'You're probably right,' said Abigail. 'You know, we must arrange something in Frances' memory. She put a lot of time in here as a volunteer.'

'Absolutely,' said Hardy. 'Maybe we could name one of the rooms after her or even the auditorium.'

'That's a good idea. And we must send some flowers and a card to Malcolm. It's—'

Abigail was interrupted by a knock at the door, and Oldroyd entered.

'Hello, everybody,' he said in his jovial manner. Oldroyd was determined to remain upbeat and not convey his anxiety about Blake and the lack of progress in the case to other people. 'It's good to see you back and this place functioning again. Everything's fine as long as you keep away from upstairs. That's a crime scene and will be out of bounds for a while yet.'

'We understand,' said Abigail. 'We're obviously really upset about Frances Hughes.'

Oldroyd nodded. 'Yes, I appreciate that it's very distressing. It appears that you were right to give us that warning. I'm sorry that we were too late to do anything to protect her. Were any of you aware of any enemies she might have had?'

They all shook their heads.

'She was a lovely woman, Chief Inspector,' said Abigail. 'I can't imagine why anyone would wish to hurt her.'

'Well, we're working hard to catch whoever is doing this,' continued Oldroyd. 'I wanted to ask you all about something else. It's concerning that Victorian building up on the Chevin. You know, Chevin Towers, I think it's called.'

'What about it, Chief Inspector?' asked Dylan. 'I might be able to tell you something. I think I've lived here longer than Abigail and Hillary, and I'm in the local history group.'

'My detective sergeant and I were walking up the Chevin on Saturday and we came across it. It's a large building, isn't it? And it seems to have been empty for a long time. Do you know anything about its recent history?'

'You're right, Chief Inspector – it's been deserted for a while. About thirty years, in fact. It was built in the eighteen-sixties for Robert Hammond – a wealthy mill owner in Bradford. Then it was some kind of private school for a while, and it was last used as a children's home back in the nineteen-nineties. When that closed, no one seemed interested in taking it on. The costs of running it will be huge and it probably needs a lot of work doing to it. I wish someone would have a go; it's a fine building but it seems to loom over the town at the moment. It must have looked magnificent at one time.'

This was intriguing news to Oldroyd. 'Do you know anything about why the children's home closed?' he asked.

'Not really, it was all a bit hush-hush and mysterious. There were rumours that some bad things had happened there.'

'What kind of things?'

Dylan shrugged. 'I don't know, but I presume it was something to do with mistreatment of the children. It was shut down very quickly and the children moved elsewhere.'

'Do you know anybody who worked there or was associated with it in any way?'

Dylan thought for a moment. 'It was a long time ago, Chief Inspector, but someone once told me that Frances Hughes had some kind of connection with it – although I can't remember what. She never talked about it and I never asked her anything. I didn't want to dredge things up. It's ancient history really and it's a kind of dark secret in the town. Older people who remember it happening won't talk about it.'

Maybe it's not so ancient after all, thought Oldroyd as he turned to the others. 'Did she ever mention that to either of you?'

Abigail shook her head. Hillary looked away and seemed very uncomfortable. Oldroyd noted with some curiosity that she'd said nothing during the whole of this conversation. 'Well, thank you very much. That's been extremely helpful.'

Oldroyd returned to the robing room, where Steph and DC David Hall were waiting. Hall reported back on the work that he and the other officers had been doing.

'We've got all the statements in, sir, and we've checked them. No one seems to have noticed anything unusual about the behaviour of the victims in the time before the murders. The account of the first victim's final movements, as stated by his wife and friend in the pub, seems to be correct. It supports the idea that he must have been attacked on his way to the pub. We've investigated and questioned this friend and there's nothing suspicious there.

'Malcolm Hughes' friend confirmed that he was with him all afternoon in Harrogate. It's conceivable that he could have murdered his wife when he returned, but that would leave us with the problem of what he did with her body. Also, if we're thinking of him as the killer, what is his motive for murdering the two victims and arranging the bodies as he did?

'We've also checked the phone records of both victims. There was nothing of interest on Lowell's phone. On Hughes' phone, there was the call made to Abigail Wilson, as she reported to you, but nothing else of note.'

'Good work,' said Oldroyd. 'Well, I've just been talking to Dylan Hardy in the office. He seems to be something of an expert on local history.' He turned to Steph. 'Chevin Towers – that old mansion we were looking at – was used as a children's home in the nineteen-nineties and apparently it shut down rather abruptly for undisclosed reasons, but probably due to some abuse of the children. Also, Hardy thinks that Frances Hughes had some connection with the place. It's a tenuous link at the moment, but if Lowell also has a link to that building, whatever happened there could have provided a motive for these crimes.'

'You mean if someone was badly treated there, sir? And they're taking their revenge?'

'Exactly. If our killer isn't Blake, it could be a victim of the abuse or maybe a parent or other relative of someone who was abused.'

'Do you have any idea who it might be, sir?' asked Hall.

'None, I'm afraid. I'm going to get DC Warner to look into it. She's our expert researcher at the Harrogate station. It's a lead and we have to follow it.'

'I'll ask around locally, sir, and see if I can uncover anything about the place. I've lived here most of my life and that place has always been empty. It's a familiar landmark in the town but nobody talks about it. It must have a history.'

Oldroyd nodded and smiled. At last, there was a glimmer of hope in the investigation. Could they link Blake to Chevin Towers in some way? Then his phone rang: *unknown number*.

'Ah, Chief Inspector,' Blake said, on the other end of the call. 'I thought I'd give you another friendly reminder that I'm still here, just so you don't start to think I've forgotten my plan for us to be reunited.' Oldroyd took a deep breath; he had been expecting another call like this.

'Don't worry, I know our relationship is far too strong for you to abandon me,' he said, trying to humour Blake in the hope that he might relax and give something away.

Blake giggled with delight. 'Oh, Chief Inspector, I just love our little conversations. It's going to be rather sad when you're no longer around. I know you're a literary man and it's always seemed to me that you play Sherlock Holmes so well to my Professor Moriarty, only in our version it's Moriarty who is going to win in the end.'

'Well, I'll have to disagree with you on that. By the way, you know we've had another murder in Otley.'

'Yes, doesn't everyone? It sounds like you're having to work hard.'

'Indeed. Have you ever had anything to do with a children's home in Otley?'

'A children's home? Not me, I'm afraid. I had a nice upbringing – too good, some people might say. My parents always gave me exactly what I wanted. Maybe that was their mistake. Ever since, I've taken what I want.' He laughed. 'And I deserve it. You have to believe in yourself, don't you, Chief Inspector?'

'So, are you comfortable where you are hiding?' asked Oldroyd.

'Another nice try, Chief Inspector. Fishing around for details of where I might be, are you? All I'm going to say to you on that is that I'm about to get a little closer to you, so you can look forward to our next – and final – encounter.'

'I will, and with keen anticipation.'

Blake laughed again. 'This questioning is beginning to feel too much like old times, so I think I'll be off. Bye for now and remember: *dulce vindicta*.' He ended the call.

Oldroyd was taken aback. What? Blake using Latin? What did it mean? That he was indeed the Otley murderer? He related the message to Steph, who was also surprised.

'I know *dolce* is sweet in Italian, sir, so I take it this means *revenge is sweet.*'

'It does, but it's more than likely that Blake is playing with us, me in particular. I spoke about the word *vindicta* at the last press conference so it's out there now. He probably saw me speaking on television. He can't resist calling to tease me about that, of course, which meant he gave away a little bit of information. He told me that he was getting closer. That ties in with him contacting Bryson in Harrogate, though he doesn't know we're aware of that. Let's hope that Andy's scheme works.'

'Yes, sir,' said Steph, who would be relieved when that was over.

'In the meantime,' continued Oldroyd, 'there are a couple of people I want to speak to who might be able to shed some light on this Chevin Towers business.'

～

At Philip Bryson's house in Harrogate, the atmosphere was tense. Andy was rehearsing various scenarios in his mind and trying to anticipate what might go wrong with the plan to recapture Blake. There were armed officers hidden throughout the house. Andy himself was going to be behind the door to the pantry; he would emerge after Blake had been shown into the living room, check that other officers were ready to move in and then give the signal. They were not expecting Blake to be wielding a weapon. DC Hardiman, in plain clothes, was outside in an unmarked car.

Bryson, not surprisingly, was nervous about the whole thing and needed constant reassurance that he would be safe.

Bryson had arranged that Blake would arrive at about one o'clock, and so everyone was in position by twelve thirty. Bryson sat in the living room fidgeting, while the officers remained quietly in their positions. Andy was waiting in the hall.

One o'clock came and went with no sign of Blake, but there was no particular concern. He was probably running late. But at two o'clock, Bryson was getting jumpy and said he felt physically sick. He put his head round the door of the living room. 'I don't know what's happening. I said one o'clock and explained where the house was. He seemed keen about it. I'm not lying; I wouldn't mess you around.'

'Don't worry,' said Andy. 'I believe you. Something must have gone wrong. Let's just be patient.' He called Hardiman. 'Any sign of anything out there?'

'No, Sarge. The street's deserted. Nobody around at all. Unless he's going to climb over the garden wall.'

'OK. We've got the back covered as well.'

Reluctantly Bryson returned to the living room where he tried to concentrate on reading a book. Andy checked all the windows but saw nothing.

One of the armed officers whispered from the stairs, 'Is anything happening, Sarge?'

'Not yet – just stay at your post.' Andy was feeling increasingly frustrated, a feeling which intensified as the disappointing afternoon progressed. At four o'clock, he decided to abandon the operation. DC Hardiman had still not seen anything in the street.

'I don't know what's happened, but we can't all stay here any longer,' he said to Bryson. 'I'm going to leave one officer here until late this evening. If Blake arrives after that, ring the number I gave you immediately. You don't even need to say anything; I'll see your number come up and we'll be round here very quickly.'

Bryson agreed, but looked as if he now thought that the whole idea had been a bad one. Had Blake got wind somehow? If so, he could be in danger.

Andy was very glum as he drove back to Harrogate station with DC Hardiman. Not only had he failed to capture Blake, but he now had to tell Oldroyd that his arch enemy was still at large. It was humiliating.

Hillary Sands worked part-time at the Courthouse, and on certain afternoons she joined her husband at the antiques shop. It was normally quiet; the shop was never very busy. In the antiques trade you relied on occasional sales of expensive items in order to make a living.

Hillary sat in a chair behind the wooden table that acted as a counter, fiddling nervously with a brass ornament. Jeremy looked at her warily. She'd been even more withdrawn and restless since the second murder.

'How are you feeling?' he asked.

'Not good. I don't know what to do. I just can't believe it, but at that press conference I heard the chief inspector say that Frances Hughes had the same word written on her forehead as the body in the Courthouse. That means that if all this is to do with what happened at the home, she must have been involved and that's why she was killed. I just can't believe it. She seemed such a nice woman. The chief inspector came in to talk to us after the press conference and I just couldn't say anything. I think he noticed.'

Jeremy sat next to her. 'Look, I've told you. You're jumping to conclusions. There's no direct link to the home, is there? You're just assuming that there is one. You just said the word yourself: *if.*'

Hillary dropped the brass ornament on to the table with a clatter. Jeremy put his hand over hers.

'I just feel it's connected . . . but I don't know what to do if . . .' Her eyes roved around the room then stopped at a glass cabinet full of small china figures. She pointed to one. 'Jeremy, what is that?'

'Which one, love?'

'That little girl with a bag; she looks to be crying. Is that an angel over her head?'

'It's a little figurine of an orphan girl; part of a set of Victorian figures. Typical piece of sentimentality: she has her guardian angel to look after her, but that didn't make much difference in those times.'

Hillary burst into tears. Jeremy put his hand around her shoulder.

'Look, I think you need to talk to someone. How about telling Abigail everything? See what she thinks. She'll be very sympathetic and will help you to decide what to do. I think it would be good to get somebody else's opinion.'

Hillary wiped her eyes with a tissue and nodded. 'I think that's a good idea. You're right, I need to see what someone else thinks. I'll speak to her soon when I'm feeling a bit calmer.'

Four

Probably the most renowned person to come from Otley is the cabinet maker Thomas Chippendale, who was born in the town in 1718. He relocated to London as an adult and in 1754 published a book of his furniture designs, the first of its type, called The Gentleman and Cabinet-maker's Director. *These designs made Chippendale famous, as they were used throughout Europe and America. Examples of Chippendale's work can be seen in a number of stately homes in Yorkshire including Harewood House, Newby Hall, Sledmere House, Nostell Priory, Temple Newsam and Burton Constable Hall. Items of furniture made by Chippendale now sell for huge sums of money.*

McNiven's investigation into the men who had helped Blake escape from Stansfield Prison had yielded little except that – as he had initially thought – intelligence suggested they were part of an underground gang based in London, who were known to help out other criminals for a hefty price. He suspected that their involvement had ended after Blake had escaped from jail.

Clearly, Blake must have had plenty of money squirrelled away. He was probably paying some local people to hide him now.

His investigation into the internal help Blake must have had in prison had also not progressed very far. The prison authorities were not cooperating. He'd been allocated an interview room on a distant and gloomy wing of the prison building. He felt as if he had been shoved there out of sight and out of mind of Perry and the prison authorities, but this did not deter him in his dogged pursuit of an explanation as to how Blake had managed to escape, and where he might be now.

McNiven interviewed the two prison warders, Martin White and Jeffrey Peters, who were stationed on the prison wing where Blake was held. He felt that they were prime suspects as there were some unusual aspects in the way Blake had been handled on that day.

He spoke to White first, who appeared very cooperative.

'How did you find Blake as a person?' asked McNiven.

'In many ways, a model prisoner: always cheerful and cooperative. He was never disruptive or threatened violence to anybody.'

'Had his behaviour changed in any way recently?'

White shrugged his shoulders. 'Not that I noticed – you'll have to ask Jeff. He didn't like Blake, said he couldn't forget what the man had done.'

McNiven noted this. 'Blake must have communicated with people outside. How do you think he managed to do that?'

'I don't know. Blake wasn't regarded as high risk. That was obviously a big mistake. He was allowed to write letters to people, but they were always read through. I have known cases where prisoners have written letters using code words to get messages out to people though.'

'What about on the day of the escape?' continued McNiven. 'Did you notice anything unusual?'

White shook his head. 'Can't say that I did.'

'Was the level of restraint appropriate?'

'The level was consistent with his risk assessment. It's only the highest-risk inmates who would be handcuffed to an officer.'

'I see.' McNiven looked at his notes. 'Was it yourself and Jeffrey Peters who escorted Blake to the police van?'

'Yes, and I got smacked in the face for my troubles.' White pointed to a bruise on the side of his head. 'We had no idea what was going to happen. There was all that distraction. And then the car appeared and Blake just whacked me. I saw another side of him that day. But I have to admit it was very well planned.'

'Did Blake ever mention any friends outside of prison?'

'No. I got the impression that he was very much a loner. But he did once say that he had connections. I took that to mean with people in the criminal world.'

'Did he mention any names?'

'Not that I recall.'

'Was he particularly friendly with any of the other prisoners? In particular, people who've been released. We're wondering if someone that he got to know in prison is helping him now.'

White shook his head. 'I don't remember anybody. Blake was very polite to everyone but I can't say that he formed any friendships.'

McNiven ended the interview and then spoke to Jeffrey Peters. White's colleague was surly and laconic. His account of Blake's behaviour and escape was very similar to White's and McNiven learned nothing new, but he noticed that Peters did seem to have a deep dislike of Blake. Of course, there had been ample time for the two warders to get together and agree on a story that would cover their backs. Perry was probably involved in that as well. There was a big damage limitation exercise going on at Stansfield Prison.

McNiven sat in the room, thinking. He'd had a report from Andy concerning the latter's pursuit of people in the Harrogate and

Otley areas with whom Blake might be hiding. The young detective sergeant had also drawn a blank so far and unfortunately his plan to trap Blake had not worked. He was fully aware of the urgency of the situation and that his colleague Chief Inspector Oldroyd was in danger. It also seemed that there was an outside chance that the two cases were linked, and that Blake could be involved in the murders at Otley. It was complicated and they seemed far from finding the solutions to any of it. But McNiven was a dogged character, and undeterred. He had an idea about what he was going to do next.

∾

Later that day, Abigail and Dylan called in to see Malcolm Hughes. It was a personal visit and also one on behalf of the Courthouse.

Malcolm had recovered from his terrible shock sufficiently to be able to make them a cup of tea. Then he slumped back into his chair, which he'd hardly left since this nightmare began.

'Frances will be really missed at the Courthouse, Malcolm,' said Abigail as she drank her tea. 'She put in so much work, particularly as a steward for the evening performances. A lot of the volunteers don't want to do that as it means turning up at night.'

'Well, she enjoyed it,' said Malcolm. 'And she appreciated getting into the events for nothing.'

Dylan laughed. 'Well, there is that, I suppose, but I don't think that was her real motive. She was a great supporter of the Courthouse. Abigail and all the staff there want you to know that we were very grateful for what she did.'

Malcolm nodded, blinking away tears.

'Have the police treated you well, Malcolm?' asked Abigail.

'Yes, that chief inspector, he's very kind but he's extremely sharp as well. He obviously has me down as a suspect – not surprising, I suppose. Most people who are murdered are killed by somebody they know.' He closed his eyes for a moment. 'They came to talk to me again on Saturday.' An agonised look passed across his face. 'The worst thing is all this horrible stuff of her body being placed with those . . . those scarecrow figures and having that word written on her forehead. What did that mean? I can't bear to think about it.' He started to shed a few tears and sob. Abigail went over to sit next to him and she put a hand on his arm.

'It's absolutely awful, Malcolm, but I'm sure they'll find who did it.'

'The police have been speaking to us too,' said Dylan, to change the subject. 'The chief inspector seemed very interested in Chevin Towers. I'm not sure why.'

'Oh, that place?' said Abigail. 'It gives me the creeps.'

'Chevin Towers? Isn't that the gloomy building up in the woods?' asked Malcolm, who, unlike the others, was not native to Otley.

'Yes.'

'I've walked past it. It's all shut up, isn't it? Ghostly place. Frances never mentioned anything about it to me.'

Dylan frowned. 'Maybe I'm mistaken then. I thought she once told me that she'd worked there.'

'Really? What was it when it was functioning?'

'A children's home. The chief inspector seemed particularly interested in that. It must be something to do with the fact that it closed under a cloud. I think there was some abuse of children going on. I told the chief inspector that it was all hushed up at the time.'

'That's terrible,' said Malcolm. 'Frances would never have been involved in anything like that. She never had any kids of her own, but she loved children nevertheless. The police don't think she was involved, do they?'

'I don't think so, Malcolm. They're just trying to find out as much as they can about the place.' Dylan didn't want to upset Malcolm any further. It would be better to change the subject.

'Do you have any family who can come to stay with you?' he asked.

'Not really. Frances had a sister with two children, but the family moved to Canada a while ago. I don't even know if they'll make it to the funeral.'

'If you feel really down you can always contact us.'

'Thank you, that's very kind. Frances enjoyed volunteering at the Courthouse and seeing you people and . . .' He stopped speaking, overwhelmed again at the shock of realising that his wife had gone, and that things would never be the same again. He looked out of the window. 'You know, everything reminds me of her and what I've lost. When I see the garden, the realisation rushes in on me that I will have to do the gardening by myself from now on.' He shook his head and his face crumpled. 'It's an awful prospect.'

~

Late that afternoon, Oldroyd drove into Leeds to pay a visit to his sister. As a Church of England vicar, she was a person of deep wisdom to whom Oldroyd had always looked for advice and guidance. She had suffered some hardships over the years. She and her husband David had been unable to have children, and then David had died in his fifties from cancer. Being very much on the liberal wing of the church, she had encountered resistance to her views on a variety of issues, from the church's attitude to women and gay people, to her political beliefs in relation to poverty at home and abroad. This had once brought her into serious danger but she remained undeterred and undimmed in her faith. In fact, her views were perhaps even stronger after the incident. Beneath her affable and gentle demeanour, she was a very strong person with a staunch religious faith which Oldroyd, as an agnostic, didn't share.

After several years as vicar of a rural parish in the village of Kirby Underside, between Leeds and Harrogate – which she always referred to as her 'sabbatical' – she had retired to a flat in the centre of Leeds where she was still involved in a variety of organisations and initiatives related to the church's work with the poor and homeless.

Alison was always delighted to see her brother and she gave him a big hug as she welcomed him into her flat. Outside, a police officer was on duty. Alison was a likely target of Blake as she lived locally, unlike Oldroyd's son and daughter. They sat in a cosy living room lined with bookshelves and full of house plants.

'These plants look so healthy. Why didn't we both inherit green fingers from Mum?' remarked Oldroyd enviously. 'Do you remember when I was in my flat in Harrogate and I spent a small fortune on houseplants from Harlow Carr? I swear I followed the instructions on the label but most of them were dead after a few months of my tender care.'

'I think you overwatered, Jim. Mine thrive on neglect,' said Alison, smiling as she brought in mugs of tea and some of her famous scones. She scarcely seemed aware that she was being guarded by the police.

All the same, Oldroyd felt he had to say something. 'Sis, I'm really sorry that you have to have a police guard.'

Alison waved her arm. 'Oh, don't worry about that. I knew there would be trouble when I read that dreadful man had escaped from Stansfield. I remember how he threatened you. I'm sure he'll be caught before long. How's Deborah managing with the police being around?'

'Very well, like you appear to be. But you know I hate it when my job affects the family in any way.'

Alison looked at him. 'Well, you've had that stress for many years. I know you love the job, but do you ever think it might be time to consider retiring? No one's indispensable, you know, and we've all got to retire at some point. I don't think yours is the kind of job that you could do into your seventies.'

Oldroyd shook his head. 'You're right, and Deborah says the same, but I've not given any serious thought to it yet. And at the moment it's impossible.'

'Maybe after this case you should think about it. This business in Otley is very macabre. When I heard about it, I called Jane Anderson – the local vicar. I've known her a long time.'

'Yes, I met her when the body was discovered. Nice woman, she was obviously very upset.'

'I can imagine. She was in the campaign for women's ordination as a very young woman. She's a wonderful priest and they will need her after something so awful has happened. Anyway, do you think these two cases are connected?'

'There's a strong possibility. I'm still working on the assumption that it's too much of a coincidence that Blake escapes and some shocking murders start to be committed, although others on the team are not so convinced.'

'I've seen you on television with that detective sergeant of yours. Steph, isn't it? You looked very much in control, as usual. You didn't look as if you were under so much pressure. But then people often don't until they finally crack. So be warned.'

Oldroyd was familiar with the experience of his family watching him on television. It always happened when a case gained sufficient local or even national prominence.

'I will. Actually, I wanted to ask you something about the Otley case.'

'Really? Well, I'm always happy to oblige. But you could have waited – I'm going to call round at yours tomorrow to see how Deborah's doing.'

'Yes, but I don't want to spend all evening talking about this and we have to get on with things. It's about a place called Chevin Towers. You know where I mean? It's that big Gothic-looking house halfway up the Chevin. You can see it from the centre of Otley.'

'Yes, I know it. I walked up there once with you and Dad, a long time ago.'

'Well, I've discovered that at one time there was a children's home there, quite a while ago now. It closed down in dodgy circumstances – possibly something to do with the abuse of children. I wondered if you knew anything about it. Aren't these places sometimes run under the auspices of the diocese? Or maybe somebody from the diocese was on some kind of board of governors or something?'

Alison took a deep breath as she thought back. 'Are you talking about the nineties?'

'Yes, I think so,' said Oldroyd, between mouthfuls of scone and sips of tea.

'Come to think of it, I do remember something. I was vicar of the parish of St Stephen's here in Leeds at the time. There was this chap called Ivan Johnson. He lived in the parish and worshipped at St Stephen's and he worked at the diocesan office, something to do with the Board of Social Responsibility. You know how hospitals and prisons and places like that have official visitors whose job it is to befriend inmates or patients?'

'Yes. We have custody visitors at police stations.'

'I think Ivan had some kind of function like that at Chevin Towers. I don't think the church had any direct responsibility there, but I think he paid regular visits to talk to the children and see that everything was fine and they seemed looked after. He could advocate on their behalf. I remember him telling me once that a child had asked for a suitcase because when he moved between homes or foster carers all his belongings were put into a black bin liner.'

'That is so sad.'

'Yes, well, I remember him turning up one Sunday at church looking extremely stressed, and when I asked him what was wrong, he told me that something bad had happened at a children's home he was involved with, but he couldn't say any more about it. I can't remember the name of the home now, but it was based at Chevin Towers. I'm afraid that's all I know. It took him a while to recover, and he would never talk about it. I recall looking in the press for any reports about what had happened, but information was very limited. It was announced that the place was shutting down, but no details were given. At least, I can't remember any.'

'That's OK, sis, other people I've spoken to have said the same – it was done very secretly. But that makes me more interested because I have a theory that these murders in Otley could be connected with what happened at that home.'

'I'm afraid Ivan won't be able to help you. He died several years ago. You know, I wonder now whether that was partly due to the stress he was under. He never spoke out about what happened, and I think he must have felt guilty about that.'

'That's a shame. He was probably intimidated into staying quiet.'

'You may be right. Ivan was a very quiet, mild-mannered sort of man. I think he was very good with the children, but I couldn't imagine him standing up to the people in authority and questioning them.'

'Anyway,' continued Oldroyd, 'a key piece of evidence is the writing of the word *vindicta* on the foreheads of the victims.'

Alison shuddered. 'I saw you explaining that to the press. It's an awful thing, isn't it? Revenge – and for what?'

'We don't know exactly, but at least it helps us to narrow down the motive for the killings.'

Alison frowned. 'It's an instinct that we all have: to get even with people who have hurt us, but it can lead to terrible things, which is why the Gospels are strong against it.'

'It's one of the hardest things in Christian teaching though, isn't it? Forgiving people who've done horrible things to you.'

'It is, and I would never judge anyone who couldn't do it.'

'If my theory is right, this could be someone taking revenge for things that happened a long time ago.'

Alison sat back, looking thoughtful. 'If it's something that the person has lived with for many years and it's not been dealt with, they could still harbour a violent resentment against the people who abused them. In fact, the feelings could have got worse over the years. They could believe that these people have ruined their life and they've gone unpunished. Also, that the system let them down, so why should they observe the law and the rules?'

'Yes, you're eloquently expressing what I've been thinking. The problem is we don't know who the murderer is and we don't know if they have more victims in their sights.'

'I see. That must put a lot of stress on you and your team.'

Oldroyd was silent for a few moments, reflecting on what his sister had said. Then he suddenly smiled and clapped his hands on his legs. 'Yes, but anyway, enough of that. I haven't come to depress you about the darker sides of human nature. What have you been up to recently?'

Alison smiled too. 'Oh, I'm finding it wonderful to be back in the city. I'd had enough of country village life. There's so much happening here and it's so multicultural and interesting. Do you know, Jim, Leeds isn't a massive city, but through the work I'm doing I've met people from all over the world? I'm still involved with St Bartholomew's crypt – homeless people and refugees. But I don't do church services any more. That's not where it's "at" for me, as I think people say nowadays.' She chuckled.

'I knew you'd never stop with your pastoral work.'

'No, and curiously enough, in the light of what you've been telling me, all the volunteers at St Bart's, as we call it, had to go on training about child safety. Of course I've done some of that before but it never ceases to shock me how much abuse there is and how it is often concealed. I suspect the people at that home we were talking about did everything they could to keep it all quiet.'

'I think you're right,' said Oldroyd. 'There are bad rumours about what went on there, but people might have preferred to let sleeping dogs lie, as it were, rather than confront what had happened in their own backyard.'

'Yes, and then it becomes a taboo subject. You'll have your work cut out getting information from people, but if I know you, you'll soon have it all solved anyway,' she said with a laugh.

'Hopefully, but not before tomorrow. I'll see you then.'

'OK, Jim.'

❧

Late that day, Edward Brown was walking through the centre of Otley. He loved the busy network of narrow lanes and old streets with intriguing passageways leading off some of the main roads. There was something pleasantly old-fashioned about it, with its traditional butchers' shops, greengrocers, stationers, a bookshop and small cafés. He had made it his life's work to be a prominent figure in the town, and some people said he walked around as if he owned the place. His father had been a wealthy industrialist in the area and his large inheritance, though diminished over the years by his relative idleness, meant that he had never had to work very hard for a living. Over the years he had been a town councillor, mayor, school governor and a member of the board of trustees at many local institutions. He enjoyed the status that all these positions brought.

He turned a corner and nearly walked into Hillary Sands, who was just leaving the antique shop.

'Oh! I'm sorry, Hillary. I nearly knocked you over.'

'It's fine,' replied Hillary, moving away from him, seemingly ready to walk on.

But Edward continued the conversation. 'How is everyone today at the Courthouse?'

'OK, we're doing the best we can in the circumstances.'

'Good. Well, if there's anything I can do, don't hesitate to—'

Hillary turned to him. 'Look, I don't know how the others feel, but I'd prefer it if you stayed away.'

Edward was taken aback. 'Why is that?' He looked at her searchingly. 'I've always sensed that you don't really like me.'

She gave him a hostile look. 'I know things about you, Edward. It might have been a long time ago, but some people have never forgotten. I don't know exactly what you did but it was all very nasty, and you know it.'

'What are—?'

'Don't give me any of that. You know what I'm talking about. I'm sure you're doing some very good things for the Courthouse and for the town, but I'd be grateful if you didn't come to the Courthouse when I'm working there.'

With that, she turned round and walked off, leaving Brown perplexed and worried. First the murders and now this. Why after all this time were things from the past coming back to haunt him?

∾

149

'So the whole thing turned out to be a complete waste of time.'

In their flat, Andy was telling Steph about how the trap set for Blake had not worked because he never turned up. There had been no word from Bryson to say that Blake had appeared later. They were eating dinner and, unusually for him, Andy had little appetite and was pushing the food around his plate.

'It was bloody embarrassing,' he continued. 'It was supposed to be my big moment, when I caught the famous escaped criminal and put him back behind bars, ensuring the boss and his family were safe. Huh! No chance.'

'It's really disappointing,' said Steph. 'But that's a given in the work we do, isn't it? Lines of enquiry lead nowhere. Crimes remain unsolved for years. I've read that there are some detectives who are still haunted well after they've retired by cases that they failed to solve.'

Andy took a drink of his wine. 'Yeah, I know, but this case is urgent – people's lives are at risk, including the boss.' He sighed. 'It was the fact that I'd organised it so thoroughly and got the officers with firearms set up. There we were, waiting hour after hour in that little house. It made me look a right idiot in front of them. I don't know how I'm going to face Superintendent Walker.'

Steph smiled. 'He'll understand. He's got massive experience, and he must have had his fair share of things going wrong.' She looked at him with her head on one side. 'Have you gone off the idea of promotion, then?'

'No, not entirely, but it makes you realise that when you are in charge of something the buck stops with you.'

'Well, being in charge is a two-way thing, isn't it? You get the credit when things go well and the blame when they don't. But it's a challenge. Do you want to spend all your career taking orders from other people?'

Andy grimaced. 'At this point, I don't know. Ask me again when something's gone well.'

'How is the rest of your investigation going?'

'Inspector McNiven's concentrating on the prison. He's trying to find out who helped Blake to escape. He's a good bloke to work with. He's got a sharp mind like the boss. If he discovers who it was, that person may have information about where Blake is now. And you?'

'We're not doing well at all and we have no leads. The boss is very interested in this spooky old mansion in the woods above the town that was once a children's home. He thinks that the murders are something to do with bad things that went on there, that it might explain this *vindicta*-revenge business. He's going to get Sharon to research the place. The only connection we've discovered so far is that it's possible that the second victim was involved in the children's home at some point. That's about it. We've got a long way to go and it could lead nowhere, so the great Detective Chief Inspector Oldroyd would have had a failure. So what? It can happen to anyone.'

'Does the boss still think that Blake could be involved?'

'Yeah, there's no change on that one. It's possible, but so far, we've got nothing to link him with the murders in Otley and no motive. Blake rang the boss again, and still denies any involvement. I don't think the boss believes him though.'

'It's strange, though, that the killings started after he escaped.'

'I know, but coincidences do happen. It doesn't prove anything.'

'No. Anyway, fancy going out for a drink somewhere? It'll take our minds off things. Why don't we try that new place in Leeds Dock?'

'OK. But I'll be watching you and making sure that you don't try to drown your sorrows by drinking too much.'

'Oh, you know me.'

'I do, and that's why I'll be watching you.'

～

Tuesday morning dawned fine with a bit of an autumn nip in the air. Near the bridge in Otley there is a calm section of the river near some gardens, which is used for boating in the summer. It was the end of the tourist season, and the owner of the boats was up early to begin the process of cleaning, covering, and tying them up for the winter.

It was a beautiful morning and he whistled to himself as he reached the edge of the river. The mist was clearing, and the sun was coming out. There were still some patches of low mist hanging over the water. It was a peaceful scene; some mallards moved gently across the river and a grey heron flapped silently down towards the weir. Then he noticed that someone was lying in one of the boats. This had happened before. Occasionally a homeless person would spend the night in one, but he didn't much mind this if they didn't cause any mess or damage. As he got closer, he saw that one arm was dangling inertly over the side. He leaned over and to his horror saw a man with his lifeless eyes open. There was a red mark around his neck. He also noticed that, bizarrely, there was writing on the man's forehead. He looked around frantically but there was no one nearby. Finally, he pulled out his phone and called the police.

～

At home in New Bridge, Oldroyd received an early call from DC Hall. It was the call he had feared but half expected: another body had been found and it seemed to be a murder by the same killer. He'd not yet set off for work. He was drinking tea and eating his breakfast in the kitchen. Deborah had yet to come downstairs. The toast now seemed to turn to ashes in his mouth. He sat down and sighed. Three bodies discovered and they weren't any nearer to finding who the murderer was. It must be Blake, surely? But they hadn't found any link. Why was he murdering these people and yet not trying to come for Oldroyd directly? The question still haunted him. The monster was playing with him. It was a terrible situation. The next press conference would be a very difficult one.

Deborah appeared at the door in her dressing gown and yawned.

'Who was that?' she asked casually, and then she saw his face. 'Jim, what's happened?'

'Another body's been found in Otley; seems like the same killer again.' His voice was quiet and flat; the tone suggested frustration and despair.

'Oh no, that's bad. It's what you feared, isn't it?' She put her hand on his shoulder. She knew that when there was a murderer on the rampage like this, he felt an intense pressure to catch the person responsible. He began to see it as a personal contest between him and the killer. He would really be feeling like a failure now, and that would be on top of the stress of the threat from Blake. 'You must really try not to make it a fight between you and the killer, whether it's that man Blake or not.'

Oldroyd put his face in his hands. 'I know, you've already warned me about that. I'm trying.'

'You might be in charge of the investigation, but you're not the only one who's responsible for catching the culprit. Your team play their part too and they are all experienced people. And the public generally also have a role by staying alert and reporting unusual things to the police.'

'Yes,' he murmured. 'Thanks. I know you're right, but it's still very difficult when you're in charge.' He stood up. 'I'd better get off.' He looked at her longingly. 'I'd much rather stay here with you today and do some gardening.'

She gave him a wan smile. Oldroyd knew she was thinking how it was very unusual for him to complain about having to go to work. Also, that he didn't like gardening, so if he would rather stay at home and do that, he must be feeling pretty bad.

She got up and gave him a kiss before he left. 'Take care,' she said.

～

For the third time in just a few days, Oldroyd arrived at a murder scene in Otley. The footpath at the edge of the river, where the boats were moored in a line at right angles to the water's edge, was cordoned off with blue and white tape. The mist had lifted. There were a number of people on the bridge looking over to the murder scene. He could again see Tim Groves in protective clothing stooping over a huddled form.

Oldroyd walked over the grass and greeted DC Hall, who was supervising. He was also looking pretty downcast. 'It's another one, sir – same method and same writing on the forehead. Mr Groves is examining the body.'

'Yes,' said Oldroyd laconically. 'Has the victim been identified yet?'

'No, sir.'

'Well, get on to that and the usual investigative stuff – did anybody see anything or anybody behaving strangely, you know.' He couldn't think of much else to say. He walked over to Groves, who was his usual cheery and teasing self.

'Morning, Jim,' he said as he put some kind of specimen in a plastic bag. 'Sorry to get you out of bed at this time, but it looks very much as if we've got victim three here in the gruesome sequence.' He paused, realising that this latest discovery would increase the already considerable pressure on his old colleague. 'I hesitate to ask, Jim, but how are things going? It's a very nasty case, isn't it? And in a little town like Otley of all places.'

Oldroyd frowned. At times like this he felt as if he was a young detective just starting out, who knew very little. All his experience seemed to count for nothing. It seemed that you could suffer from imposter syndrome however long you had been doing a job like this in which life and death were involved and people looked to you for answers.

'Thank you for asking, Tim, but I'm afraid progress is very slow to say the least. I . . . Good God! What?!' he suddenly shouted and stepped back.

'Jim?' said an alarmed Groves.

Oldroyd had looked down at the body while he was speaking to Groves and had seen the face.

The dead man was Adam Blake.

At this moment Steph arrived to find her boss staring down incredulously at the victim and Tim Groves giving Oldroyd a baffled look.

'Sir? What's happened?'

'It's Adam Blake,' declared Oldroyd, pointing and shaking his head. It wasn't clear whether he had heard Steph or Groves speak. 'How can . . . ?' His voice trailed off.

Steph and Groves looked down at the body.

'You mean the same Adam Blake who escaped from Stansfield Prison?' asked Groves. 'The one who's been threatening you?'

Oldroyd nodded and then spoke quietly, musing to himself. 'So, it is Moriarty who died after all.' He looked at the river. 'He didn't fall into the Reichenbach Falls, although he was quite near to going over the weir on the wharf at Otley. But if Holmes didn't dispatch him, who did?' He shook his head.

'Beg your pardon, sir?' asked Steph, bewildered by her boss's apparent ramblings, and also stunned as she attempted to take in the complex implications of this discovery.

Oldroyd didn't reply. He stooped down and looked very carefully all over the corpse, particularly at the writing on the forehead.

'How long has he been dead?' he asked Groves.

'About twenty hours, I would estimate. A bit longer than the other victims.'

Oldroyd turned to Steph. 'No wonder he didn't turn up to walk into Andy's trap. He was probably dead by then. Thanks, Tim – send me your report. We're going to have to go and think about this. It's something we never expected.' He turned and walked away, apparently distracted and ignoring Steph, who followed him back through the streets to the Courthouse.

Oldroyd said nothing on the way and Steph sensed it was not the time to engage him in any kind of conversation.

When they arrived back at the Courthouse, Oldroyd went over to the little café and ordered two coffees, which he took back across to the robing room. There was an art exhibition and a small group of visitors which he passed without registering. Steph was waiting and they both sat down.

'Bloody hell,' said Oldroyd at last, looking dazed. 'Sorry, I've been completely distracted. Talk about a bombshell – it doesn't half complicate things and no mistake. I was convinced it must be him.'

'At least you're not under threat any more, sir.'

'Probably not.' He took a deep breath and drank some coffee.

'What do you make of this situation, then, sir?' asked Steph tentatively.

Oldroyd shrugged. 'It's not entirely clear to me.'

Steph had rarely seen him so bemused. 'Surely,' she asked, 'it means that we can at least eliminate Blake as a suspect for the first two murders?'

'Maybe . . . but he's got *vindicta* written on his forehead like the other victims . . . Does that mean that Blake was involved in the children's home, despite what he said? And how? Was he a victim or an abuser? I'm convinced that place must be involved. I'll get DC Hall to look into it too. We need to find out the names of children who were in that home and the staff who worked there, but it won't be easy. We'll get Sharon Warner to try to find the records. Maybe there were two people involved in these killings and they fell out. It doesn't give us any clear answers. Anyway, I'd better call Andy.'

Like the rest of them, Andy was astonished by the news. He was in the corridor at Harrogate HQ when he got the call and he had to go into the office and sit down.

'In a boat by the river, sir?' he said, trying to get his head round it.

'Yes, strangled. And that same word written on his forehead. Been dead since yesterday.'

'Bloody hell! No wonder he didn't turn up at Bryson's house.'

'That's exactly what I said to Steph.'

There was a pause as Andy struggled to find a response. 'Well, sir, I don't know what to say. I'll get straight on to Inspector McNiven and tell him what's happened. At least he can focus now on how Blake managed to escape. There are still people to bring to justice on that one.'

'I'm sure he'll need you to continue working with him.'

'Yes, sir. I'll see what he says.'

The call ended.

'That must have been a shock for him, sir,' said Steph.

'Yes. I imagine it will feel like a big let-down after his scheme to trap Blake failed. I think he really wanted to make an impression by tracking the famous criminal down, didn't he? And of course, protecting me.'

'He did, sir. It's the first time he's been in charge of an operation like that and he wanted to succeed.'

'Of course he did – it's really good that he's so keen. You have to live with a certain amount of disappointment and frustration in this job, I'm afraid. I'm feeling it myself at the moment. There will be other opportunities for him to take a leading role and maybe it's time for him to move on and get an inspector's job.'

'He keeps talking about it, sir. Eventually I think he will . . . and maybe I will too. The problem is it's such rewarding and interesting work when we're with you that we've probably got too comfortable.'

Oldroyd laughed. 'Well, maybe I'll have to make things harder; start being very grumpy and give you difficult and boring tasks to do. Then you might want to leave.'

'Oh, please don't do that, sir,' said Steph, smiling. 'I think we're a great team. I wouldn't want anything to spoil it.'

'You're right and don't worry, I'll stay my pleasant and fascinating self.'

He sat back in his chair, closed his eyes and tried to collect his thoughts. He was still reeling from the shock of seeing Blake's body, but puzzling doubts were starting to enter his mind and his instincts were telling him that something was wrong.

The discovery of a third body had a profound effect on the population of Otley. The centre of town became noticeably quieter as people stayed at home, fearful to be out on the streets. Business owners were feeling the effects; some cafés were closing early due to lack of custom. Pupils were shepherded to and from school by anxious parents, and security on school premises was increased. The MP for the area and other local dignitaries were interviewed on television and radio.

Well-known reporters appeared from national television stations and requested interviews with Oldroyd, but he declined. Instead, he issued a number of statements and said he would hold another press conference later in the day.

Some people in the town continued to go about their daily business, refusing in a stubborn Yorkshire way to allow anything to interfere with their lives. Even so, this third murder was the topic of a hushed conversation whenever people met someone they knew in the street.

At the Courthouse, the mood had been starting to improve a little as the centre prepared to fully reopen. But this latest news had brought them down once again as the three regular employees met that morning in the office.

'Great news for a Tuesday morning,' said Dylan Hardy, trying to lighten the atmosphere a little with his sarcasm.

Hillary Sands stopped what she was doing, groaned and covered her face with her hands. 'Oh, I'm not sure I can take much more of this, and neither can the town. There's quite a close-knit community here but something like this tears it apart. It fills people full of fear and suspicion.'

'I know,' said Abigail, 'and selfishly – from our point of view – fewer people are going to want to come to our evening performances.'

'I've heard that this latest victim is the man who escaped from Stansfield Prison. You know, the man who inveigled his way into the lives of older women before killing them and taking their money,' said Dylan.

'Maybe it's not such a bad thing then; he sounds like a bit of a monster,' said Hillary.

'Yes, but what is his connection with the other two victims? He didn't even live in Otley.'

Abigail threw up her hands in a gesture of despair. 'Oh, I don't know, but let's leave it to the detectives. They've got more information than we have.' She stood up. 'I'm going to fetch us all a coffee.' She went out of the office and up the short corridor past the reception desk to the café.

The other two remained quiet for a little while. Then Hillary said, 'That escaped criminal . . . what was his name? Adam Blake, wasn't it?'

'I believe so, yes.'

'Could he have had any connection with the children's home at Chevin Towers?'

Dylan raised his eyebrows. 'Why do you ask that?'

'Because the police obviously think there is some link between these murders and that place. You put them on to that when you said that Frances was involved there.'

Abigail returned with the coffees and listened to the conversation.

'I suppose I did, but I'm not aware that this man Blake had anything to do with it. Did he have any connection with Otley at all?' Dylan looked at Hillary. 'By the way, you don't appear to like any mention of Chevin Towers. It seems to make you a bit touchy. Why's that?'

'Never mind, Dylan, it's about something that happened a long time ago. Forget it.'

'OK, but if you know anything that's relevant to these murders, Hillary, I hope you will tell the police. People like that chief inspector are very shrewd and they find everything out eventually. Then anyone who has kept information from them is in trouble.'

'Yes, Dylan, I know. There are things about this that are not easy for me. In fact, they're very upsetting. I'll work out what to do in my own time. I'd be happy if you didn't say anything to anyone.' She looked away at her computer screen.

Dylan and Abigail exchanged glances but neither said any more.

～

At Stansfield Prison, McNiven was talking to Perry in the latter's office. They had received the news that Blake had been found murdered in Otley and a bullish Perry appeared to think that this represented closure on the matter of his escape. McNiven, however, pressed on.

'Do you have any information about the men who created that diversion when Blake escaped?'

'No, but I rather think that's your area, isn't it? They were on the outside,' Perry replied complacently.

'And what about on the *inside* then – I assume you are responsible for that?' insisted McNiven, with a note of sarcasm.

'No point wasting a lot of time on that now,' said Perry breezily. 'I'm sure we've all got more important things to be getting on with. The man's dead so he's no danger to anyone. You can leave it to us to find out who, in the prison, was involved in the escape, if anyone was.'

McNiven gave Perry an icy stare. He was having none of it. 'There is no doubt about that, but we can't let this matter of collusion in the escape of an inmate drop. You know as well as I do that internal investigations like this can leave the impression that the institution has something to hide. I'm sure that you don't want that – especially if the press get wind of it. One of the staff here – *your* staff – assisted Blake in his escape. That's a very serious offence. Having spoken to a number of people and assessed the circumstances in that part of the prison, it's clear to me that it's most likely to be one of the warders who works on that wing. I've spoken to Martin White and Jeffrey Peters, and now need access to the full records for them. Are you aware of any problems with either of them in the past?'

Perry gave him a sour look. His positive mood had been punctured; McNiven was not going away. 'None at all. And I can assure you that all our staff are thoroughly vetted before they are employed here and—'

'I'm sure they are,' replied McNiven abruptly. 'But I know that you will want to continue to fully support our investigation.'

'Yes,' replied Perry through gritted teeth. 'I'll contact HR. I hope this investigation doesn't go on for too long. It's very unsettling for my staff and the inmates.'

'Just as long as we need,' said McNiven implacably.

❧

On the farm above New Bridge, George Milton was feeding his pigs. Looking after these animals, even though they would be sent for slaughter before very long, was the only thing that he cared about on the farm in his current embittered state.

'Hey, Dad!' It was his son Jake.

Milton finished emptying feed into a trough and turned. 'What?'

'I've just heard from Phil Bradley – there's been another murder in Otley.'

'Bloody hell!' said Milton, though he didn't feel too concerned about it.

'Phil said the victim was that bloke you were in prison with . . . the one who escaped. He was called Blake, wasn't he?'

'Shit!' exclaimed Milton. 'Yeah, he was.'

Jake gave him a searching look. 'You never said much about him or anything much about prison at all. Did you get on with him OK? Was he really a friend of yours?'

'What? Why the hell are you asking me that? You sound like t' police. Do you think I did him in or summat?'

'I don't know. You've been weird since you came back here from prison. I don't know what you did in there. Maybe the police are right. You helped this bloke escape, then something went wrong, and you had an argument. You were out till late last night. Where were you?'

Milton was speechless with rage. He kicked over a feeding trough, grabbed the front of his son's shirt and pulled him forward so that they were nearly touching face to face.

'So, do you think I killed the others as well? I'm a bloody serial killer, then? I ought to give you a thrashing!'

'Get off me!' shouted Jake, pulling himself free with difficulty. He was taller than his father but Milton was built like a bulldog. 'You haven't answered my question.'

'OK. I walked down to The Black Horse, stayed until closing time and then a few of us went back to Tom's place and drank a few whiskies. Then I walked back up here. How's that?' He pushed Jake, who stumbled back and banged his head on the wall of the barn.

'Watch it!' exclaimed Jake.

'It might knock some sense into you. Imagine, a son of mine thinks I'm a murderer.'

'I didn't say you were. It's just that you're so bitter and angry all t' time that I don't know what you might do – especially after t' police came. They must suspect you.'

'They think I helped Blake escape, but it's all rubbish. And I didn't kill him, right?'

'OK, OK,' said Jake, and walked off rubbing his head and thinking. He needed to speak to his brother. They were going to have to do something about the situation if his father went on behaving like this.

Milton went back to feeding his pigs and reflected on the news that his son had given him. He had no sympathy for that bastard Blake who deserved all he got. He smiled to himself. If the police came, he had a watertight alibi. And anyway, he was too clever for them. They'd never stick anything on him again.

~

As Oldroyd predicted, the third press conference was even more difficult than the previous ones. It was rare for him to have to face the press for the third time concerning a particular case. He usually had it all wrapped up before that was necessary. It felt like another defeat.

He spoke to them again outside the Courthouse with Steph and DC Hall at his side. There were more reporters, microphones and cameras than ever before – and a huge clamour of people trying to ask questions. Oldroyd kept to his rule never to answer questions until he had said what he wanted to say first.

'No doubt you will have already heard,' he began, with some irony undetected by the baying crowd, 'that a third body has been discovered in this town. We have reason to believe that the same person is responsible for this murder as for the murders of Tony Lowell and Frances Hughes. The body was found in an unusual place, the method of killing – strangulation with a ligature – was the same and the word *vindicta* was written on the victim's forehead.'

He had their attention now, all right. There was no doubt in their minds that some vicious and deranged serial killer was at work in the small town. It was an absolute dream for the tabloids and Oldroyd could already see the headlines: *Sleepy Yorkshire Town Terrorised by Mad Killer, Beautiful Market Town Shocked by Third Gruesome Murder, Who is Next? The Shocking Question Being Asked in Yorkshire Murder Town.* But although a lot of them were absolutely loving it, he knew that there would be a hostile onslaught of questions to him about why the killer was still at large. For the moment, he continued.

'I can confirm that the victim was Adam Blake, a convicted murderer who recently escaped from Stansfield Prison.' He braced himself for the loud calls of surprise, which duly came. The crowd surged forward and threatened to engulf him. Police officers had to pull them back.

He wondered how they would now amend their melodramatic headlines. Perhaps: *Murder Mayhem: Escaped Killer Strangled to Death in Murder Town* or *Third Victim in Otley is Recently Escaped Criminal. Can Town Ever Recover?*

He struggled on. 'So, as usual, we would like to speak to anyone who saw any unusual activity last night, especially by the rowing boats on the river, just over the bridge from the centre. I'll take questions now.'

'How come Adam Blake was in Otley, Chief Inspector?' asked the closest reporter. 'Was it to have a pop at you? We've heard that he wanted to get his revenge on you for putting him away. You must have been scared.'

Oldroyd had half expected that this would come up. It was too dramatic a story for them not to pursue it. It suggested further impactful headlines: *Bitter Rivalry Between Famous Detective and Infamous Criminal Finally Comes to an End.*

But Oldroyd wasn't going to go into too much detail on this. It was a distraction from the urgent issue of tracking the murderer down. 'OK, it's true that Blake swore to get revenge on me after his sentencing, so that could be why he remained in the area. Of course, it's not certain that he was murdered here. His body could have been brought to Otley after.'

'Why would anyone do that?' asked a TV reporter.

'Because it would appear that these murders are part of a sequence. This body, like those of the other victims, was brought to the crime scene and staged.'

'You mean the murderer is making some kind of statement through the crime scene?'

'Probably. We're working on what the message might be.'

'It's weird stuff, Chief Inspector,' commented another. 'How is the investigation going? Are you any nearer to catching this person?'

Oldroyd gritted his teeth and faced them defiantly. 'We are not expecting an imminent arrest, but I would remind you that the first body was discovered only five days ago. Going by the word that has been written on each of the victims, this is a campaign of revenge for something. It has clearly been planned in advance and is being executed deliberately at speed so that we have much less chance of tracking the person down before they have finished.'

'Revenge for what, Chief Inspector?'

Again, it was frustrating to Oldroyd that he could not give a clear answer – but at least if he mentioned Chevin Towers, that might jog someone's memory, and they might come forward with useful information.

'We're not sure about that yet, but we have a theory, and it is only a theory at this point, that the murders may have something to do with events some time ago at Chevin Towers – a Victorian mansion in the woods above the town here. A children's home operated there in the nineteen-nineties. So I'll ask that if anyone has any information about that children's home would they please come forward.' This caused some excitement: this story was getting better and better – gruesome murders, revenge, now a sinister mansion and child abuse.

'Do you mean that children were abused there, Chief Inspector?'

'I can't confirm that, but it appears likely. We have discovered that the home was closed quite abruptly, and a veil of secrecy was cast around it. The result is that information is very scarce, but we have some of our best researchers looking into it. If abuse there was concealed, we may well have our motive, if not yet the perpetrator.'

'Is anyone else at risk, Chief Inspector?' This was always the big one and always difficult to answer.

'I've already said that we don't believe that this is a random killer, but that everyone should take care. The killer is targeting their victims carefully. If we're right that these crimes relate to what happened at Chevin Towers, then there may be someone involved with the children's home who realises that they may be at risk. If that is so, they need to come forward immediately both for their own protection and for the valuable information that they can provide us with.'

Oldroyd knew that this was further wonderful material for them. They would all be thinking that Christmas had come early. Now they had a spooky Gothic mansion to add to the mix, inspiring yet another series of headlines: *Are Events at this Ghostly Old Mansion Behind the Terrible Series of Murders in Otley?* and *True Gothic Horror in Quiet Market Town.*

The truth was that he was so desperate for leads that he had to get all this out to the public, even if it meant dealing with such exaggeration. He had to hope that the lurid headlines might prompt someone to come forward with new information.

～

Back in the Courthouse, Oldroyd collapsed into a chair, exhausted with the strain of conducting the press conference.

While he recovered, Steph went out briefly to buy some sandwiches at a local independent bakery. The streets were very quiet and the staff in the bakery were standing around in the empty shop and pleased to see a customer. The smell of fresh bread wafted out from the ovens at the back of the shop and the counters had a mix of traditional and more modern cakes, tarts and squares. Steph's eyes lingered on the wonderful variety on display, all made on site: sticky Yorkshire parkin . . . and Yorkshire curd tart: a Yorkshire delicacy made from curds, currants and spices.

Oldroyd, she knew, was trying to avoid sweet things at lunchtime but Steph decided he needed a treat, and Yorkshire curd tart sounded just the thing to cheer him up. When she returned with the food, he was thrilled. The smell of the hot bacon tea cake and the sight of the curd tart improved his mood considerably.

As they ate it all, they again considered where they were with the case.

'Where do we go from here, sir?' asked Steph, as she ate her hummus and red pepper wrap. 'We still have no direct leads, do we?'

'No,' replied Oldroyd, taking a sumptuous bite out of his bacon tea cake. 'As I said at the press conference, the killer appears to have planned all this in advance, and they are several steps ahead of us all the time. We're waiting for more information either from DC Warner or from somebody who comes forward. I also need to contact Tim Groves. I want him to take a closer look at Blake's body.'

'Why's that, sir?'

'There are things that puzzle me about that last murder. I'll tell you more when Tim has reported back.'

Steph smiled. She was familiar with this quirk of Oldroyd's methodology. Sometimes he wouldn't share his thoughts until he was sure about an idea and had evidence to back him up.

'I thought you handled the press well, sir, as always. You didn't show any of the strain that we're under. There's nothing worse than trying to catch an elusive criminal who could strike again at any time.'

'You're right, but—'

Oldroyd's phone rang. It was Tom Walker. The pressure was unrelenting but at least his boss was normally very supportive.

'Hello, Jim. Well, it's a rum do in Otley, isn't it? Three people killed and the latest one is Blake, of all people? What the hell is going on?'

'I wish I knew, Tom. We're working on it very hard but – as I was telling the press just now – it's all happened very quickly, which means we've had hardly any time to locate any suspects. It's been very well planned and the perpetrator's been ahead of us. But don't worry, we'll crack it.'

'I know you will, but I've had you-know-who on the phone, asking about the case, who was on it, etc.' This was a reference to Matthew Watkins. 'It's to be expected, I suppose. He only gets interested when it looks as if we're having difficulties that might reflect badly on West Yorkshire Police and tarnish his bloody reputation. Never mind the fact that people are risking their lives chasing these killers down. And sometimes facing the consequences for years. Look at you with Blake. At least you won't have to worry about him any more. But anyway' – Oldroyd could imagine him waving his hand dismissively to symbolically obliterate Watkins – 'you've got full support from me. I know what a great job you and your team do in the field, and I won't take a word against you from that ridiculous fake.'

'Thanks, Tom.'

'I'll leave you to get on with it. I know it's a lot of pressure, so let me know if you want more help. You've got Stephanie Johnson, haven't you? Young Carter is still working with McNiven, but he should be available for you soon if you need him now that Blake's no longer a problem. Best of luck, and don't worry about

Watkins – I'm more than a match for him and I think he's a little bit frightened of me.' He chuckled. 'He bloody should be.'

~

That afternoon, Andy arrived at Stansfield police station. Stansfield was on the very northern limit of the West Riding Police area. The police station was a grand Victorian red brick building on the edge of the town and not far from the prison.

Andy reported to McNiven's office, which was very tidy and well organised, reflecting McNiven's rational and scrupulous approach to his job. The inspector sat upright behind his desk. He wore steel-rimmed glasses and had a neatly trimmed moustache. Andy sat on the other side of the desk.

'So, all our efforts to recapture Blake alive have been in vain; we've merely been left with his body,' observed McNiven drily.

'That's right, sir. Half of our investigation has been closed down, but I think Chief Inspector Oldroyd's work on the murders in Otley has become more complicated.'

'Yes, I can see that; it's very unfortunate. But we'll have to leave him to it because, as you indicate, we have the other part of our investigation to complete: who helped Blake to escape?'

'How's that progressing, sir?'

McNiven smiled. 'Some good news on that front, I think. We have made progress, despite some resistance from James Perry, the governor of the prison. It was clear that the main suspects must be the warders who worked on the wing where Blake had his cell, as they would have got to know him. Questioning them revealed nothing, so I looked into their backgrounds. They both had unblemished records, so I've widened the search to other warders who might've had contact with Blake. But still no joy.

'The most popular theory was that Blake had offered some kind of financial inducement to whoever helped him to escape. So I checked credit ratings and things like that to see if any of them had any money problems. This also yielded nothing, and I began to think that maybe we'd got the whole thing the wrong way round. I think Blake's murder has proved me right.'

'What do you mean, sir?'

'Instead of making money out of helping Blake to escape, what if someone wanted to spring him from prison in order to get their hands on him, so to speak – someone who had reason to hate him?'

Andy realised what McNiven was suggesting. 'You mean a relative of one of the people that Blake murdered.'

McNiven grinned and nodded. 'Exactly. Look at this.'

He pushed a folder of documents towards Andy. Inside were copies of newspaper reports of one of Blake's most heinous crimes. He had befriended an isolated and lonely old lady and persuaded her to change her will before poisoning her and making it look like suicide.

'Look at this one and at the photograph,' said McNiven, pulling one from the pile.

Andy read the account, written before Blake's involvement came to light, of the sad death of Mrs Marjorie Barnes, a widow, who had never been able to adjust to the loss of her husband. She had taken her own life when 'the balance of her mind was disturbed' as the old phrase from coroners' reports went. It wasn't until Oldroyd's investigation linked her death with Blake's activities that it was revealed as murder.

There was a photograph of her smiling with a young man by her side.

'The caption says, *Mrs Barnes with her nephew, Martin White*. That's the name of one of the warders in charge of Blake. I've checked and it is the same person.'

Andy whistled. 'Well done, sir. So we've got a suspect and a motive. Do you really think he killed Blake?'

'Very likely. So, what we have to do now is search his house for evidence that Blake has been there and if we do, that would clinch it, though of course he may not have taken Blake there.'

'Right, sir – that sounds good. I'm eager for some success in this case after the fiasco at Otley.'

'Yes, that was unfortunate. But the likely reason Blake didn't turn up was that he was dead – a very good reason, I think. Your idea was a perfectly sound one.'

'Thank you, sir,' replied Andy, smiling. 'That's exactly what Chief Inspector Oldroyd said, but it didn't seem much consolation at the time.'

'No, but you'll get over it.' McNiven thought for a moment. 'You know, I'm not sure how Blake could really fit into the sequence of the murders at Otley, from what I've heard, but we'll leave that to DCI Oldroyd. He usually gets it right in the end, doesn't he?'

'He does, sir,' replied Andy, knowing how difficult a case the Otley murders was, even for a detective with Oldroyd's talents.

∼

Edward Brown sat at home endlessly turning things over in his mind and becoming more anguished and agitated. He'd always been very disciplined with alcohol, but he had a glass of whisky by his side now, even though it was the middle of the afternoon. He'd drunk half a bottle since he got up.

He'd thought long about the dilemma that Frances Hughes must have been in before she was murdered. She must have recognised somebody, and realised the danger. Why hadn't she contacted and warned him? Maybe she was about to do so when she was killed. Where had she seen this person? Was it in the streets of Otley? Or maybe on the media coverage of the first murder? He scrolled through various sites trying to find some of that coverage, but he didn't recognise anyone from the photographs and short videos that he found.

He took a drink of his whisky and found that his arm was shaking a little. He understood what she must have gone through. They'd all sworn to keep the secret. It wasn't easy to violate that promise, but now he was beginning to think that maybe he'd handled it wrongly. After what Hillary Sands had said to him, it could be that things were leaking out. The truth couldn't be concealed forever. It would probably be better for him if he told the police rather than waiting for them to find out. But after so long it was difficult to make that move. There were very serious things for which he could be held responsible.

But what to make of this latest murder? He'd never had any contact with this man Blake. How did he fit the pattern? Were the police any nearer to solving the mystery? He finished his whisky and poured another. It was hopeless; he couldn't make any sense of it but felt too paralysed to take any action. There was no one that he could turn to for help.

As the light began to fade in the late afternoon, he finally got up to check that all the doors were locked in a desperate attempt to feel safer.

~

When Abigail Wilson picked her two children up from school, she found them in a state of high excitement. They came bouncing out of the building.

'Mum!' shouted Jonathan, the eldest. 'There's been another murder! You didn't tell us!'

Abigail had been shocked to hear the news of the body found by the river and had agreed with Dave to say nothing to the children for fear of frightening them. That appeared to be something that she needn't have worried about. It was quite the contrary: it had been all over the school and they were loving every minute of it!

'Shush, Jonathan!' she said, giving him an angry look.

'We've been playing murderers in the playground – watching people go past the school who might know something, and then making notes about them.'

'I'll bet the teachers weren't very pleased about that.'

'No, but we might take it to the police. We might have seen the killer and—'

'Everybody thought I was the best at dying when I'd been stabbed,' Mary butted in, not wanting to be left out.

Jonathan was scornful. 'You and your friends were rubbish. You don't just fall over backwards when you've been stabbed. You have to clutch yourself because of the awful wound, groan and fall down like this.' He put a hand on his chest, let out a moan and collapsed slowly and melodramatically to the ground.

Abigail shook her head but had to suppress a smile. 'Get up, Jonathan. I've told you two before, it's not something to enjoy when somebody has been killed.'

'Yeah, but can we go down to the river, Mum, and see where it happened? Greg said his dad's going to take him and his sister. He said there's a boat full of blood and you can see where the body was lying – a red shape on the ground.'

'Ahh!' screamed Mary, but in a way that showed she would love to see it.

'There's no such thing as a boat full of blood down there,' said Abigail. 'And we're not going anywhere near the river. It's not a very nice thing to do, and anyway the police will not let anyone walk where it happened. They put tape around the area and you can't cross it.'

'That's not fair,' said Mary and she stamped her foot.

'Idiot!' called out Jonathan, changing his attitude to upstage his little sister. 'They won't let you go there because you might touch the evidence. Oh, but if they let me and Greg in we might find something that the police have missed on the body.' He grabbed hold of Mary and pretended to examine her all over.

'Stop it!' she yelled. 'Mum, tell him!'

'OK, you two, let's go home. They will have taken the body away a long time ago and you've had enough excitement for one day.'

'Well, it will be a relief not to have armed police officers around the place. It made me feel tense all the time.' Deborah was talking to Alison, who had called round to see how she was coping. Alison had given up her car when she moved to Leeds, but luckily there was a train station at New Bridge with a direct link to Leeds.

'And very intrusive,' added Alison.

'We've still managed to do things. Jim always hides the stress he is under very well. Too well, I think. And I also believe they take him for granted at police HQ. I know he likes Superintendent Walker and it's good to get on with your boss, but they seem to forget that he's not getting any younger.'

'I was saying something very similar to him yesterday when he called round. In fact, I mentioned the R-word.'

Deborah laughed. 'That was brave of you. I've raised it a few times, but he won't really engage with the idea. I think he is afraid that he would be bored if he gave up police work. Although it's stressful, he gets a buzz out of it and I don't think he knows where he would get that if he retired.'

'Hmm. I'm sure you're right. I think we need to work on him. Everybody has to face the fact of change in their life at some point. I'm sure we can help him to find out what he could do and how he could adjust.'

There was the noise of the outside door opening and then slow footsteps in the hall. Oldroyd walked wearily into the room.

'Well, talk of the devil,' said Deborah. 'Have your ears been burning?'

'What better subject could there be?' said Oldroyd with a flourish of mock conceitedness, trying to be light-hearted. 'Let me guess your conclusions: he's clever, he's entertaining, he's wonderful company, he's—'

'A stubborn and arrogant so-and-so,' interjected Alison, and they all laughed.

'Despite your insults, I'm glad you're here. You told me that you were coming round to check on Deborah.'

'Yes, and it's been lovely to see her.'

'Well, I'm glad that the death of Blake means that neither of you are under threat any more; not that I ever thought you really were. It was me Blake wanted. But something he didn't foresee has happened, and now things have changed.'

Oldroyd went into the kitchen and made some tea for everyone. When he returned, he asked Alison if she would stay for dinner. Deborah also wanted her to stay.

'Well, that's really kind and I'd love to, but I'd better get back. I've got an early start tomorrow. I'm going to visit my friend Marie who is the bishop of a diocese in the north-east. I'm fascinated to discover how she's doing. How about Friday evening? I can make it then.'

'That will be great,' said Deborah.

'I expect your friend will be finding her job difficult, like many of us do,' replied Oldroyd with a twinkle in his eye, suggesting that he had worked out what they had been talking about before he arrived. 'But remember it's often not possible to achieve worthwhile things without enduring some stress.'

'You're right, Jim. But I also know for a fact that she's set herself a limit. She's announced that she's going to retire in two years' time.'

Oldroyd nodded and drank some tea. 'Good for her and I hope it works out well. It's easier for some people than for others.'

'Yes, Jim, but don't think you've heard the last of this. We're on your case and it's for your own good. Surely what you've been going through recently has made you think a bit about the future?'

Oldroyd held up his hands. 'OK, fine, I understand what you are saying, but I can't think about it at the moment. It was a relief to see the end of Blake, but we still have a very tricky investigation in Otley. Lives may still be at risk.'

'That's a huge responsibility, and exactly the thing we're concerned about. You've endured a lot of stress working on cases like this over the years, more than your fair share, and maybe it's time . . .' said Alison, but decided not to press the issue now. 'Anyway, how's it going over there?'

'Not exactly smoothly, but I'm confident that we'll move forward soon. Once we find out a little bit more about Chevin Towers. There's someone I need to speak to who may know something useful.'

'Who's that, then, Jim?'

'It's a journalist I've known for a long time. He's semi-retired now, but would have been active at the time of the problems at Chevin Towers. He was always a good source of hard-to-get information.'

'If bad things were happening to children at that place,' said Deborah, 'why has it been hushed up all these years?'

'I suspect part of the answer is that they were different times, and abuse of children was just not taken as seriously as it is now.

Also, I think there was a pretty determined effort to keep it all quiet and the police were persuaded to stay out of it.'

'Ugh, it sounds awful.'

'Yes. And at the end of all this, if there's a big inquiry, it might be that poor Otley becomes notorious for where abuse of children took place and was not prevented. But I hope not.'

Five

Otley had mixed fortunes during the medieval period. After the Norman conquest, much of the area was laid to waste and many people starved to death as part of William the Conqueror's cruel scorched earth policy, known as the Harrying of the North. The Saxon church was replaced by a Norman one and English aristocrats in the region were replaced by Normans. But by the thirteenth century, Otley was beginning to prosper. The church granted so called 'burgage' plots of land to attract merchants and tradespeople. In addition to farming, there was quarrying of stone for building and the manufacture of potash from bracken, which was used to make soap.

Early next morning, Andy and McNiven were sitting in an unmarked police car parked down the shabby street in Stansfield where Martin White lived in a small rather rundown semi-detached house. There was another car parked behind them.

McNiven looked across at the house. 'I've examined the rotas at the prison. He was on the late shift last night, so he'll be in there now, probably asleep.' He checked that the officers in the other car were ready, then they all moved swiftly across the road and McNiven rapped smartly on the front door. 'Police! Open up!'

he shouted and continued to bang on the door, which was soon opened by a dazed Martin White.

'What's going on?'

'Martin White, I'm arresting you on suspicion of aiding a prisoner, Adam Blake, to escape from custody, and also for the suspected murder of the said Adam Blake. You do not have to say anything, but it may harm your defence if you do not mention, when questioned, something which you later rely on in court. Anything you do say may be given in evidence. We also have a warrant to search these premises as we suspect that they have been used as the hideout of the aforesaid escaped prisoner.'

White's face crumpled with shock and incomprehension. 'But—'

McNiven ignored him, beckoning other officers into the house while he detained White. It turned out to be a swift and satisfactory operation. There was abundant evidence that White had recently had a lodger. White was then bundled into a police car and taken to Stansfield police station.

∼

This was also the day that saw Oldroyd finally make some significant progress in the Otley investigation. As soon as he arrived at the Courthouse, he received a call from Tim Groves, who he'd contacted the day before to ask for more information. Steph was there and he put his phone on speaker.

'I think you're right, Jim, but I must confess I didn't notice it. I'm sending you some close-up pictures of the foreheads of the three victims. They're a bit grisly but I know that you're used to it. I'm not a handwriting expert, but once you look closely, it's clear that the way the word *vindicta* has been written on Blake's forehead is not the same as the writing on the other two. Not obviously so at first glance, but the word on the foreheads of the first victims is almost identically written, while the third is significantly different, not the same hand.'

Groves paused briefly before continuing, 'I take it this means you think the killer of the first two victims was not the person who killed Blake?'

Oldroyd glanced at Steph, who was listening carefully.

'Exactly. Remember, what was written on the foreheads of those first two victims has been in the public domain since my second media conference. It could easily have been copied by someone who wanted to hide Blake's death as part of that pattern.'

'Yes, I can see that,' said Groves.

Oldroyd continued, 'I was also puzzled by the place where the body was dumped. After our discovery about the children's home at Chevin Towers, we've been working on the idea that the killer might be taking revenge for things that happened there. If that is the case, it's likely that by leaving a body in a prison cell he's probably telling us that being in that home was like being in prison. That horrible tableau with the scarecrow children suggests a family – a family that betrayed children? Or a family life that they never had? We don't know, but it leaves us a problem with where Blake's body was left. I can't see any connection between a boat on the river and whatever happened at Chevin Towers. Maybe there is a link that will emerge later, but I'm inclined to think that a different killer staged the murder to look like the other two. The problem for them is that they didn't quite get it right. They were probably going entirely on what I said at the press conference, which was not very detailed.'

'Well, that's complicated stuff, Jim. I'll leave you to it. Bye for now.' Groves ended the call, giving the impression that he was happy to remain with his clinical investigations and leave the puzzles of motive and psychology to his colleague.

'My God, sir,' said Steph. 'Does this mean that we are now looking for two murderers?'

'Yes, but I think one of them may have just been captured by Andy and his team.'

～

McNiven and Andy faced Martin White across a table in the interview room at Stansfield police station. White had a duty solicitor sitting next to him. He looked tired but not particularly anguished.

The team of police officers who had examined White's house had discovered evidence that someone had been staying in the spare room. They had taken fingerprints and removed items to be checked for DNA. It was only a matter of time before the material was linked to Blake. White knew that the game was up and had already made a brief confession.

'So,' began McNiven, 'I want you to take me through everything that happened. The more honest and upfront you are, the better it will be for you.' He produced the photograph of White with his aunt. 'I think it was all about your aunt, and what Blake did to her, wasn't it?'

White nodded and his composure seemed to falter as he looked at the photograph. He wiped some tears from his eyes and a police officer in attendance gave him a tissue.

'Yes,' he said finally, making a big effort to pull himself together. 'My mother died when I was two, and my father found it hard to cope. I was the youngest by several years. My brother and sister left home when they were in their teens, but I was looked after by my auntie. I loved her.' He briefly broke down again and the detectives waited patiently. 'She and her husband Bill didn't have any children and they sort of half adopted me. They ran a small farm and I stayed there at weekends and school holidays. I loved it – helping to look after the animals and cycling around the farmyard.

'Uncle Bill died of a heart attack when I was fifteen, leaving Auntie Marjorie by herself. She sold the farm and bought a cottage nearby. It was in a very isolated hamlet, but she didn't want to live in a town or even a large village. She was used to being a long way from things. I don't think she realised that it wouldn't be the same without her husband.

'I moved away for a while doing various jobs in York before I trained to be a prison warder. When I visited, I sensed that she was quite lonely, but I couldn't persuade her to move again. She said that she was too old and couldn't be bothered.'

White paused and took a drink of water. He took a deep breath before continuing. 'One day, she greeted me at the door, and I noticed she was very cheerful. More than she had been in a long time. Of course, I was pleased, so I asked her what had happened. She told me to come in and introduced me to a good-looking man, who she called Neville Broadbent. Of course I would later find out his name was Adam Blake. He was much younger than her. I didn't know much about him then, but I felt uneasy. There was something cold about him, but my aunt couldn't see it. It was obvious that she thought he was wonderful; it was Neville this and Neville that.'

'Did that make you feel angry?' asked McNiven.

White frowned. 'I suppose it did in a way, but mainly I was very concerned about where this man had sprung from and what his intentions were. Apparently, he'd called at the house one day posing as an insurance salesman. He must have immediately set to work on her. I suspected straight away that he was some kind of fortune hunter, though I didn't know just how sinister and dangerous he was. My aunt was well off. She had sold the farm for a lot of money and her small cottage had been relatively cheap. When I saw how kind and charming he was to her and how she loved the attention, the alarm bells started ringing in my head.

'But what could I say? I realised that she wouldn't take kindly to any criticism of him let alone any implication that he was intending to take her money from her. So I didn't say anything.' He lowered his head. 'I regret that now, but I didn't want to do anything that would lead to any bad feeling between us. I couldn't bear the idea. My dad had died by this time, my brother was in Australia and my sister down in London. She was the only family I had left and the person I felt closest to in the world.' He stopped speaking again and appeared troubled.

Andy was finding it very difficult not to feel sympathetic towards him. It was a moving story.

'Please carry on,' said McNiven.

White took a deep breath. 'I had a busy life in York. I had a girlfriend, though we split up later, and I was working hard to pay the mortgage on a flat. And to be honest, it upset me to visit her because he was always there. I suppose I just hoped that she would see the truth about him.'

He paused again as if he was coming to a very difficult part of the story. 'Then the police turned up at my apartment in York one morning and said that my aunt was dead. Her body had been found in the river near to her house. They said she'd left a note saying that she was lonely and depressed. I knew straight away what happened. She may have been a bit lonely, but she would never have killed herself. She was never seriously depressed. They wanted me to come and identify her, and to verify that the note was in her handwriting. So I did. It was definitely her and the note seemed to be in her writing, but I never believed it.'

'What happened with "Neville" then?' asked McNiven.

'He turned up a couple of days after she'd been found; said he'd been visiting a friend in Leeds. He put on a superb act of being grief stricken. Of course, he denied all the allegations that I'd made and remained calm and courteous throughout. He said that recently she had seemed very depressed and he blamed himself for leaving her when she obviously needed him.

'The police seemed to be completely taken in. They didn't investigate her death properly at all. The verdict was suicide. The friend in Leeds verified that he had been visiting and there was no evidence to link him with the death even though the police confirmed that they thought it was an unusual relationship.

'So there he was, weeping at the funeral, and as soon as he got his hands on his money, he disappeared. I just felt awful – angry, full of grief and also guilty. I think that's why the relationship with my girlfriend ended.'

'When did you learn the truth about Blake?'

'I think it was about three years later when he was finally caught and that detective from Harrogate—'

'Chief Inspector Oldroyd,' interposed Andy with some pride.

'Yes. Thank God for him. He was the one who realised that my aunt had been murdered and also that Blake had committed a series of these crimes and had changed his identity many times.' He stopped talking suddenly, took in a deep gulp of air. 'That bastard!' he cried.

'Steady,' said McNiven.

'OK.' White held up his hand, paused and took another drink of water while he composed himself. 'The police found lots of material about his murders, including some letters in my aunt's handwriting which he'd used to practise forging that suicide note. Luckily my aunt had been buried and not cremated. Her body was exhumed and small traces of a sedative were found. She'd died from drowning but what Chief Inspector Oldroyd said was that, probably, Blake put a small amount of the sedative in her drink and then suggested they take a walk. When she became drowsy, he pushed her in.'

McNiven shook his head, then continued. 'And you planned to take your revenge?'

'Not straight away. Blake was jailed for life and sent to a prison in the south of England. I thought that was the end of it. I got on with my life and eventually got the job at Stansfield Prison. Things changed a couple of years ago when Blake was moved to Stansfield. I never expected this to happen, and I wondered if he would remember me. He'd not been there long when I came face to face with him in the prison dining area, but he showed no recognition at all. It was about fifteen years since he'd seen me, and I was young at that time. My appearance had changed a lot.'

'So you saw you might have an opportunity for revenge?'

'Yes. I wanted to do it in a way that humiliated him and gave him a taste of his own medicine. I was going to get him to trust me and then utterly betray him.

'I began by getting a transfer on to the wing where he was held. Then slowly I began to drop hints to him about how people could escape if they had help on the inside. I could see that he was interested, and it came to the point where he made me an offer. He said he had lots of money stashed away that the police had never found, and he would pay me a big sum if I helped him to escape. I pretended that I thought it was too dangerous and let him think he was persuading me. Eventually I agreed to help him get out and provide him with a safe place afterwards. He said he would pay me fifty thousand pounds.' White laughed. 'I don't know whether he would have done or not; he didn't realise that I wasn't at all interested in the money.

'I smuggled a mobile phone into the prison for him so that he could arrange for a gang to create a diversion outside the prison and bring a car to pick him up. His chance to enact his escape came when he was going to be taken to the court at Leeds. Before the officers came to escort him from his cell to the police van,

I gave him a key to the handcuffs they put on him. I think our procedures were very lax with a criminal like Blake. He didn't have any restraints to his legs and he wasn't cuffed to either of the officers.' He looked at McNiven, who shrugged his shoulders.

'You know the rest. The gang created the planned diversion, Blake broke away from his escort, hit me as part of the act and got in the escape car. Then he could get his handcuffs off.'

'And they took him to your house?' asked Andy.

'Not straight away, they destroyed the getaway car, hid until dark, and then brought him, making sure that no one saw him come in.'

'But then things took an unexpected turn?'

'Yes. I planned to kill him and dispose of his body somewhere far away.' He looked up with a distant expression on his face. 'But once he was there in my house, I enjoyed having power over him. I found I didn't want to end it straight away.' He smiled. 'Blake completely trusted me by then. I think the prospect of escape had put him off his guard. He started to talk about how he was going to get revenge on Chief Inspector Oldroyd who had unmasked him as a ruthless serial killer of older women. He used the phone I got for him to call Oldroyd – I don't know how he got the number, it must have been through his contacts – and threatened him. This was something that I was never going to allow to happen. He didn't know, but I was very grateful to Oldroyd for exposing Blake.'

'So you changed your plan?'

White frowned. 'I got too clever. Things had gone so smoothly up till then. I was following what was going on in Otley and I thought, why not present this murder as part of that series? That would put people completely off the trail. So I took Blake by surprise and strangled him. When I had the rope round his neck, I told him who I was. That I was avenging my aunt. He struggled but I was too strong for him.'

Andy looked down to see that both of White's fists were clenched. White paused and took a deep breath before continuing.

'I'd read about the word being written on the victims' foreheads, so I did the same with Blake. It was appropriate for me to write that on him; it was revenge for my aunt. Then I took the body to Otley and placed it in a boat by the river. Ironically, I didn't want to cause problems for Chief Inspector Oldroyd, but I suspect he won't have been taken in anyway.' He looked at McNiven. 'I never thought that you would be on to me so soon.'

'No,' replied McNiven. 'It was just a hunch I had, that the motive for Blake's murder might be a different sort of revenge to the other murders. Luckily, I found that picture of you with your aunt quite quickly.'

'You're a lot sharper than the people at Stansfield Prison,' said White. 'I don't think they would ever have made the connection.'

Secretly, McNiven agreed. Perry and his slack systems were going to be in a lot of trouble – just as Walker had predicted. There was silence for a few moments. It was one of those cases that inevitably aroused mixed feelings towards the perpetrator. Some people would even have argued that White was doing the public a service by getting rid of Blake. No more taxpayers' money would be wasted on keeping that evil man alive in prison.

This wasn't McNiven's view.

'We understand how you felt about Blake,' he said. 'But it's never acceptable to take the law into your own hands as you did and commit murder. Nevertheless, you've been very open about everything and, as I told you at the beginning, that will be very much in your favour when your case comes to trial.'

White shrugged his shoulders. 'I knew you'd catch me in the end,' he said. 'But I just wanted justice for my aunt.'

McNiven nodded and then turned to the duty officer. 'OK, take him away.'

'Thank you for your help with this case,' said McNiven when he and Andy were back in the office. 'We'll wrap up everything here and you can get off back to Harrogate. I'll leave you to report back to Chief Inspector Oldroyd.'

'OK, sir, and thank you.'

McNiven looked at him with wise, perceptive eyes. 'You've done a very good job, Andy – you've obviously learned a lot working with DCI Oldroyd. Have you thought about moving on and up? You seem to me to have the right experience and personality.'

Andy was wrong-footed. He hadn't expected this, and wondered for a moment if his boss had been talking to McNiven.

'Oh well . . . yes, sir, I have as it happens. I'll probably have a look round soon and see what's on offer.'

'Good, well, I'm sure you'll get a very good reference from DCI Oldroyd, but if you want someone else to write nice things about you, just let me know.'

'Thanks again, sir.'

On the drive back, Andy felt very pleased that McNiven had been so positive about him. He also reflected on what he'd learned from the experience of being in charge of at least part of a serious investigation. He'd found out that things could go wrong and that the buck stopped with you. He had a lot more to learn about being in charge. But how else could you learn other than by doing it? On the whole it had been a very interesting experience and it made him think hard about his future career.

~

Jake Milton was still convinced that his father was up to something. He had seriously wondered whether Adam Blake was being concealed on the farm, such was his father's hostility to the police and his general shiftiness. However, the police had found nothing.

And he had now searched all possible places on the farm himself – including outlying barns – where a person might be hidden, but had also drawn a blank.

When the news came through that Blake had been murdered, he'd confronted his father directly, only to receive an aggressive and vehement denial.

Later, while his father was occupied with the pigs, Jake called Ian into the house and explained what was worrying him. The brothers were close in age and so much alike physically that they could be twins. Ian had always looked up to Jake as his older brother.

'You know what he's been like since he came back from prison,' Jake began. 'Bitter, not saying much, sitting around smoking and doing nothing except looking after those bloody pigs.'

Ian shrugged. 'What about it? It doesn't bother me. I can't relate to him as well as you. It was bloody awful living here with him. He was as grumpy as hell; never did anything around the house or any cooking. He's never had much time for me. He knows that I think he was an idiot to do what he did and go to jail for it. He knew that using those chemicals was illegal.'

'Yes, I agree, but we don't want him to drag the reputation of this farm down even further. It's time we took control of things.'

'What do you mean?'

'There's something definitely wrong. I can tell by his shifty attitude. I thought he might be hiding that escaped criminal here: Adam Blake. He got to know him in prison.'

'Dad? I don't think he'd ever do that even to get back at the police. He doesn't like any strangers on the farm.'

'He might have done it for money – he's always short of that – but anyway, Blake's dead now.' He looked at Ian. 'It crossed my mind that Dad might have been involved in that. When I asked him some questions about it he nearly bit my head off.'

'Well, I don't blame him. I can't see Dad killing anybody.'

Jake nodded. 'I agree, but he does have a temper and there's definitely something shady going on. I think we need to search the farm very carefully. I think he's hiding something.'

Ian frowned. 'What?'

'I don't know, but I think it might be something that would get him and us into a lot of trouble if the police found it.'

'Oh, I don't know, surely he doesn't want to get into trouble again.' Ian was about to leave but Jake grasped his arm.

'Look, it's our future at stake. We want to take this farm forward, don't we? We don't want him to ruin it for us. Remember how hard we had to work when he was in prison. This is our farm now as much as his. Anyway, he's going into Harrogate tomorrow afternoon; that's our chance to search the place.'

'OK.' Ian sighed but nodded, and then went out back to his work in the fields.

Jake sat for a moment as sadness washed over him. He caught sight of a family photograph on the sideboard. He and Ian were little boys, and his mother and father – both so young – looked happy together. Where had things gone wrong with their father? When they were that age, they had looked up to him and enjoyed helping him with jobs on the farm. They'd both wanted to work with him when they were grown up, and they'd never wavered from that. He'd taught them everything they knew about farming. But since their mother died things had gone sour. There was a period when his father could not really cope with looking after them and they felt neglected. Now he was an adult he realised that his father had been depressed and angry about losing his wife, and because he couldn't deal with it, he'd taken it out on his sons.

He frowned. They had not maintained their relationship with their father when he'd gone to prison. They had been embarrassed by it all at the time – young men who only felt the shame of seeing their dad locked up. They rarely went to see him as they felt intimidated by the idea of going into the prison building. They'd just managed to keep the farm going with help and advice from other local farmers. They learned a lot, but their father's absence meant that their relationship with him weakened, and when he came home, he was more isolated and his behaviour became strange.

Jake stood up, ready to go back to work himself. It was very complicated. Whether their relationship could ever be repaired was unclear, but he felt that, despite everything, it was vital that the current problem was tackled, otherwise there might be trouble with the police again.

~

After the arrest of White, DC Hardiman returned to Harrogate in order to join DC Warner in doing research for Oldroyd and Steph. He'd already learned a lot from her about how to access various useful archives and how to search in them. It was tough work; you needed to be very dogged and patient when lines of enquiry petered out and you had to move on to something else. On the whole, he preferred working out in the field.

He'd just got back to Harrogate HQ when Sharon called him over. She'd found something and was so excited about it that she didn't ask him how things had gone at Stansfield.

'Alan – look at this.'

Hardiman stared at her screen and saw that she was researching in local newspaper archives from a period around thirty years ago. She'd found something about Chevin Towers in reports of the time and had also unearthed an unusual archive.

'Wow! At last! Something concrete. That should be useful to DC Oldroyd.'

'Yes, I'm going to get on to him right away. Oh, sorry – I meant to ask: how did things go over there?'

'We arrested the warder who helped Blake escape. I think that's the end of that case.' He smiled at her. 'I'll be able to spend more time helping you now.'

She smiled back at him. 'Good.'

~

Dylan Hardy was not working at the Courthouse that day. It was quite a relief to have a day at home after the stress of recent times. It gave him a chance to do some of his artwork. He had set up the smaller of his two bedrooms as an artist's studio where he had all his paints and an easel. The window offered a view over a cobbled yard. The walls were covered with his paintings.

He put on BBC Radio 3 for classical music as he got his materials together. His aim today was to finish a painting he'd started several days ago. The radio was playing a symphony by Shostakovich as he began work. He reflected on the trauma of the last week as he applied paint to the canvas.

The truth was that, although he tried his best to be sympathetic to people who were experiencing difficult things, he was really a loner who preferred his own company and found the messy feelings associated with relationships difficult. This had been the case since his childhood, which had not been easy. He had no family and no close ties to anyone. Working part-time at the Courthouse with two other people was about his limit in terms of social interaction. It helped that Hillary and Abigail were very easy to get on with, and it did him good to spend time with them. It prevented him from becoming socially isolated, which he knew was a danger. He also made brief visits to the local pub and made an effort to talk to people. Here you could be friendly without having to get close to anybody. He'd progressed to being able to join the darts team, although he sometimes found this stressful.

People were complicated – emotionally demanding and difficult to trust. Luckily, he had three interests which he found calming and fulfilling: painting, walking the countryside, and historical research. He knew more about certain things than he'd admitted to the police, but he just did not want to get involved in the investigation. It was too taxing for him.

After a while he took a break and made some tea. When he came back to the studio, he had a close look at the picture he was producing. It was a landscape in his usual style – which was to emphasise the drama and turbulence in a scene with broad brush strokes and dark colours. It was a painting of Chevin Towers, darkly sinister amidst a wild Chevin Wood.

Oldroyd was at the Courthouse, having a long phone conversation with Andy, who had returned to McNiven's office after the interview with White was over. Andy explained about the arrest of White.

'Well done to yourself and Inspector McNiven,' said Oldroyd.

'Thank you, sir, but it was the inspector who made the breakthrough connecting White with one of Blake's victims.'

'Don't underestimate what you did. In an investigation, all the possibilities have to be followed through, including the ones that don't lead anywhere. You did a thorough job, and it wasn't your fault that Blake was dead before he could get to Bryson's house. He certainly would have gone if White hadn't intervened.'

'Thanks, sir.'

'So, Blake was bumped off by a relative of one of his victims? I suppose there's some crude justice there, even if in a civilised society we can't encourage people to take their own revenge like that.'

'That's exactly what Inspector McNiven said, sir.'

'I'd already concluded for various reasons that Blake's murder was not connected to the previous two. What you've discovered confirms that, and also that Blake was even more unlikely to be involved in the first murders.'

'Are you any nearer to finding out who committed those, sir?'

'No, but Steph and I believe that they are bound up with something that happened in the past at a children's home near here called Chevin Towers.'

'Yes, sir. Steph was telling me about it. It sounds like a place from a horror movie.'

'We're waiting for more information, but in the meantime, I think we're going to have to go back up there and take another look ourselves.'

'If you're going up at night, sir . . . rather you than me,' laughed Andy.

'Don't worry – Steph will protect me.'

'OK, sir.'

Oldroyd ended the call. He had put his phone on speaker so Steph could listen in.

'So, the case of Adam Blake is over, sir?'

'Well, he's dead so he can't go back to prison, they've caught his killer, and in the absence of any link between him and the events in Otley, I think it is.'

'At least we can concentrate on our case completely now, sir.'

'Yes.'

'Are we going back to Chevin Towers again?'

'I think we have to.'

'Don't worry,' she said with a smile. 'I'll protect you from the ghosts and ghoulies.'

'Thanks,' said Oldroyd and put a finger to his lips. 'But let's keep quiet about it. We haven't got time to go through the official channels and get a warrant to search the place. People's lives are at stake. We should—' His phone buzzed with a message. It was from Sharon Warner. She had finally found something about Chevin Towers. He called her immediately and put his phone on speaker again.

'It's taken a while, sir, but I've found some material about that children's home. There are some local newspaper articles from nineteen-ninety-four. The first reports state that the home was closing under unspecified circumstances. No one was available to make any comments. There are a few more articles speculating about what happened but in the absence of any facts, they seem to have dropped the story very quickly.

'I've also managed to unearth a very obscure archive about private children's homes, going right back to the nineteen-thirties. There is a brief entry about Chevin Towers and one photograph. Luckily, it's dated nineteen-ninety-two, so not long before it closed, and the period we're interested in. It's a black and white photograph showing a large group of people, adults and children. I assume it's all the staff and the kids they looked after. Anyway, I'm going to send copies of all the newspaper reports and the page from the archive to Sergeant Johnson's laptop. I think you said you didn't have yours with you, sir?'

'That's right,' said Oldroyd and grimaced at Steph. He didn't think he would ever manage to get into the routine of having all his electronic devices with him. 'Good work,' he said to Sharon, and he and Steph waited for the material to come through.

'I don't think you do too badly with modern tech, sir . . . for someone of your generation,' she said with a twinkle in her eye.

'Don't be so patronising,' replied Oldroyd, laughing.

The newspaper reports revealed virtually nothing they didn't already know, as Sharon had said, but the photograph was very interesting. The group was standing outside a building immediately recognisable as Chevin Towers in better, smarter days. Below the photograph, a brief text included the names of the staff members. Frances Hughes was there and clearly recognisable, though obviously a lot younger. A second person was even more intriguing.

'Look at this,' said Oldroyd, pointing at the photograph. 'That is clearly the person we know as Tony Lowell – the first victim. But here his name is recorded as Alex Abelman.'

'Yes, sir, I agree – it's him.'

'So, from this I think we are a little bit nearer to understanding what probably happened. Abelman or "Lowell" was involved in something serious enough for him to have to change his name and appearance. Look, he has long hair in the photograph and it's blond. There's no moustache. Remember his wife said that he had been away from this area for some time before he returned and before she met him; long enough to disappear out of people's memories. And look at this.' He pointed to the name of the children's home at the top of the page. 'Chevin Towers Children's Home: *Cura Personalis.* They had a Latin motto. Is that connected to the word written on the foreheads of the victims?'

'What does it mean, sir?'

'Something like, *care of the person*, I think. Hmm. Except they didn't, did they?'

'What, sir?'

'Look after the children in their care.' He looked up and thought for a moment, then put the photograph down. He remembered at the last press conference a reporter had mentioned their school motto. It had somehow resonated with Oldroyd, and now he was realising why. 'Anyway, at long last, after having no leads, we've suddenly got some things to follow up.' Oldroyd was animated for the first time in days. 'First of all, I need to get straight back to DC Warner.'

He called the number. 'Again, excellent work, extremely useful. You are a wonderful researcher,' he said to Sharon, and Steph smiled as she imagined Sharon beaming with the praise. 'Now, I want you to try to find out more about the person in the photograph called Alex Abelman, because he, under the name of Tony Lowell, is our first victim. Also see if there's any way you can find out about any of the children in the photograph, and anything about Frances Hughes, our second victim, who is also in the picture. And, finally, anything more you can discover about the home in that period. Good, thanks.' He ended the call and turned to Steph. 'This makes it all the more vital that we go back to that place and see what we can find.' Now it was his eyes that twinkled. 'And we're going to do it tonight; there's no time to waste.'

~

The tension in Otley was almost palpable. Some people were watching TV news and listening to local radio almost continuously. Neighbours were checking on old people and those who lived alone. The streets were noticeably quieter than normal and fewer people were prepared to go out by themselves; there was the general feeling of terror that a serial killer might be on the rampage and DCI Oldroyd's reassurances that the killings were not random did little to calm the atmosphere.

At the Wilson household, however, Jonathan and Mary were becoming more and more excited and were not the least bit frightened by what had happened. Abigail was torn between wanting to laugh at them and being pleased that they were not scared, and remonstrating with them that they shouldn't be enjoying something awful like people being killed. But to them it was a huge game.

'Our gang beat everyone today,' announced Jonathan proudly as he raced around the room, blasting imaginary people with his toy gun. His mother had resisted buying him a gun but found that he simply used a piece of wood instead. She ended up buying Mary one too; at least that meant she was sticking to her principles of equality of treatment if not to those of her pacifism.

Mary ignored him and said to her mother, 'Anne Darnley's dad told her that the body had writing on it. Ugh! How could you write on a dead body?!'

Jonathan went right up to his sister and said into her face, 'What if it came back to life and got hold of the pen and wrote on its own face?'

Mary screamed.

'Jonathan! That's enough. You'll be giving her nightmares.'

Jonathan ignored his mother and challenged his sister. 'I dare you to walk down to the river when it's dark and sit in the boat where the body was found.'

'Jonathan! I said that's enough. She'll do no such thing, and neither will you. You're both safe here with me and Dad, but I'm afraid you're not allowed to go outside beyond the garden and play by yourselves, not even with your friends, until the police have caught the person who's doing these terrible things.'

Jonathan's face fell. 'But . . . That's not fair!' he cried. 'Josh Stephenson's coming and we're going to cycle around and look for evidence.'

'Oh no you're not, Jonathan. You're—' There was a knock at the door. Abigail felt nervous; who was it? 'Someone's here – now just go to your rooms and play quietly.'

Obediently, Mary went upstairs with Jonathan sulking behind her, hitting each step with his gun.

When Abigail tentatively opened the door, she was surprised to see Hillary Sands, who looked anxious.

'Is this a bad time, Abi?' Hillary asked.

'No, Dave's not back yet and the kids are playing upstairs.'

'Can I come in? There's something I need to talk to you about urgently. I've been trying to summon up the courage to come to see you for a couple of days.'

Abigail looked alarmed. 'Hillary, what's the matter? Of course, come in.'

She led her colleague into the living room, and they sat down. She looked at Hillary's strained face. 'What's all this about? I noticed you haven't been yourself recently, but I thought it was just because of all that's happened.'

Hillary was sitting up, looking agitated. 'It is to do with what's happened. I think I know what's behind these murders. Maybe not who, but I know why they're doing it.'

Abigail was stunned. 'Really?'

'Yes, it's about things that happened a long time ago. I can't prove anything, but I want to know if you think I should go to the police.'

~

That evening there was a clear sky with a large harvest moon which could be glimpsed through the trees on the dark slopes of the Chevin. Oldroyd and Steph climbed carefully up the same path that they had ascended just a few days ago. The woods seemed much more sinister at night. It was very quiet apart from the occasional rustling in the trees. Was it a squirrel? Or a person? Oldroyd shone his torch into the trees, taking his eye off the path for a few seconds. He caught his foot on a tree root and fell headlong on to the path. 'Blast!'

'Sir, are you alright?' Steph rushed towards him, worried that her boss might be injured, and how they'd explain what had happened if he was. They shouldn't have been there without backup.

'I'm OK, just winded, and my arms are covered in mud. Let's carry on.'

When they reached Chevin Towers, the deserted Gothic mansion was truly terrifying in the moonlight. They had a brief look around to check that no one was there before contemplating how they might get inside the building.

'It shouldn't be too difficult,' said Oldroyd, keeping his voice down. 'I think the best bet is to force one of those long windows on the ground floor.' He had brought a crowbar for the purpose and they each had a powerful torch. He placed the bar under the window catch and prised it off. Fragments of rotten window frame came away with it, making more noise than Oldroyd had intended. He froze, then swung his torch around. There was nothing nearby except for two points of moving light – what were they?

'It's a fox, sir,' said Steph as the animal, whose eyes had been caught by the torchlight, moved quickly away, its splendid bushy tail just visible behind it.

'Phew, that's a relief!' Followed by Steph, Oldroyd climbed through the window.

'What exactly do you hope we might find, sir?'

'Anything that might give us a clue as to what went on here and who was involved.'

They were in a large room with some gym equipment, which may have acted as a kind of play space for the children and would probably have originally been a ballroom. The ceilings and walls were richly decorated with flaking plaster work. The floor was thick with dust and pieces of the fallen plaster. There was no furniture other than a few overturned chairs in one corner.

The detectives raked the walls and floors with their torches. On one side there was some grubby and fading graffiti, which was probably the work of local kids who'd managed to get inside the building some time ago.

'Ghostly in here, sir. Andy was right. Glad I'm not by myself, even if I am a police officer and supposed to be fearless.'

'Me too,' Oldroyd chuckled. 'There's not much in here; let's try some of the other rooms.' They walked across the floor and opened the creaking door to enter a passageway from which several doors exited.

'This is more like it,' said Oldroyd quietly. 'These look as if they could have been offices, and that's where we might find something.' He was right that there was a series of small rooms. Most of them were disappointingly empty – there were certainly no desks or filing cabinets full of vital information. A thorough job had been made of stripping out everything. They got to the last room on the corridor. Oldroyd opened the door. There was a swift scurrying noise, which came as a shock after the quiet. Steph had to contain the urge to scream.

'Mice,' said Oldroyd.

Steph had faced real dangers in her police career calmly and with courage, but mice and rats triggered the flight response in her. She took two deep breaths and kept her torch directed at the walls. She didn't want to see the creatures on the floor.

At first this room seemed just as empty as the others, but then Oldroyd's torch picked out some papers scattered on the floor. He picked them up, and he and Steph looked at them together. Some of the sheets contained lists and figures, some seemed to be pages pulled out of some kind of yearbook as there were comments on activities undertaken. On one page there was a photograph of an event that looked like a sports day. Children were running on a track with the house in the background. It must have been a space now overgrown with trees and bushes. Another photograph showed prizes being presented, presumably to the winners of races.

'Sir, look at that,' said Steph excitedly, pointing to the man in the photograph who was presenting the awards. It was Edward

Brown smiling into the camera, younger but recognisable. And the caption confirmed it. *Governor Mr Edward Brown Presents First Prize in the Long Jump to Gordon Haigh.*

'So, he was involved here as well,' said Oldroyd.

'Yes, sir . . . but doesn't that put him in danger? He could become the third victim.'

'You're right. Surely he must know that. Why didn't he or Frances Hughes contact us? They must have realised what was going on when Lowell – or Abelman, to be exact – was killed and that word, *vindicta*, was written on the body. It suggests that what happened here must have been very serious and they had some kind of pact with each other never to reveal anything.'

'And they managed to cover it up?'

'Yes, someone must have had some influence where it counted. I mean . . .' Oldroyd froze. Steph breathed in sharply. They'd both heard a noise which wasn't the mice. It was a bang that seemed to come from underground.

'Over there!' whispered Oldroyd. They walked back down the corridor and towards a door. There was a glow of light at the bottom and they could now hear a scraping noise below them. 'This must be the entrance to the cellar. It sounds like someone's digging down there.'

Steph took a deep breath and told herself that she didn't believe in ghosts and that she was a confident, imperturbable police officer. She glanced at Oldroyd's face and saw that his expression was very grave, and his brow was furrowed. He slowly opened the door to reveal stone steps going down steeply past dirty, crumbling whitewashed walls into a deep, cold cellar. The glow of light was stronger and the scraping sound became louder. They were about to carefully descend when Oldroyd dropped his torch, which crashed on to the steps.

The scraping immediately stopped, and the light below went out. Before the detectives could react, there was the sound of someone running up towards them. Steph's torch picked out a figure dressed in black with a balaclava over their head – and wielding a spade. Whoever it was ran quickly up the steps like a horrible black spider from a funnel web.

'Watch out, sir!' cried Steph. The figure raised the spade and Oldroyd shrank back. They didn't strike, but threw down the weapon and ran off, footsteps echoing along the corridor.

Steph set off in pursuit, but Oldroyd called out, 'Don't bother.' She rejoined him. He continued in a low voice: 'Whoever they are, they know this place better than we do. They'll be away in no time and we've no backup to conduct a proper search. And remember this is all unofficial; we shouldn't really be here. Let's go down and see what they were doing.'

Oldroyd picked up his torch, and they slowly descended the steps into the dark and cold. At the bottom was a large room with a stone floor. The walls and ceiling were covered with old spiderwebs and large sections of plaster had collapsed on to the floor. Smaller rooms led off to the left and right. Some were completely blackened and had clearly been coal stores in the past. The air was very chilly and damp.

At the far end of the room they found where the digging had taken place. Some of the stone slabs had been lifted and soil underneath dug out. Oldroyd crouched down and shone his torch over the hole.

'My God, look at this!' His voice was hoarse with shock. Steph looked down and put her hand to her mouth. There were bones and a skull protruding out of the soil. They were small but looked human.

They continued to gaze down into this horror for a few moments, unable to move.

'Oh my God, sir! What is this?' Steph finally said.

'If it's what I think it is, it might give us more insight into the motive for these killings. We've been thinking for a while that some kind of abuse went on at the children's home. Maybe the abuse went too far.'

Steph took a sharp intake of breath. 'You mean a child died, and was buried here?'

'It's beginning to look that way to me. And it's clear that our murderer suspected that a body had been buried and was trying to find it.' He looked around the gloomy and hideous room with an expression of extreme repulsion. 'God, this is an awful place!'

'Sir, here!' Steph, not wanting to look at the bones any more, was exploring the rest of the room. Oldroyd walked over to where she was. There was a broken wooden chair with some remnants of ropes tied on to it.

'What's all this about, sir?'

'Don't ask. I can't bear to think about it.'

The next morning, Oldroyd and Steph were back early at Chevin Towers, which presented a completely different scene in the daylight. Several cars – including police cars – were parked near the house, which was cordoned off by blue and white police tape. The big front door had been forced and police officers were coming and going.

Downstairs, the cellar was much less frightening in the daytime. Shafts of light from small windows partially lit the room, which seemed to be full of people. A team of SOCOs was examining the area and the remains of the chair for any evidence of what had taken place, and anything that might have been left by the person Oldroyd and Steph had disturbed.

Powerful electric lights had been set up near to where the buried body had been discovered and a team of forensic archaeologists in protective clothing were working carefully to excavate the remains.

Oldroyd, who rarely saw a team like this at work, watched curiously. It was slow going, and clearly they would have no results from their investigation for a while.

Steph came up behind him. 'Grisly stuff, isn't it, sir?'

'Yes, and it looks as if it takes a lot of patience too. I think they're all going to be here for quite a while – there's no point us staying. I'll just have a quick word with them.' He went over and spoke to the senior member of the archaeological team as Steph looked around the room again and shuddered as she remembered the events of the previous night. The horror of the case seemed to be deepening.

'They're pretty sure that the remains are those of a child,' Oldroyd said, coming back. 'Maybe about eleven or twelve years old. They can't confirm the sex or how long the body has been there, but they've promised to work quickly as this discovery is part of a murder inquiry.'

Steph shuddered again. 'Rather them than me, sir. It's all a bit ghoulish. I've never liked bones and skulls.'

Oldroyd glanced at the skeleton slowly emerging from the soil beneath the stone slab. 'I suppose so. But I think I'd prefer that to Tim Groves' work with the recently dead. At least with this there's no rotting flesh, bloated bodies and terrible smells.'

'Ugh! Sir, let's go before I'm sick!' Steph looked pale, and Oldroyd chuckled.

'You go back to the Courthouse. I've got to visit someone I've been meaning to speak to for a while now. Go outside and get some fresh air and sunshine; it's terrible down here.'

~

When Oldroyd left Chevin Towers, he drove around the outskirts of the town into the surrounding countryside in the direction of Ilkley and then up a narrow-walled lane. This led to a barn conversion set in the glorious landscape which rose up to Burley Moor in the distance. He parked outside, got out and knocked on the door, which was opened by a man with longish grey hair and beard dressed rather flamboyantly in red corduroy trousers with braces and a blue shirt.

'Ah, Jim!' he exclaimed, shaking Oldroyd's hand enthusiastically. 'Come in! It's been too long!'

'Hello, Harry. How are you?' replied Oldroyd, and walked through the solid wooden doorway. He entered a big room with a large open ceiling with old wooden rafters. The walls were lined with tall bookshelves all crammed with books and files. It was like a small library in a college. Harry Davidson had enjoyed a long career as a journalist in the Yorkshire area, mostly freelance and specialising in investigating scandals and mysteries. He always seemed to be able to access information that was closed off to the police, and some detectives found him a nuisance. However, he and Oldroyd had developed a close relationship over the years based on trust and an admiration for each other's skills. Harry was semi-retired now but Oldroyd doubted that he would ever be able to retire completely.

'Sit down,' he said, in a voice in which the accent was less marked than Oldroyd's. Harry had been privately educated but had later renounced the system as elitist. He had some experience of investigating child abuse in schools. 'Do you fancy a whisky? Oh no, I suppose you're on duty.'

'I'm afraid so. Just a glass of water will be fine.'

Harry went into the kitchen and returned with the water and a tumbler of dark peaty-looking whisky. Oldroyd sat down on a large, comfortable but rather dusty sofa. He noticed that the windows were dirty and the carpet badly needed vacuum cleaning. Harry had never married and had a rather cavalier attitude to housework.

He sat back casually in another sofa opposite Oldroyd. 'You mentioned the Chevin Towers children's home when you called me. I presume it's something to do with this case you're on at the moment. We don't expect things like this to happen in a place like Otley, do we? Anyway, how can I help? I've done a bit of research in my archives,' he said with a smile, and pointed to a pocket wallet on the coffee table between them.

'Anything you know about the place will be useful.'

'Hmm . . .' Harry picked up the wallet and leafed through the papers inside. 'It's a difficult one. What happened was very skilfully hushed up. That man Edward Brown was like a puppet master: he pulled strings all over the place. It was easier to do in those days. He was a class above, so to speak, and people didn't ask questions of people like him. He was well connected. He inherited a big family business; he knew people in high places in the police, councillors, owners of newspapers, you know. He was in some kind of lodge with them all and they scratched each other's backs.'

'So, what was it all about, Harry?'

'Child abuse, of course. But it was thirty years ago, before society was properly aware of that kind of thing. If children were naughty they deserved to be punished, was the thinking, and not enough questions were asked about just how badly some of them were treated, let alone whether paedophiles had access to them in these residential places. Of course, I took a keen interest, having suffered some of it first hand at a terrible private boarding school: being caned for very little provocation until there were marks on your arse, and sometimes made to go without food. Thankfully nobody molested me, although there were some dodgy people on the staff.'

'Tell me what happened at Chevin Towers.'

Harry frowned as if the memories were unpleasant. He took a drink of his whisky.

'The place was run by a charitable trust, not by the local authority. But local councils did place children in that home. Rumours started to circulate about bad things going on there, but everybody involved was tight lipped. I assume they'd all been warned not to say anything by Brown and the other governors.

'Then, quite suddenly, there was a dramatic development. It was announced that the home was closing, virtually immediately, and the children would be taken to other places. They couldn't escape press interest, but said it was due to financial difficulties and denied there were any other kind of problems. Unluckily for them, I had some contacts who knew people who worked there and were prepared to talk.'

'What did you find out?' asked Oldroyd, knowing better than to ask Harry for the names of his sources.

'Apparently there was a member of staff who was a real sadist. He was taking it upon himself to sort out all the badly behaved kids and doing some very nasty things. Some of the children were orphans but many had been taken from their families by social services and placed there for their protection, which is ironic. Children from those kinds of backgrounds can be difficult. Their lives have often been traumatic. You need to have well-trained and dedicated staff, and it seems that a number of them were finding it hard to cope and were grateful for his help.'

'Did you find out what had brought things to a head?'

'Partly. One of my informants said that kids were being locked up in a cellar and beaten.'

'Bloody hell! That ties in with what we've found.' Oldroyd leaned forward, eager for more information. 'The crucial thing is, did you manage to get any names? We know that Frances Hughes, the second murder victim, worked there, and we know about Brown . . . But who else?'

Harry picked up the document wallet again. 'These are from one of my sources. They told me the name of one of the boys who had been particularly badly treated.' He looked at the sheet of paper. 'The boy was Trevor Hattersley. They also divulged the name of the member of staff who was abusing the children. It was Alex Abelman.'

Oldroyd nodded. 'Abelman was the first murder victim, but he was going under the name of Tony Lowell. The name Trevor Hattersley hasn't come up – but I wonder if he's going under a different name too. That's excellent, Harry, thanks a lot.'

'Glad to be of service,' said Harry. He read some more of the notes. 'Things are coming back to me now. I remember thinking that something else must have happened for the home to be abandoned like that so abruptly. The physical abuse had been going on for some time and nobody had stopped it.'

'Did you hear anything about a child dying?'

'What?!' Harry whistled. 'No, but that would explain the haste. A dead child? What did they do with the body?'

'We think they buried it in the cellar. We were searching at night in there and we disturbed someone digging a body up.'

'Good God! And you went in there at night? You old bugger. I bet that was so that you didn't have to get permission. You're as unorthodox as I am in your methods.'

Oldroyd grinned. 'Well, you've got to bend the rules a bit sometimes. Luckily my boss turns a blind eye on things like that if I get the desired results.'

Harry laughed and poured himself another whisky. 'You're sure you won't have one?'

Oldroyd got up. 'I'd love to, Harry – but, as you say, I'm on duty. And I need to get back. I need to speak to Edward Brown urgently. Thanks again.'

'You're welcome. I hope that someone is brought to justice for what happened at that place. I think it was one of the worst things I ever investigated, partly because of the cover-up. No newspaper would run with the story at the time. We just didn't have enough hard evidence and it all faded away.'

'That must have been difficult.'

'Oh yes, but it happens a lot. I can't tell you the number of incidents that remain unresolved because the people involved have never been prosecuted. It's our privilege as reporters to access information that doesn't get to you lot . . . but it can be very frustrating because we can't always do anything with it.' He paused and took another drink of whisky. 'You know, the terrible truth is that people in those days didn't really care about children that didn't belong to anybody. It was all about the family. But what if you didn't have one? You were right at the bottom of society, especially if you were illegitimate.'

'Hmm,' mused Oldroyd. 'Do you think it's changed since then?'

'We like to think so, don't we? But sadly, I'm not so sure.'

～

At the Courthouse, Abigail Wilson and Hillary Sands were waiting for the arrival of the detectives. Hillary was very nervous, but determined to go through with it. Abigail had heard her story, was in no doubt that she should go to the police, and offered to accompany her.

Soon after Steph and Oldroyd had arrived and gone into the robing room, the two women came over from the main building.

Oldroyd was telling Steph what he had learned from Harry Davidson when there was a knock on the door.

'Sorry to disturb you,' said Abigail to Oldroyd, 'but Hillary has some important information relevant to the case. It's difficult stuff for her to talk about.'

This surprised Oldroyd but he was also pleased that at last people were coming forward with information. 'I see. Please take a seat. Can I get you anything?'

'I think we're OK, thanks. Hillary just wants to get this over with.' They sat down at a table opposite the detectives. Hillary was fiddling nervously with a handkerchief.

'What I've got to say concerns Edward Brown. He's a member of the committee here and I know you've spoken to him at least once.'

'Yes,' said Oldroyd.

'Years ago, he was a governor at the Chevin Towers Children's Home.'

Oldroyd nodded. 'Yes, we found that out yesterday.'

Hillary was relieved to hear this. The police seemed to be on the same page, which would make her task easier. 'Well, when that place shut down, something bad had happened and I'm sure that he was involved in some kind of cover-up.'

'Why do you think that?'

Hillary hesitated and glanced at Abigail before continuing. 'You see, I had a relative who was in that home in the last years before it shut.' She stopped and seemed to be struggling to continue. She dabbed her eyes with the handkerchief.

'Go on,' said Oldroyd gently.

'Her name was Susan – Susan Thomas. She was my cousin and a few years younger than me. My aunt was my mother's sister, and they lived near to us in Otley. Susan and I were always good friends. My aunt was divorced and had problems with alcohol.

She couldn't work, and had no money, so she agreed to put Susan into the home until she could turn her life around. My mother wanted to take Susan in, but there were four of us already and it just wasn't possible.

'I used to walk up to Chevin Towers to see her. I thought it was a very gloomy building but there were nice gardens and places to play. We mostly stayed outside; she seemed to prefer that. It was very isolated, and I don't think the children mixed much with other kids in the area except at school. Susan didn't seem happy. She had been a pleasant, bubbly child before she went in there, but now she was morose and quiet. To be honest, it felt like visiting someone in prison.'

She paused again, then looked at Steph and Oldroyd, who were listening very attentively to what she had to say.

'Things went from bad to worse for Susan. My aunt died. Her liver had packed in. So there seemed no prospect of Susan getting out of the home. One day . . .' She stopped again and started to cry.

'Take your time,' said Oldroyd.

'I went to see her. We walked around the grounds a bit and then I heard this terrible shouting coming from the house. It seemed to be a member of the staff having a real go at one of the kids. Then there was a cracking sound and a cry, as if a child was being beaten with a cane or something. When Susan heard it, she looked terrified and suddenly she flung her arms around me and pleaded with me to take her away from there.

'I was shocked. I asked her what was wrong, why didn't she like it there. She looked at me and across at the house and seemed too frightened to say anything. Then she gestured for me to go behind a tree with her. She made me promise not to tell anyone about what she was going to say. She said that the grown-ups there did nasty things to the children, like hitting them a lot and locking them up. Everybody was frightened. There was one adult in particular called

Mr Abelman; they were all scared of him. Then she said that they had all been warned not to say anything about what went on at the home – that if they did, they would be severely punished. As she was speaking, she was constantly glancing over nervously towards the house.

'I didn't know what to do. I was only fifteen and it was all very confusing. I said I couldn't take her with me, and she started to cry. It was horrible. I said I had to go but I would come to see her again soon. When I got home, I didn't say anything to my parents. I thought something bad would happen to Susan if I did.' She shook her head and looked anguished. 'I really wish I had done now. It's haunted me all these years.'

'It was very hard for you then, being so young, but you are telling us now, aren't you? It's never too late to unburden yourself of something like this.'

Hillary nodded. 'Susan stayed in the home until she was sixteen, and then she moved to some council-run flats for young people in Leeds. By this time, I didn't see much of her. On my last visits she seemed increasingly withdrawn and not really pleased to see me any more. I don't know whether she felt that I had let her down or was just depressed by living there.

'I got married to Jeremy when I was quite young, and we had two children. They're grown up and left home now, but if you've had kids, you know what it's like when they're little – they take over your life. I just didn't have much time to give to Susan.' She closed her eyes and shook her head. 'I really regret that now. I rang her occasionally over the years, but never got much response. She'd gone to college but dropped out. I don't know what she was doing but I think there were drugs involved. Eventually she stopped answering my calls and I got worried. I tracked her to a rundown shared house in Hyde Park. I'll never forget that when I got there it was the middle of the afternoon and she was laid on the bed in this dirty room and I hardly recognised her: she was thin and pale with black marks around her eyes.

'I think she was pleased to see me. I tried to get her to talk. I knew that all her troubles related to her time at the home, and I wanted her to tell me about it. I thought it would do her good to let it out. There was still fear in her face when I mentioned Chevin Towers. I pleaded with her to tell me what had happened there, and I remember distinctly what she said: "I can't tell you, you don't understand; you've never had the chair."'

Oldroyd looked up and glanced at Steph. 'Did she tell you what she meant by that?' he asked.

'No. She wouldn't say any more. I took it that it must have been something dreadful that she couldn't bring herself to talk about. How can people do that to children?' Hillary wiped her eyes again and Abigail put a hand on her shoulder. 'Not long after that she was dead.' Hillary broke down and started to weep. The others waited for her to recover.

'It was a drug overdose; whether it was deliberate or not they said was unclear. Obviously I was devastated and felt guilty. I thought I could have done more for her. I tried to find out about the home at Chevin Towers, but it was almost impossible; a ring of secrecy had been thrown around it. The only thing I did find out, talking to people locally, was that Edward Brown had been some kind of governor of the place in those final years. I believe he must have known something of what was going on there, but what could I do? I had no evidence, and he was a more powerful person than I was. The very fact that he stayed in this area shows that he felt secure. I didn't believe the police would take me seriously. This was before all the scandals about child abuse in institutions around the country had come out. Things were being hushed up all over the place.'

'So, I take it that it's recent events that have prompted you to speak out?'

'Yes. When these murders started to happen – and the word *vindicta* was written on the victims – I started to wonder if it was revenge for things that had happened at the home. I still found it difficult to bring myself to say anything and I had no real evidence. Brown is on the committee at the Courthouse, so I felt he had some kind of power over me, as he had over those children. Anyway, I'm talking to you now. I'm sorry I didn't come forward before.'

Oldroyd nodded. 'I can understand how difficult it was for you to come and speak to us. I think you felt the same way as the children in the home, like your cousin: too frightened to speak up.'

'Yes. There's one more thing. What's happened recently has brought all my anger back. I saw Edward Brown in the centre of the town here and told him I knew things about him. I shouldn't have said that.'

Oldroyd smiled. 'Don't worry – we were already on to Mr Brown. We recently discovered that he was a governor at the home, and we know he participated in some kind of cover-up. He's now at risk from whoever is behind these murders. Police officers have been dispatched to his house and we'll be talking to him again shortly. Your story will help us in our investigation. Perhaps it might give us a way to make him open up about what happened.'

'Can you think of anything else that Susan told you about that home, however trivial it seems? Did she ever mention Frances Hughes?' asked Steph.

'No. It's obvious now that Frances was involved, but Susan never named her. As you say, I think she was too frightened.'

'Yes. Tragically, if a child experiences that level of terror, it tends to stay with them into adult life and it's a very difficult thing to overcome.' Oldroyd looked at her and smiled. 'You mustn't blame yourself. You didn't inflict any of this on her and you were too young to have stopped it. It wasn't your responsibility.'

Hillary nodded but didn't look entirely convinced. 'I've always wanted to see some kind of justice for Susan. It sounds awful but if these people who have been murdered were responsible for abusing those children – and Susan was only one of many – I have to say I don't feel sorry for them.'

Oldroyd thanked her again, understanding how she felt – sometimes the line between the law and justice could seem incomprehensible to people at the centre of such terrible events – and the two women went back into the main building.

Steph looked very grave. 'God, sir, this is getting worse and worse. What on earth did that poor girl mean by having "had the chair"? Do you think it was the chair that we found in that cellar?'

Oldroyd sighed and shook his head. 'Unfortunately, I think there's every chance that was the chair she meant. Obviously, something very traumatic happened in that cellar. I think at the least children must have been tied up there and left in the dark and cold, but maybe worse.' He closed his eyes and shook his head again vigorously, as if trying to erase the images that came into his mind. 'I need a strong coffee after that, and then we need to go to speak to Edward Brown.'

Steph was still considering the new information. 'I think you're right, sir. Tony Lowell was Alex Abelman – but who is Trevor Hattersley, and where is he now?'

'That's what we've got to find out, and quickly,' replied Oldroyd grimly.

~

The atmosphere was very tense at Edward Brown's house. DC David Hall had arranged for a police constable to remain there until they decided how best to protect Brown, maybe by moving him to a safe location.

Brown felt more at ease now but found conversation with the young PC difficult. He continued to sit in the same chair, sipping whisky from time to time. He tried to read a book but found it difficult to concentrate and kept going over to the window to check the garden. He should be safe now, but all the past was going to be raked up by the police as they investigated the murders. How on earth was he going to protect the reputation he had been building up all these years?

He had not been sleeping well at night. He was just nodding off in the chair when there was a knock at the back door, and he jerked awake. The PC in the kitchen called through. 'Stay where you are, sir.'

When the PC opened the door, there was no one there. He stepped outside and looked around one side of the house. As soon as his back was turned, a figure came up behind him and struck him over the head with a wooden mallet. He fell to the ground unconscious.

Brown rushed to his feet, but was met by the attacker dressed head to toe in black. They closed the door and brandished a long, sharp knife. Brown's legs went weak with panic.

'Mr Edward Brown,' the figure taunted, pulling off the balaclava. 'Trevor Hattersley is the name, but I don't expect that you remember me. We weren't important to you, were we? Just awkward little kids who deserved what they got for making trouble. That bastard Abelman made our lives hell, but at least I'm here, unlike Liam Quinn. Do you remember him, Mr Brown?'

'Look,' said Brown in desperation, 'I didn't do anything to you or anyone else.'

The man laughed. 'Oh no! You just covered up for the people who did and made sure that we could never get any justice. Anyway, we can't stay here. You're coming with me. Don't try anything stupid – or you'll get this knife straight into your back.'

Six

In the nineteenth century, while remaining a country town surrounded by farmland and woodland, Otley took on a second identity as a small industrial centre. A cotton mill and weaving shed were built by the river in the late eighteenth century. By the mid-nineteenth century, 500 inhabitants were employed in two worsted mills, a paper mill, and other mills. A tannery was established too. Terraced housing was built and a railway opened in 1865. The Wharfedale Printing Machine was developed in Otley by William Dawson and David Payne, and by 1900 the printing machinery trade employed over 2,000 people in seven machine shops.

At the farm high above New Bridge, Jake and Ian Milton were taking the opportunity of their father's absence to search the farm. For what, they were not entirely sure, but Jake was determined to get to the bottom of what his father was up to.

Ian went into the loft space of the farmhouse, while Jake took another look in some of the outbuildings, including the two field barns. They still used the barns to house the small herd of cattle in the winter, but at the moment they were empty apart from birds. When he entered one of the barns, he saw the twiggy remains of wood pigeon nests and the neat mud constructions of house martin nests in corners and under the eaves. A barn owl was perched on a stone ledge, but it immediately flew off through an opening high up in the wall.

Jake looked around, but there was nothing but dried cow manure and straw. His father was cunning. Maybe he had hidden whatever it was much closer to the house, where you wouldn't expect it. He walked back down to the farm. The view across the slopes of lower Wharfedale was beautiful. He'd been brought up in this place, and only left to study agriculture at university. Ian had studied at a lower level at the local college. Their father had poured scorn on studying, saying it wasn't necessary. He'd learned everything from his father through working on the farm.

Jake wanted, along with his brother, to inherit the farm from their father in good condition. They were ready to implement forward-looking organic and green policies which their father rejected. Without these changes the farm would struggle and things would be made even worse if there was further trouble with the law.

Ian joined him. 'There's nothing up there. Are you sure he's got something? We've looked everywhere.'

'Yes. He's a crafty old sod.' They walked into a small outbuilding that was used as storage. Jake's eyes rested on a large pile of plastic bags containing pig food. They'd already searched the building, but Jake felt that something was wrong.

'Hold on,' he said. 'That's a lot of pig food. Let's pull some away. I'll bet he's got something concealed underneath.'

Jake was right. Once they removed a couple of layers of the pig food, they discovered bags underneath containing something else.

'Bloody hell!' said Ian. 'The stupid . . .' He couldn't finish the sentence.

'Shit!' said his brother. 'We need to have this out with him once and for all. And from now on we have to take control here. Our future is at stake.'

∾

Abigail Wilson was in the office at the Courthouse. She had sent Hillary home to rest after her trauma of telling Oldroyd about her cousin Susan. Dylan was in the office but there was not much conversation between them. It was also difficult to concentrate on work. The atmosphere was still so tense everywhere in the town and it was hard not to think about the murders all the time.

She sat back in her chair and rubbed her eyes. 'How are you feeling, Dylan?' she asked.

'Hard to focus, isn't it? With everything that's gone on,' he replied, pausing his work for a moment.

'I know. Do you feel, you know, safe?'

'Walking around the streets, yes . . . but to tell you the truth, I've had new locks fitted to my external doors at home. All this business makes you think about security, doesn't it? How are you and the family?'

Abigail had to laugh. 'Obviously Dave and I are worried, but the kids are having a great time. It's a huge adventure to them. If I didn't stop him, Jonathan would be here with his friends offering to do some detective work for the police.'

Dylan laughed. 'They might welcome it. It's been a difficult case for them. You can see the stress on the face of that chief inspector.'

Abigail continued, 'As for Mary, she loves the scariness of it. Jonathan keeps telling her horrific details and she screams, but I think she actually likes it.'

'It's not real for them, is it? They can have fantasy games with it and enjoy being frightened.' He paused and sighed. 'It's for us that it's real in all its horror.'

~

In the robing room, DC David Hall brought the news that Brown had been abducted. Oldroyd sat down and banged his fist on the table. Steph frowned, recognising his devastation and self-blame.

'Damn! We should have taken more care. Did we only have one officer there?'

'Yes, sir,' replied a sheepish David Hall. 'It's normally sufficient for house protection for one person, sir. We haven't really got the officers to spare to send more than one.'

'Yes, I know. I'm not blaming you,' Oldroyd said. 'Clearly, this killer is determined and ruthless. But it's deeply frustrating – how on earth are we going to find out where he was taken before it's too late?'

'I don't know, sir,' said Hall.

Oldroyd stood up. 'I can't just sit here.' He looked around the room and through the open door to the main building. His brow was furrowed. 'Maybe we need to go back to the very beginning; there could be a clue here that we've missed.' He walked out. Steph didn't follow him; she sensed he wanted to be by himself to think.

Oldroyd strode into the main building and looked carefully around the entrance, the steps up which the body must have been dragged or carried, and the cell where the body was found. Then he came back down and went into the courtroom itself, where judges had sat and where musicians and comedians now performed. He noticed the smell of new paint. Suddenly he had an idea. He went swiftly to the Courthouse office. Abigail looked up, startled, as Oldroyd burst in.

'Sorry to interrupt,' he said. 'But I notice that the courtroom has been painted recently.'

'Yes,' replied Abigail. 'Scott Evans, a local chap – he's been decorating different bits of the centre for a while now.'

'And does he come and go as he likes? Did—'

Abigail leaped to her feet, realising in a flash what Oldroyd was getting at and recalling something of vital importance. 'Oh my God, yes! I remember. He asked me a few weeks ago if he could borrow the keys so that he could come in on Sunday when we're normally closed. He gave them back to me the following week. But he could have had a set made at a locksmith's.' She looked at Oldroyd. 'So you think the murderer could be Scott? You think he didn't break in because he had a key. I'm so sorry – how could I not even have thought of that?'

'Don't worry,' Oldroyd said. 'It happens a lot with people doing their jobs in the background: you hardly notice them . . . and in time you even forget they're there. He didn't register in your mind as a member of the Courthouse staff. I only thought about this when I realised someone had been painting inside the Courthouse, and that we hadn't even asked who that had been. Now . . . Where does he live?'

'I can give you his address, but I just can't imagine Scott doing anything like that. I hope I'm not getting him into trouble.'

'Don't worry. It may not be him, but we have to follow this up. Please bring me his details as soon as you can – I'll be in our office.'

Oldroyd returned to the robing room just as DC David Hall entered, looking harassed. He clearly felt somewhat responsible for the abduction of Edward Brown.

'I've got some more information, sir,' Hall said. 'Our PC will be OK, I think, although he's been taken to hospital to have treatment for concussion. We've been out talking to people in

Edward Brown's street, where two people saw a van parked nearby at about the time he must have been taken.'

'I don't suppose anybody got the number plate?'

'No, but one person said they thought it looked like a decorator's van.'

Oldroyd felt like punching the air. At last, they could be getting close to identifying the killer. 'Excellent! We've already had information that makes Scott Evans – a decorator they use here – a suspect. We just need his address and then we'll get over there.'

'Here we go, sir,' said Hall, looking up from his phone. 'Twenty-four Duke Street. That's off the Leeds Road.'

'Good! Let's go!' Oldroyd and Steph almost ran across the forecourt to their car, passing a bemused Abigail Wilson who was holding a piece of paper with the promised address on.

'Thanks, but we've got it!' shouted Oldroyd as he got into the car and they sped away.

~

Edward Brown was tied to a wooden chair in a back room at Hattersley's house with a gag in his mouth. The house was an end terrace with a garage at the side where the van was parked, beside a back alley.

Brown's abductor stood in front of him, but Brown still didn't recognise him.

Hattersley had shed all the light-hearted cheeriness with which he had conducted himself at the Courthouse. He looked at Brown with snarling contempt and his eyes shone with hatred. He still brandished the terrifying knife but showed no inclination, as yet, to use it. He seemed to be enjoying the process of playing with his victim for a while.

'You're the third person to sit in that chair,' he said. 'How does it feel?' Brown grunted through the gag and Hattersley laughed. 'I know you can't answer, but you have to listen. Abelman was the first. I can't tell you how satisfying it was to make him suffer in the same way that he made so many kids – tying them to the chair in that cellar and leaving them in the dark. Have you any idea what it feels like, as a child, to be left in a place like that and then beaten?' He leaned towards Brown with his knife and seemed about to cut him but then sat back down again. 'I enjoyed strangling him slowly. That bloody sadist got a taste of his own medicine.

'Then there was Hughes. She never gave us any punishment directly, of course; she was far too weak to do that. But any kid she couldn't deal with, she sent to Abelman, knowing full well what he'd do. She was in a right state when I got her here, but as I said to her, how did she think kids felt when Abelman got them in the cellar? I suppose she pretended it wasn't happening.' His eyes blazed for a moment as terrible memories came into his mind. 'But it was. And then she helped to cover it up and left us all damaged.' He went up to Brown, grasped his hair, pulled his head back and put the knife to his throat. Brown tried to cry out. Hattersley pulled back, laughing.

'You're OK for a little while longer. Blood is too messy, I—'

Suddenly there was loud knocking at the door and shouting. It was the voice of DC Hall. 'Police! Scott Evans, we know you are in the house and have reason to believe that you are keeping a person there against their will. The building is surrounded. Open the front door and walk out with your hands raised.'

'Shit!' exclaimed Hattersley. He went over to the window to peep out and saw police officers in the road outside. He was indeed trapped. For a moment he had a recurrence of the terrible feelings he and other kids experienced when they had been tied to that chair and locked in the cellar. And then his strength seemed to drain out of him and he felt a strange peace. He had got revenge on the sadists who had done so much damage to him and the other kids in that awful place, including that poor kid Liam Quinn. He'd always known that it was likely that he would be caught, which is why he'd acted so quickly. Not quite quickly enough, he thought, looking at Brown. The bastard would escape death, but his reputation would surely be destroyed, and that would be devastating for someone like him.

Calmly, Hattersley went to the back door, opened it and stepped out with his arms raised. It was over now.

～

Oldroyd and Steph faced Trevor Hattersley – AKA Scott Evans – in an interview room at Otley police station. A duty solicitor was next to Hattersley, who sat up in his chair with his arms folded, looking strangely calm and defiant. He had readily confessed to the murders of Alex Abelman and Frances Hughes.

'Let's talk about Chevin Towers and your time there,' continued Oldroyd.

Hattersley shifted uncomfortably, clearly finding it difficult to think about that place.

'OK,' he began, and spoke in a halting manner as he retrieved the painful memories of his childhood. 'My dad didn't hang around for very long after I was born, so my mum had to bring me up by herself in Leeds. The stress of it all led her to have problems with drugs and she couldn't cope. She put me in care. I was shunted around from place to place for a while until I ended up at the Towers. Spooky Towers, we used to call it. It was a big, gloomy, rambling place, freezing cold in winter. We slept in these big, echoing dormitories, one for girls and one for boys; young kids, we were terrified at night. It was like something out of Victorian times.

'We were taken down to local schools in Otley in the daytime but in the evening and at weekends we were stuck up there and had little contact with the outside world. Discipline was very strict; we had all these routines about mealtimes, doing homework and lots of jobs around the place. They didn't seem to employ any domestic staff apart from in the kitchens. We did all the cleaning, and a lot of the laundry too. They took a pride in it, said we were learning to look after ourselves. Actually, we were just used as free labour.' He paused and looked at Steph and Oldroyd before he echoed what Harry Davidson had said. 'In those days nobody seemed to care about what happened to children like us. Chevin Towers was good for the public because we were all hidden away from view, and they could forget about the fact that not all children lived in a nice family with loving parents.'

Steph frowned. She remembered her own upbringing, which had not been without the problems brought by an alcoholic father, but she had always felt secure and loved by her mother. To have to live as a kid in a place like Chevin Towers without the warmth of family life: it made her shudder.

'I take it that things got gradually worse while you were there,' said Oldroyd.

Hattersley nodded. 'It was when Abelman arrived. I think they chose him because he was a hard bastard. A lot of the kids, including me, didn't behave well, but do you wonder in the circumstances? I expect that the staff who lived in found it particularly hard; they were sort of on duty twenty-four hours a day and some of them like that Frances Hughes couldn't cope, even though she was technically in charge of the place as the senior warden.

'I think Abelman had been some kind of sports teacher, or maybe even a coach. He was big and strong, and enjoyed handing it out to kids. He was definitely a sadist. He used to have a smile on his face when he was hitting you or pulling you across the room by your hair. He seemed to be in charge of the place. I think the other staff were frightened of him too, but we were absolutely terrified.

'He told us that we were all a bunch of hooligans who didn't know how to behave, and he was going to make us change. He introduced all kinds of rules, and punishments if you didn't follow them. It started with making you miss meals or banning you from the television room, and then people were caned. But the worst . . .' He stopped and couldn't continue for a moment and put a hand up to his head.

'The worst was the chair. If you were a repeat offender – and some of the so-called crimes were very minor, like putting your feet up on the sofa or making too much noise at mealtimes – he would take you down into the cellar and tie you to a wooden chair. You would be left in the total dark and cold. Sometimes you would be left overnight.' Tears were coming into his eyes at the memory.

'I can't tell you how horrendous it was to be tied up in that cellar. It happened to most of us in the end and every single person was traumatised. It was so frightening and desolate. You felt that you'd been left to die, and nobody cared. I've seen tough-looking kids reduced to snivelling wrecks. Sometimes we used to hear the shouts and screams from kids who were down there. If Abelman heard them, they were left there for longer.' He paused and shuddered. A look of contempt came on to his face. 'That Hughes. She was supposed to be in charge and looking after us. She gave Abelman free rein to do what the hell he wanted. She just looked after herself.'

'Did you tell anyone about what was going on, like your teachers at school?'

'We were too scared. We didn't think that they would believe us. And if they had contacted the home, goodness knows what Abelman would have done to punish us. There was this guy who used to come and visit from a church.'

That must have been Ivan, thought Oldroyd.

'He used to ask us if we were happy and stuff like that. We were told not to say much to him, but he must have picked up that there were problems. I don't think he was the type to ask difficult questions. He looked as if he was frightened of the staff too.'

'How long were you at Chevin Towers?'

'Three years. I was nine when I went and twelve when it was shut down. I was sent back to Leeds.'

'I presume it was closed because a child died?'

Abelman looked at Oldroyd with some respect. 'You're right. You've followed up on our encounter the other night. I wasn't only trying to get revenge. I also wanted to prove that Liam died, and that they hid his body. I found some remains in the cellar where I thought he would have been buried. It's up to you lot to prove that it was him.'

'We will. Who was this boy?' asked Steph.

Abelman took a deep breath. 'Liam Quinn. His family originally came from Cork, I think, but he didn't seem to have any contact with them any more. I don't know whether they went back to Ireland and left him or what. That kid suffered terribly. We used to tease him about his Irish accent.' Hattersley stopped and his face looked anguished. 'I'm so sorry about that now, but we were only kids ourselves – and not happy ones. Brown and the others were lucky there: a kid died who nobody would come looking for. I don't know exactly what happened or how they covered it up, but Liam had done something and was taken to the cellar. Next day we noticed that the staff looked worried and were whispering to each other. Liam never reappeared and it was then that we were told that the home was going to close.'

'What exactly did they say to you?'

'We were all taken into the big room on the ground floor. Brown, Hughes and Abelman were there, looking extremely serious. The image is seared into my memory. They were the three people responsible for what happened, and they were the people I was determined to make pay.

'Brown told us that Liam Quinn had been taken ill and he'd gone home to Ireland. He said that is what we should say if anyone asked us about him. If we didn't, we would get into trouble. He and Abelman glared at us. Brown said that the same thing applied to the way we'd been treated in the home. His staff had always done their very best for us and he didn't expect to hear that anybody had said bad words about them. If anybody had ever been punished, then they must have deserved it. He followed this up with another threat.

'He told us that we would now be separated and sent to new places to live, but we must not think that we could not be found if necessary. It was no use believing that it would be safe to say bad things about Chevin Towers, because he and the others would know, and they would come and get us. Everything would be OK if we stayed quiet and didn't talk about our time in Chevin Towers.'

Steph grimaced and looked down. How terrified the kids must have been.

Hattersley continued. 'It shows how strong a grip they had on us that I don't think anybody has ever spoken out. We were afraid, particularly of Abelman. He was a monster and we believed that he really would find us if we didn't do as we were told, wherever we were.' He paused. 'I know it's ridiculous, but if you've suffered such terror as a child, it's hard to get that threat out of your mind.'

'I think it's very understandable,' remarked Oldroyd. 'What happened to you after you left the home?'

Hattersley fidgeted in the chair and shrugged his shoulders. 'It was hard, even though I wasn't being brutally treated any more. I was moved to a children's home in Leeds with a few of those who'd been at Chevin Towers, but we didn't have much to do with each other. I suppose we reminded one another about what had happened. We never talked about it because of the fear that had been put into us. It might have been different if we'd had happy times together.

'I did badly at school. I left at sixteen and got work as an apprentice with a painter and decorator. But I couldn't settle to any job. All my relationships failed. I emigrated to Australia – trying to run away from everything, I suppose – but it was no different there and eventually I came back.

'I'd kept up with my painting and decorating, and managed to earn a living that way in different parts of West Yorkshire. I tended to stay away from Otley because of the awful memories. Then one day I saw a picture of Edward Brown in a local newspaper. He was wearing a gold chain. He was now the mayor of Otley or something.' Hattersley stopped and anger blazed in his eyes again. 'I tore up the newspaper in a rage. How could this man be a public figure and honoured after what he'd done? The injustice of it broke me. I'd spent years not thinking about Chevin Towers, but now I just had to get revenge somehow.

'I tried to find out who else from the home was still around. The only other member of the staff I could trace was Frances Hughes. She and her husband were running a care home for old people not far from Otley. I spent a lot of time stalking them. I often got very close, but she didn't recognise me now that I was an adult. It might not have gone any further than that, except I was doing a job in Menston when I saw Abelman. You could have knocked me over with a feather. He also had the gall to be still living near the site of all his abuse of us. It showed how arrogant he was and sure that none of the kids would ever speak out. He'd changed his appearance and, I found out later, his name, but I recognised him. It was all I could do to stop myself attacking him in the street.'

'So you developed a plan to get even?'

'Yes. I wanted to get all three of them and pay them back for ruining the lives of those kids, including me. I couldn't believe they were still in this area. It made it all worse somehow that they had no fear of ever being brought to justice and had their reputations intact. I knew I would have to work fast once I had started because if the connection with Chevin Towers was discovered, people would be on the alert.' He looked at Oldroyd. 'The first two were easy. It was very gratifying when they both finally recognised me before I killed them. I was glad to see the fear in their eyes. They must have seen that fear so many times in the eyes of the children that they abused but it never stopped them. But then you caught up with me before I could finish Brown.'

'You must have known that we would track you down in the end. You were actually leaving clues, weren't you, in the way you left the bodies?'

Hattersley smiled for the first time. 'I did that to publicly humiliate them, and hint at what they'd done to children. I wanted to get away with it if I could, so I didn't leave anything linking me to the killings.' He looked at Oldroyd. 'I knew the odds were against me – even more so when I found out that you were the one leading the investigation. But I was prepared to risk being caught to do what I did.'

'But did you also think that people might follow the clues, to finally reveal what happened at Chevin Towers?'

Hattersley shook his head. 'I don't know about that. I just wanted to get revenge on the people who made the children suffer. I was doing it for all the kids who had to endure living there.'

'So, am I right in thinking that leaving Abelman in the cell at the Courthouse was referring to how he had locked kids up in the cellar?'

'Yes. I think all the kids ended up down there at least once. It was a way of terrorising us all.'

'And you had a set of keys to the external door copied when you borrowed them?'

'Yes, no one suspected anything. I did that a while before I killed Abelman so that no one would make the connection, but it seems like someone did remember in the end. When I left the building, I locked the door behind me. I didn't want anyone to go in there, steal things and cause more trouble.'

Oldroyd nodded. He'd thought something like this from the first day.

'Go on,' he said.

'I think Hughes realised what was going on. She probably recognised Abelman from the photographs in the newspapers, but I was too quick for her.' He glanced at Oldroyd. 'I was nearly too quick for you as well, with Brown.'

'You were. So, placing Frances Hughes with those scarecrow children was saying something about the fact the children were betrayed by a person who should have been looking after them.'

'Yes, they had no parents, no family life, and they weren't safe. I think she should have been like a mother and protected us, but she didn't.'

'What would you have done with Edward Brown?'

'Put him on a swing at a children's playground. The kids at Chevin Towers had their childhood taken from them.'

'Why did you write *vindicta* on them? We know it was all about revenge, but why Latin?'

Hattersley laughed grimly. 'I found out that the home had a motto: *Cura Personalis*. I looked it up and it means *care of the person* or something. A fancy bit of Latin and it was a sick joke, so I replied with *vindicta* – vengeance.'

Oldroyd nodded as his hunch was proved correct. He looked at Hattersley before he continued. 'And how do you feel now? Do you feel satisfied that you took vengeance?'

Hattersley swallowed. 'It could never be enough. They ruined everyone's lives, and a kid died – murdered. They were never brought to justice. There are a lot more victims out there. And I don't know what happened to them.' Hattersley stopped and looked down. 'I'm not really a bad person.'

Oldroyd wondered how to respond to that. 'Despite killing two people, and abducting and planning to kill another?'

'They deserved it. It was justice. I couldn't let them get away with what they'd done.'

Oldroyd looked at him with a mixture of compassion and revulsion. There was one more thing he wanted to ask.

'Did you know a girl called Susan Thomas? She must have been in there about the same time as you.'

Hattersley looked up, shocked. 'Sue? Yes, yes, I did. What happened to her? She was one of my best friends, but I never saw her again after we left the home.'

'It wasn't good, I'm afraid,' said Oldroyd kindly, and he explained how Susan had died from a drug overdose.

'Sue? No!' exclaimed Hattersley and he burst into tears. Clearly more, very vivid memories had come back. Oldroyd hoped there were happier memories of friendship too, of how they had tried to support each other in a dark place. But now it all appeared to be engulfed by the same sadness, bitterness and despair that seemed to engulf everyone associated with Chevin Towers Children's Home. Oldroyd left him to recover as he and Steph went quietly out of the room.

～

George Milton didn't arrive back at the farm from Harrogate until late on the Thursday evening, and he was quite drunk after an evening with some friends. He walked up across the fields from the station and went straight to bed, so his sons did not have a chance to confront him. On Friday morning, however, they were waiting for him when he came downstairs. They were both sitting at the large kitchen table beside the fire.

Milton scratched his head and looked at them, sensing that something was up.

'What's going on, then?' he growled. 'What are you two doing in here? You should be out working.'

'Sit down, Dad. I'll get you a cup of tea,' said Jake. He went to put the kettle on. Milton sat, looking suspiciously at Ian, but didn't say anything. Jake brought over the tea and sat opposite his father. He took a deep breath and began.

'We found it, Dad.'

'Found what?' growled Milton.

'The bags of pesticide hidden under the pig food.'

Milton glared at his son defiantly. 'So what? Do you think I'm going to let anybody tell me what to do on me own farm?'

Jake leaned over the table. 'You haven't learned anything, have you? Even though you went to jail. I think it's just made you more stubborn. That pesticide is banned by law because it's dangerous – dangerous to wildlife and to humans.'

'Who says so?' Milton pointed his finger at Jake. 'I'll tell you who. Bloody scientists and environment nutcases who don't have to work a farm and make money on it.'

'So it doesn't bother you that this stuff leaches out into the rivers and streams? Poisoning the water and killing fish?'

'Does it hell – it's all exaggerated. I've never put much on. It all gets diluted in t' rivers.'

Jake looked up in a gesture of despair. 'Not before it's killed the fish and . . . Oh I give up. Where did you get it anyway?'

'There's a bloke in Ripon who supplies us. I think he gets it from Romania or somewhere.'

'"Us?" You mean there are other farmers using this stuff?' asked Ian.

'Course there are. I'm not the only one who won't be told what to do.'

'I see,' said Jake. 'It's the bloke who supplies the pig food, isn't it? The bags of pesticide are hidden underneath when it's delivered.'

Milton shrugged.

The brothers shook their heads. 'Whatever you think, Dad,' said Ian, 'the fact is it's against the law to use it. If the police find any more of this stuff here, not only will you go to prison again – and for longer this time – but the farm will probably get shut down or something. Me and Jake are not putting up with it any more.'

The young men stood up and Milton looked from one to the other.

'What are you talking about, you arrogant young buggers? You'll do as I tell you, like you always have.'

'No, Dad,' said Jake calmly. 'We're taking over here now. You can't be trusted and it's our future that's at stake.'

'What? I . . . You've got a bloody nerve. I built this farm up. It was nearly bankrupt in your grandfather's time.'

'Yes, Dad, you did, and we're grateful for that. But it's not exactly in a great state now, is it? Parts of it are falling to bits; it needs money spending on it.'

'Huh!' scoffed Milton. 'And where are you gonna get that from?'

'We'll take out a loan,' said Ian.

'Debt! You'll get yourself into debt.'

'We have to do it if this farm's going to have a future. And the way you're behaving now is endangering this farm's future, Dad, so we're going to be in charge, and you can concentrate on the pigs.'

Milton leaned forward as if he was going to make a grab for Jake, who pulled back.

'If you cause any more trouble, the police will have to get involved. That's not something we want, Dad, but things are going to have to change here. Look at you, you can scarcely take care of yourself. We need to get you a cleaner to come in regularly, get this house sorted out.'

Milton stood up to face his sons. He spluttered with anger and continued to glare frantically from one to the other. But their faces were implacable, and he suddenly realised that they had overtaken him. They seemed to tower above him and were now stronger and more capable than he was. His authority had gone. He sat down again; his head bowed over the table, and he seemed to shrink into a weakened old man who had no choice but to accept his fate.

Much to his disgust, Edward Brown had been arrested on suspicion of child cruelty and aiding a murderer. He was brought to Otley police station after he had been treated in hospital for shock and minor wounds and spent the night at home. He was brought into an interview room where he refused to cooperate until his solicitor arrived.

Oldroyd and Steph came into the room.

'What's going on? Why have I been arrested? You have no evidence against me!' His tone was still arrogant, but his appearance was somewhat dishevelled and he seemed nervous and uncertain after his brush with death.

'Good morning,' said Oldroyd, ignoring what Brown had said. 'I'm glad to see you unharmed and that we reached you in time before you suffered the same fate as Alex Abelman and Frances Hughes.'

'Well, I'm glad about that too,' said Brown. He looked at Oldroyd disdainfully, but his hand shook a little as he spoke. 'That

Hattersley's a complete nutcase. I had no idea that he'd come back to this area. He was always very difficult at the home, according to the staff who worked with him at the time.'

Oldroyd looked at him sternly. 'Before you go any further down that road,' he said in the commanding voice which cowed most of his interviewees, 'terrible though Hattersley's crimes were, they were not without provocation, were they? We want to know a lot more about what went on at that home, and in particular we want to know about Liam Quinn – what happened to him and why his body is buried in the cellar at Chevin Towers. I advise you to cooperate. In the end, you could be facing a murder charge.'

This abrupt and powerful speech had an impact on Brown. His eyes widened and his mouth almost dropped open. But then he sneered at his interrogator and pulled himself together, clearly thinking he was not going to be beaten by an upstart like Oldroyd.

He looked at his solicitor who said, 'Chief Inspector, I think you need to withdraw that last statement, unless you have any evidence. You are trying to intimidate my client. Has this body even been formally identified?'

Oldroyd smiled and continued to address Brown. 'We're very confident that the body will prove to be that of Liam Quinn, so it's going to save us a lot of time if you tell us what you know about it, plus all the other brutal things that happened up there which you helped to conceal.'

'You don't have to say anything,' said the solicitor, but Brown overruled him. He knew they would get to the truth in the end, but he believed he could justify what he'd done. Nevertheless it wasn't easy revisiting what had happened all those years ago.

'They came to me in a panic,' he began, speaking slowly as the memories he'd suppressed for so long came back. There was no more arrogance or disdain in his voice but instead regret mixed with self-justification.

'Who are "they"?'

'Frances Hughes and Abelman. This boy Quinn had been punished, and he'd died.'

'I presume by "punishment" you mean being tied to a wooden chair in a dark cellar?'

'I don't know anything about that. I left punishments to the staff at the home. It was their responsibility to maintain order.'

'By whatever means possible? You chose not to be aware of what they were doing, didn't you? Are you saying you didn't know that staff were virtually torturing children?'

'That's a bit extreme, Chief Inspector. Some of those children were very difficult and needed firm discipline. Abelman took it upon himself to take charge when it came to the worst offenders, but I didn't realise that he had gone as far as he did. Children should never have been left in a cellar like that. On this occasion they found the boy dead and still strapped to a chair. When they looked at his medical records, they found he had a history of asthma, so he probably died of an attack brought on by anxiety, I suppose.'

'That's outrageous! No one checked his medical records before that? You, in your senior role, were responsible for making sure that proper procedures were in place, and you should have known that physical abuse and neglect were going on. You seem to have been unaware of what was actually happening there – how do you know Liam Quinn hadn't been beaten and the injuries caused his death?'

'Chief Inspector, no one who worked at Chevin Towers would have behaved so brutally. I know because I was involved in interviewing and appointing them all.'

Oldroyd shook his head sceptically. 'So, what did you tell them to do?'

Brown paused. Again, his solicitor warned him that he didn't need to say anything.

Ignoring the warning, Brown continued to talk. He seemed unconcerned about implicating himself. 'I knew that this was the end for the home. If any of this had ever come out, the place would have been in very serious trouble. They told me that this boy came from Ireland, that his parents had gone back, and there was no trace of them. Abelman buried the body and I began the process of shutting the home down. The place was on its last legs anyway. The trustees were all old and I easily persuaded them that we didn't have the resources to continue. In retrospect, it was a bad idea to have a children's home on that site. It was too remote, too big and not welcoming for children.

'I got the staff together; there weren't many. Only Frances and Abelman knew what had happened to Quinn, and I said the boy had been sent back to Ireland. They were all offered a redundancy package, but they had to sign a gagging clause.'

'I understand you also frightened all the children into keeping quiet?'

'I didn't want them telling all kinds of stories. Children exaggerate things and you can't trust them.'

Steph was incensed by this. 'That's one of the big problems with child abuse, isn't it, Mr Brown? People sometimes don't listen to or believe children's accounts of what happened to them, and the abusers get away with it.'

Brown looked defiant. 'We wanted to avoid a big inquiry with police and officials all over the place. That boy's death was an accident but I'm sure many people would have liked to have said that we were responsible.'

'Well, weren't you?' continued Steph. 'He must have been terrified in that cellar and it must have triggered his asthma. And the very fact that your staff didn't even know that he suffered from that condition shows criminal neglect.'

Brown waved a dismissive hand at her. 'Things were different in those days. There were fewer rules and regulations. We made sure all the children were moved on to good accommodation.'

'Yes, they were, and—' Steph was angry and nearly out of her seat. Oldroyd raised a hand to restrain her, and she sat back again.

Oldroyd continued. 'How can you justify filling kids full of terror for life just to save your skin?'

Brown shrugged.

Oldroyd leaned towards him. 'We know at least one of those kids in addition to Hattersley never recovered from their experiences in that home and died from a drug overdose when they were still quite young. They were all too frightened and mixed up to say anything after Abelman had worked on them. I wonder what happened to the rest? Do you ever think about it? Is it on your conscience?'

Brown drew himself up. He was accepting nothing. 'The person most responsible for the treatment of those children is now dead. And Frances didn't really have enough experience for the job. We'd put her in charge of the pastoral side of things when the previous person left abruptly, but I accept it was a mistake. She let Abelman control things. I know she regretted what happened. She was a personal friend of mine and a good woman.'

Oldroyd frowned at him. 'How did you prevent the police from finding out what happened there? We know that you were in a position to exert influence and I suspect that you had contacts in the police too, didn't you?'

Brown smiled and looked at Oldroyd with condescension. 'I knew people high up in the force and I had a word. There was nothing to be gained by getting the police involved. That's how power worked then, Chief Inspector, and that's how it still works.' He gave Oldroyd yet another arrogant and self-satisfied look, and his lip curled.

Steph was clearly seething with anger, but managed to contain herself.

Oldroyd looked at Brown with contempt. The man thought the normal rules didn't apply to him. He considered himself above the law, as enforced by petty bureaucrats like police detectives. This was exactly the kind of thing that enraged Superintendent Walker when he had to deal with Matthew Watkins, who also had connections with powerful local people. It was sleazy, undemocratic and led to people escaping justice.

He'd had enough of Brown's evasive and arrogant answers. 'The charges against you stand: at least conspiring to prevent a lawful and decent burial and involvement in child abuse. We'll be talking to you again before long.' He pointed at Brown, his eyes flashed and his face took on the hawkish expression that intimidated most criminals he interviewed. His voice was harsh as he said, 'Make no mistake about it. I will ensure that these charges stick and you will go down. I don't care who you think will pull strings for you.'

Brown returned Oldroyd's gaze but he shifted uncomfortably, and both Oldroyd and Steph detected for the first time a suggestion of fear and uncertainty.

Oldroyd continued to fix Brown with his gaze and then shook his head. 'There's one thing I don't understand. You don't seem to have had any concern about the welfare of children, so why did you get involved with Chevin Towers in the first place?'

'I was asked to join the board of governors and I thought it my duty to serve.'

'And are you proud of what you did?'

Brown tried to maintain his defiance, but his voice was less confident. 'I've always followed the call of duty. Let's say things didn't work out exactly as I would have liked, but I did my best.'

And you avoided anything negative that would damage your reputation, thought Oldroyd, but he didn't say anything. He'd had enough of the man. 'Take him out,' he called to the police officer on duty. When Brown walked away, his figure was bowed, and he suddenly looked much older than the man who had entered the room.

~

When Brown had gone, Oldroyd and Steph stayed in the interview room, trying to process what they had heard.

'It almost makes you wish we hadn't got to him in time, doesn't it?' observed Oldroyd with grim humour.

'It does, sir. I think he was just as guilty as the others. What about that stuff about not informing the police? Isn't that corruption?'

'Yes, it will all be investigated, but I think we'll find that most of the people are no longer around. I know what you mean about him being responsible, though he would never admit it. There was a kind of moral hierarchy, wasn't there? Abelman, the worst one, administered the brutal punishment. Hughes, as far as we know, didn't do anything violent, but she was in charge of the place, knew what was happening and colluded with Abelman. Brown was still further removed and claimed not to know what was happening at all until he was called in about Liam's death. But he interfered with the process of justice and instigated a cover-up in order to protect his reputation, despite what he said about just tidying things up and saving a lot of trouble. But, as you say, they were all involved, and some people would argue equally guilty.'

'I'm sorry I nearly lost control, sir. I find it difficult to deal with anything that involves cruelty to children.'

'I know. Don't worry, I was very angry too. I sometimes wonder what it must be like for social workers dealing with children at risk all the time.'

243

Steph shook her head but didn't reply.

Oldroyd gave a big sigh, slapped his knees and got up. 'Well, that's about it, I suppose. There's a lot of work to do wrapping things up but we can leave that to DC Hall and this team. They seem to be a very efficient lot.'

He often felt a sense of anticlimax at the end of a tense and dramatic case like this. But this time, other feelings came up: disgust at what had happened to those children and frustration at not being able to do anything about it. And a sense that justice had not really been properly administered: Abelman and Hughes were dead, but had never been put on trial to face up to what they had done. At least Brown would have to face the music and the destruction of his reputation.

The detectives left the police station and walked through Market Place. It was market day again and the town was returning to normal as news of the arrest filtered through and the threat of danger was lifted. There was a tangible sense of relief as people wandered amongst stalls, stopping to chat and have a laugh.

'Everything will come out about the home now, won't it, sir?' said Steph as they walked down one of the ancient ginnels and across the road to the Courthouse.

'Yes, big time. And, as with a lot of these things, it will be too late to stop what happened to those poor kids. There will be a big inquiry, which will go on for years, into the home and what happened there. Now that any threat of retribution has gone, other people – including former staff and children – will come forward to testify. Questions will be asked about why the local authority, the police and the board of trustees didn't do more. It will be a huge scandal and the press will have a field day holding this or that person responsible. At least they will be off our backs now that we've solved the murder case.'

'Will any good come out of it, sir?'

'We can only hope so,' said Oldroyd, raising his hands in a gesture of scepticism. 'The problem is, we've seen so many of these inquiries over the years into terrible cases of abuse and people saying "never again". But unfortunately similar things continue to happen. We never seem to get to the core of the problem and invest properly in the solutions.' They arrived at the Courthouse and went into the robing room. The table was covered with papers and used coffee cups. 'Anyway,' Oldroyd continued, 'that's me on my political high horse. We'd better just finish off, clear up here and get back to Harrogate.'

∼

Abigail Wilson, Hillary Sands and Dylan Hardy were in the Courthouse office. They were still finding it difficult to concentrate on work, despite the good news that the 'reign of terror' – as one tabloid had called it – was over, and they were sitting having a coffee together. With Abigail's encouragement, Hillary had told Dylan about Susan and her experiences at Chevin Towers. It was better to tell him now before the inquiry made everything public.

Hillary's feelings about the resolution of the case were complex. 'I'm glad the truth is going to come out at last,' she said. 'And I find it difficult to feel any sympathy for the two who were murdered, especially Abelman, who was a nasty sadist. At least Susan will get some recognition for what she went through, and surely Brown will go to prison for a long time. He deserves it.'

'I never felt that he was really interested in the Courthouse,' said Dylan. 'I think it was all about his own status as a local dignitary on the board of everything.'

'It's amazing how quickly people forget things,' said Abigail. 'He still got invited by those organisations, despite what had happened.'

'He did a very good job of covering his tracks and presenting his behaviour as positive: he was the man who took the difficult decision to close down a failing children's home, and he did it very efficiently and with compassion and so on.'

'Huh!' sneered Hillary. 'Unfortunately, you're right; people still look up to characters like him, who present themselves as very respectable and civic minded.' She shook her head. 'I still find it hard to believe that Frances was involved in that abuse. It was so unlike her.'

'I'm not trying to excuse her,' said Abigail, looking at Hillary. 'But I think in her case she was in a situation that she couldn't deal with. She was too inexperienced to be in charge of running a place like that and she turned to Abelman to enforce order and discipline. Then it got out of control.'

'Maybe,' said Hillary. 'But I can't forgive her for being involved in treating children so badly.'

'Well, the Courthouse will be looking for a new chair of trustees,' observed Abigail. 'And I hope they get a better one this time.' She looked at her two colleagues and smiled. 'I think we should try to cheer up now. We're bound to get a lot of support here after what's happened. We'll also get some of the ghoulish types who want to see where the body was. As they say: there's no such thing as bad publicity.'

'True,' said Dylan. 'Now it's all over I'll tell you a secret. I thought at one time that the police might suspect me.'

'Dylan?! Why?' exclaimed Abigail.

'Well, because I'm a bit of a loner and I knew a lot about Chevin Towers, more than I told them, actually. I found some information years ago in newspaper archives about the place and I've always been fascinated by it.'

'Why didn't you tell the police?'

Dylan shrugged. 'It wasn't much, and I just didn't want to draw attention to myself. I've even painted a picture of it recently as an atmospheric Gothic place, and I think the police would have found that interesting. I've never told you this, but I was in care myself for a time as a child. I identify with the kids who were in that place, but I'd rather forget all about it. I knew the police would find out all the information they needed in the end.'

'Dylan, that's very sad. We never knew,' said Hillary.

'No, well, not to worry. I manage OK these days. I'm just glad the investigation is over.'

'Aren't we all,' said Abigail. 'The only people who aren't pleased are my two. They've got so into the idea of murders and police investigations that they looked quite sad when I told them that the police had arrested the person who had been killing people.' They all laughed. 'When my son came home today, he said it had been very boring at school. The teachers had told them they couldn't play at being murderers and police officers any more as it was all getting out of hand. I think they let them play like that for a while so that they could express some of their feelings, but now it's over, the teachers have had enough.'

'I can imagine,' said Hillary, still laughing.

There was a knock at the door. Oldroyd and Steph entered. 'Just popping in to say cheerio and thank you for your hospitality and cooperation. You made it very easy and convenient for us to work from here.'

'You're welcome,' said Abigail.

'I'm sorry again that you had to go through so much trauma – finding a body here, and now losing a volunteer and your chair of trustees.' Oldroyd looked at Hillary. 'I think at least you will be experiencing some welcome release after all these years for your feelings about your cousin.'

'Thank you,' said Hillary. 'We were just talking about it and about the Courthouse. I think *release* is the right word. There's been something nasty which has been concealed and festered for a long time in this town. What happened has brought it out into the open. Now we can all begin to heal.'

'I've just been saying how I've always found Chevin Towers fascinating, Chief Inspector,' said Dylan. 'But it is a gloomy building, looming over the town like that, and not to everyone's taste. I didn't know it held such awful secrets. After what's happened, I think they should demolish it.'

Oldroyd agreed. He and Steph were just about to leave when Oldroyd's phone rang. It was Tom Walker. His voice was much more upbeat than on the first day of the investigation when he had told Oldroyd that Blake had escaped.

'I see I need to congratulate you yet again on a fine piece of work,' he said.

'Thanks, Tom.'

'It was damned complicated, wasn't it, with Adam Blake being on the run at the same time? Young Carter did well with the Stansfield people; McNiven put in a great report for him. At least that's the end of any threat from Blake. I won't be shedding any tears about him going the same way as his victims. Of course, there's an almighty row blowing up at Stansfield Prison now we know Blake's escape was an inside job. It's typical of what happens when you get somebody like that James Perry in charge. Weak and useless; all PR and no substance. He reminds me so much of Watkins.'

Oldroyd shut his eyes in anticipation of the familiar tirade against the chief constable.

'You won't believe this, but I've just had him on the phone asking about the man you arrested, Edward Brown. "Were we sure we had the right man?" I tell you . . . sometimes I don't know how

I stop myself from losing it with him. I told him straight that the people we had working on the case were some of our best detectives and I would always trust them to get it right. He had no answer to that, of course, because he knows bugger all about what's going on in the real world of policing, even though he's meant to be in charge.

'Actually, it won't be anything to do with whether or not he thinks you're any good. As I told you before, he'll probably know this Brown character from some kind of lodge or something that they're both in. You know, where they cover for each other? It disgusts me.'

Oldroyd stayed quiet.

'It was a nasty business up at Chevin Towers too, wasn't it? I've always found that a creepy building, to be honest. I'm not surprised that it all happened there. One of the victims got his revenge on two of the perpetrators, didn't he? I know we shouldn't approve of things like that – but it's hard not to feel some sympathy, isn't it? Especially as there didn't seem to be any chance that justice was going to be achieved in any other way. I think I would feel the same in the circumstances.'

'Me too, Tom. It was scandalous how things were covered up. Children's lives were ruined. There's going to be a big scandal and inquiry there too, as well as at Stansfield.'

'Yes, it's terrible how people will try to hide what they've done. And they often seem to get away with it, although you can be sure that Perry will be dismissed for his shabby behaviour. Anyway, once again, well done! And I'll see you back here in Harrogate tomorrow. I know you've had Stephanie Johnson with you and DC Warner doing research; excellent officers. And Carter did well assisting McNiven. Watkins has no idea how lucky he is with the people he's got.'

With that he rang off. The tirade against the chief constable hadn't lasted very long and Walker had once more shown that underneath the gruff exterior he was a man who could empathise. Again, as on many occasions after difficult investigations, Oldroyd reflected that, despite his faults, Walker was a good boss to have.

'Well, sir, we did it again. It was tricky but we got there,' said Steph.

'I'm glad you said "we". It's always a team effort. I have to confess I didn't feel at my best in this one. There was too much going on with Blake escaping at the same time as these murders in Otley. It was hard to concentrate on what was going on here.'

'Of course, sir. You and your family could have been in danger.'

'Yes. I could have been sharper on that key business, though. I thought that somebody might have stolen a set of keys to the Courthouse and maybe had them copied to be used later, but for some reason I didn't consider that somebody could have borrowed them. I should have asked about that and it might have jogged her memory earlier.'

'Well, I didn't think of it either, sir. And maybe she would have remembered if she hadn't been so stressed after finding that body. We all make mistakes, so don't beat yourself up about it.'

Oldroyd gave her an affectionate smile. 'You're maturing into a very wise person,' he said. 'And I remember you as a young lass straight from school. It's great to see how you and Andy have come on. By the way, how has he found this Stansfield case and the responsibility he had?'

'He's enjoyed it, sir. Although he didn't take it very well when his plan to trap Blake went wrong.'

'Well, there we are; the same as me. It can be tough when you're in charge and things aren't going well. You tend to blame yourself and it doesn't matter how long you've been doing the job.'

Steph nodded. 'I can see that, sir. It's a long learning process, isn't it?'

'It is.' Oldroyd sighed. 'OK. Well, it's just about over here now, but there's one more visit I have to make. You can get back to Harrogate. Let's see how your partner's getting on.'

~

'How could she, Chief Inspector? How could she? It's not the woman I knew.'

Oldroyd sat opposite Malcolm Hughes, who was devastated to find out about his wife's involvement in the abuse at Chevin Towers. Oldroyd was familiar with this scenario: the shock, distress and sheer incomprehension of the relatives of people discovered to have committed terrible crimes.

'Edward Brown told us that she always regretted what had happened at the home. Remember, she didn't administer any of the brutal punishment. I think she just couldn't deal with the challenging behaviour of some of the children and turned in desperation to Abelman. She was supposed to be in charge, but she couldn't cope. She wasn't very old and lacked experience. The committee should never have appointed her to that role. I think the death of that boy must have haunted her.'

'Why did Hattersley kill her if she was not as much to blame?'

'Because she was still around here and he saw her. Frances, Brown and Abelman were the people on whom he took revenge. It could have been someone else from the home if they'd still been in the area. Remember he was seriously damaged by what had happened to him. But also try not to be too hard on your wife. There was nothing sadistic about her, unlike Abelman. I think her work in the care homes that you ran together was a kind of reparation. She realised that she wasn't cut out for working with children so turned to working with old people instead.'

'She was very good at it, Chief Inspector. All those old people loved her.' He shed a tear and reached for a tissue.

'I'd stay with that memory of her and all the good work you did together. After all, we've all done things that we regret, haven't we?'

'Yes, but why didn't she tell me about it?'

'I think the most common reasons why a person like your wife keeps past secrets are shame and embarrassment at what they did, and a fear that they will lose the good opinion of someone who is precious to them. I'm sure she felt a certain amount of guilt for not telling you. It was a private thing for her, not, I'm afraid, like Edward Brown. For him it was all about preserving his public reputation.'

Hughes looked at Oldroyd and he smiled weakly. 'Thank you, Chief Inspector. I'm sure you're right. I'll do my best to remember Frances in a positive way.'

~

When she got home to the flat in Leeds, Steph was exhausted. She had expended a great deal of physical and emotional energy on the case and now she flopped. Although it was Friday evening, she had no desire to go out anywhere. After telling Andy about what happened, she had a long bath and then relaxed on the sofa with a glass of wine beside her on the coffee table. After a while, Andy sat down in an armchair with a can of beer and saw that Steph was nodding off.

'Hey, too early to be going to sleep!' he called out with a laugh.

Steph opened her eyes. 'Oh, sorry. I'm absolutely knackered. It's been one of the most draining cases I've ever worked on. Disturbing, too.'

'Yeah, I'll bet,' he said. 'It's bad when kids are involved, isn't it?'

'Exactly. Anyway, now your case is over, how are you feeling about your first experience of taking charge of things?'

Andy took a drink from his can. 'Well, it was a mixed bag, to be honest, but as you said, that's the way things are. You won't get it right all the time. It did make me think – yeah, I can do this. I felt I had much more experience than the younger officers I was working with. They looked up to me for leadership.'

Steph clapped. 'Hurray! Time to look out for inspectors' jobs.'

'I think so, but what about you?'

'I can't think about it just at this moment, but, yes, I think I'm ready too. But it would have to be the right job in the right place. I don't want us to move to some place we don't like just for promotion.'

'No, I agree. Anyway, what are we going to do about food? Why don't we order some pizzas?'

'Good idea,' she replied and laughed. 'You never go long without thinking about your belly, do you?'

'Well, a big hunky chap like me needs proper feeding.'

'Is that right? Well, don't turn into a chap with a big belly; you won't be hunky or healthy then.' She put her foot across and prodded him in his stomach. 'It's time you worked out a bit more. You should join a gym and drink less beer – especially less beer. You know what I think about that.'

Andy nodded. He understood that Steph was very sensitive about alcohol abuse after her experience of her family and her father.

'Yeah, perhaps. Maybe we could go running together. I see lots of people running up along the canal towpath. Don't the boss and his partner do those parkruns in Harrogate?'

'Right, you're on. We'll go to the one at Roundhay Park tomorrow morning, nine o'clock.'

'Whoa, wait! That's a bit sudden!'

'No time like the present, especially if you're going to look for jobs. You don't want to be the Colossal Inspector Carter, do you? You'd be like Derek Fenton.'

'Bloody hell! Don't compare me to that slimebag!'

Fenton had been a DI at Harrogate HQ. He'd been dismissed for gross misconduct, sexual harassment and inappropriate behaviour after Steph and some other women officers had produced evidence that brought him down.

Steph laughed. 'Well, I'm warning you. You don't want to decline into an unhealthy middle age.'

Andy finished his beer. 'OK, you've made your point. Maybe we should just have some grilled chicken and salad instead of pizzas.'

'OK, I'm happy with that.' She got up and went over to sit on his knee. 'And don't forget, I'll love you just the same whether you become an inspector or stay a sergeant.' There was the usual teasing note in her voice.

'But not if I get overweight,' replied Andy, and suddenly he lunged at her, grabbed her around the middle and started to tickle her with his thumbs.

'No, Andy!' she shrieked, writhed and laughed. 'Stop it!'

'No way. You deserve it for comparing me to Fenton.'

Like Steph, Oldroyd was very tired when he arrived home that evening. He was pleased when he remembered that Alison was coming round for a meal. He enjoyed talking to Deborah and Alison when he reached the end of a case. It was a kind of debriefing. He was able to reflect on the moral and psychological issues that had been raised. His job was not just about collecting information and interviewing people; it was about moral and human dilemmas.

The food was vegetarian, but he didn't mind. It was Friday night, and he was able to drink red wine – although not too much, as it was parkrun the next day. He and Deborah were confining their drinking to weekends as part of their drive to live more healthily. As they ate their Mexican bean burritos with salsa, green salad and grated cheese, he filled them in on more details of the two cases.

'So, in the end it was all about revenge: *vindicta*. Revenge on Blake from a relative of one of his victims, and revenge on the people who abused children at Chevin Towers by someone who suffered there. Also Blake's thankfully unsuccessful attempt to get revenge on me. Did I tell you that he compared me to Sherlock Holmes and himself to Moriarty?'

'No!' exclaimed Deborah. 'How weird!'

'Well, there was something in it, in the sense that I think he had a certain amount of respect for me as I had tracked him down, but he regarded himself as my intellectual equal as it were, and in a fight to the end, just as Holmes and Moriarty were locked in a death struggle that only ended at the Reichenbach Falls.' Oldroyd laughed. 'In this case, Holmes prevailed, but somebody else finished Moriarty off.'

'Jim, what an extraordinary flight of literary fancy!' exclaimed Alison with a laugh.

'Not only that, I'm afraid. I had the Sherlock Holmes stories in my mind when we realised that the person who had brought the body to the Courthouse was probably a decorator: someone inconsequential, in the background and almost invisible. It was just like *A Study in Scarlet,* where the murderer turns out to be a cabbie.' He took a sip of wine. 'Anyway, to get back to revenge, it can be a very powerful motive, can't it?'

'Indeed,' replied Alison. 'It's one of the most difficult parts of the Gospel. It's very natural to feel that you want to get your

255

own back on someone who has mistreated you. You want justice. But Jesus tries to get us to a higher level: forgiveness. There's an old saying, isn't there? An eye for an eye leaves us all blind. But forgiveness can be really hard, especially if you're dealing with terrible things like murder and child abuse.'

'I agree,' said Deborah. 'The problem with deep bitterness, hatred and a desire for vengeance, understandable though they often are, is that they end up destroying the person who has them. I would always try to help someone to let go of those feelings for their own benefit.'

'I must admit,' said Oldroyd, 'Steph and I felt very ambiguous about it at the end. This man Hattersley and the other children in that home were very badly treated and it was all covered up. I certainly understood how Hattersley felt. Interestingly, my chief superintendent, Tom Walker, said the same – and he's a tough old character.'

'People are especially affected by cruelty when there are children involved,' said Alison. 'It's the innocence, defencelessness and the abuse of power by adults that's really shocking.'

Oldroyd got up and started to clear the plates away. Deborah brought in a dessert of lemon cheesecake. Oldroyd almost sighed with contentment. After a case like the one they'd just concluded, it was important to recognise how lucky you were in life.

'I think in that home,' continued Deborah, 'the bad things that those children went through were made worse by the fact that no adults ever came in to put things right and they were left to deal with it by themselves right into adulthood. Sadly, I think many of them probably ended up feeling that it was their fault, that somehow they deserved the treatment they got. There doesn't appear to have been any good adult role model. No one ever helped them to process what they'd been through and reassure them that they were not to blame. You say there's going to be a big inquiry; it will be interesting to see how those kids fared in adult life, assuming some will come forward. Unfortunately, I'll bet in many cases it wasn't very well.'

'Besides Hattersley himself, who obviously never recovered, we know of at least one person who got into drugs and died young.'

'Tragic,' said Alison, shaking her head.

After the meal they went into the sitting room for coffee. Deborah was telling Alison about *The Mousetrap*.

'Do you know, I've never seen it, even though it's so famous,' remarked Alison.

'Neither had I before we went. It was a wonderful period piece with a cunning plot twist.'

Oldroyd sipped his coffee and smiled. 'Yes, I enjoyed it a lot. But what I didn't tell you at the time was that it gave me some ideas about the case.'

'Really? What?'

'Well, Agatha Christie based the plot on the real-life story of the O'Neill brothers who, in 1945, were fostered out to a Shropshire farmer and his wife, where they suffered terrible abuse. They were starved and beaten and one of them died. I began to wonder if something similar was behind these Otley murders. We were struggling to establish any connection between the victims, then Stephanie Johnson and I went back up to Chevin Towers and we saw some evidence that children had been abused there at some point in the past. It was just a hunch, but it turned out to be right.'

'Good heavens! When you're on a case, your brain never stops working, does it?' said Alison.

'I suppose not, particularly in one like this where the pressure to find the perpetrator is intense. You're on full alert all the time, searching for clues in everything that you see and do. That's why I'm exhausted now,' he said, lounging back in his chair and closing his eyes.

'Well, don't go to sleep on us now,' said Deborah. 'But you do need to take a rest after all that. After parkrun tomorrow, we'll go for a nice long walk in the Dales.'

'That sounds good,' said Oldroyd, still with his eyes shut and his hands behind his head. 'But it sounds a lot to do parkrun and then a long walk. What if we just do the walk and have a bit of a lie-in first? Then you could bring me breakfast in bed. Surely I've deserved that after my recent exertions?'

'Jim!' said Deborah, and Alison laughed.

ACKNOWLEDGEMENTS

I continue to be supported by my family, friends and the Otley Writers' Group. Members of the latter will recognise the detectives' incident room or 'office' as the robing room where we hold our meetings. The Otley Courthouse is a vibrant arts centre run by local people, many of whom are volunteers, including me!

Otley is a bustling place with a long history. I have mostly described the town as it is. The only major change is to The White House. This famous landmark in Otley has a long history as a farm, café and visitor centre. I hope the residents of Otley will forgive me for turning this pleasant building into the dark Gothic horror of Chevin Towers! The children's home sited there in the story is entirely fictional.

Similarly, I hope the members of the Bridge United Reformed Church will forgive me for basing St Saviour's church and the scarecrows on the excellent scarecrow display at their church, which is becoming an annual event in the town!

The West Riding Police Force is a fictional force based on the old West Riding boundary. Harrogate was part of the old West Riding, although it is in today's North Yorkshire Constabulary.

ABOUT THE AUTHOR

John R. Ellis has lived in Yorkshire for most of his life and has spent many years exploring Yorkshire's diverse landscapes, history, language and communities. He recently retired after a career in teaching, mostly in further education in the Leeds area. In addition to the Yorkshire Murder Mystery series, he writes poetry, ghost stories and biography. He has completed a screenplay about the last years of the poet Edward Thomas and a work of faction about the extraordinary life of his Irish mother-in-law. He is currently working (slowly!) on his memoirs of growing up in a working-class area of Huddersfield in the 1950s and 1960s.

Follow the Author on Amazon

If you enjoyed this book, follow J. R. Ellis on Amazon to be notified when the author releases a new book!

To do this, please follow these instructions:

Desktop:

1) Search for the author's name on Amazon or in the Amazon App.
2) Click on the author's name to arrive on their Amazon page.
3) Click the 'Follow' button.

Mobile and Tablet:

1) Search for the author's name on Amazon or in the Amazon App.
2) Click on one of the author's books.
3) Click on the author's name to arrive on their Amazon page.
4) Click the 'Follow' button.

Kindle eReader and Kindle App:

If you enjoyed this book on a Kindle eReader or in the Kindle App, you will find the author 'Follow' button after the last page.